PROFILE

What Reviewers Say About Jackie D's Work

Elimination

"This book ramps up the spy-craft, which I always love. Dylan and Emma even have to go undercover as a couple to cover their tracks, and that's a trope I can always get behind. This is a fun series about strong, capable woman who love their country, careers, and each other, and in the end, it's just a ton of fun."—*Love Bytes: LGBTQ Book Reviews*

Spellbound—*Co-authored with Jean Copeland*

"The story is a mixture of history and present day, fantasy and real life, and is really well done. I especially liked the biting humor that pops up occasionally. The characters are vibrant and likable (except the bad guys who are really nasty). There is a good deal of angst with both romances, but a lot of 'aww' moments as well."
—*Rainbow Reflections*

"*Spellbound* is a very exciting read, fast-paced, thrilling, funny too. …The authors mix politics and the fight against patriarchy with time travel and witch fights with brilliant results." —*Jude in the Stars*

"[T]he themes and contextual events in this book were very poignant in relation to the current political climate in the United States. The fashion in which existing prejudices related to race, socioeconomic status, and gender were manipulated to cause discord were staggering, but also a reflection of the current state of things here in the USA. I really enjoyed this aspect of the book and I am so glad that I read it when I did."—*Mermaid Reviews*

The Rise of the Resistance

"I was really impressed by Jackie D's story and felt it had a truth and reality to it. She brought to life an America where things had gone badly wrong, but she gave me hope that all was not lost. The world she has imagined was compelling and the characters were so well developed."—*Kitty Kat's Book Review Blog*

"Jackie D explores how racist, homophobic, xenophobic leaders manage to seize, manipulate, and maintain power."—*Celestial Books*

"The best thing about the writing is the seamless blending of two very different genres. First we have the uber action packed main plot, but it is blended artfully with the second romantic plot so that the two never feel tacked on. More often than not, I prefer my dystopian novels to be lighter on the romance and my romance to be light on the action, but I really enjoyed seeing them play out alongside one another in this book."—*Lesbian Review*

Infiltration—*Lambda Literary Award Finalist*

"Quick question, where has this author been my entire life? …If you are looking for a romantic book that has mystery and thriller qualities then this is your book."—*Fantastic Book Reviews*

"This book is an action-packed romance, filled with cool characters and a few totally uncool bad guys. The book is well written, the story is engaging, and Jackie D did a great job of reeling the reader in and holding your attention to the very end."—*Romantic Reader Blog*

Lands End

"This is a great summer holiday read—likeable characters, great chemistry between the leads, interesting and unusual premise, well written dialogue, an excellent romance without any unnecessary angst. I really connected with both leads, and enjoyed the secondary characters. The attraction between Amy and Lena was palpable and the romantic storyline was paced really well."—Melina Bickard, Librarian, Waterloo Library (London)

Lucy's Chance

"Add a bit of conflict, add a bit of angst, a deranged killer, and you have a really good read. What this book is is a great escape. You have a few hours to decompress from real-life's craziness, and enjoy a quality story with interesting characters. Well, minus the psychopath murderer, but you know what I mean."—*Romantic Reader Blog*

Pursuit

"This book is a dynamic fast-moving adventure that keeps you on the edge of your seat the whole time…enough romance for you to swoon and enough action to keep you fully engaged. Great read, you don't want to miss this one."—*Romantic Reader Blog*

Visit us at www.boldstrokesbooks.com

By the Author

The After Dark Series

Infiltration

Pursuit

Elimination

Lands End

Lucy's Chance

The Rise of the Resistance: Phoenix One

VIP

Profile

Books with other Authors

Spellbound—Jackie D and Jean Copeland

Swift Vengeance—Jackie D, Jean Copeland, and Erin Zak

PROFILE

by
Jackie D

2022

PROFILE

ISBN 13: 978-1-63679-282-8

This Trade Paperback Original Is Published By
Bold Strokes Books, Inc.
P.O. Box 249
Valley Falls, NY 12185

First Edition: December 2022

CREDITS
EDITORS: VICTORIA VILLASEÑOR AND CINDY CRESAP
PRODUCTION DESIGN: SUSAN RAMUNDO
COVER DESIGN BY TAMMY SEIDICK

Acknowledgments

Thank you, Vic Villasenor and Cindy Cresap, for always taking such care with my words and ideas. Thank you to Bold Strokes for doing this with me ten times. Unyielding love and affection for all the friendships in my life, which have taught me endless lessons in love, loyalty, and admiration. You're all an inspiration. Great big thanks to my wife and son. You two have given me more reasons to be thankful than I deserve. Finally, to my mom and sister—I love you.

Dedication

For Terri.
Thank you for helping to create the best person
I've ever known. You live in her.

CHAPTER ONE

There are very few things Alex Derby hates more than pomp and circumstance—yet here she is, sitting in a crowded room listening to colleagues pat themselves on the back under the veil of fundraising.

"How much longer do we need to endure this bullshit?"

Hunter Nagle smiles and shakes his head before leaning closer. "Come on, Derby. It's for a good cause." He shrugs and motions to the corner of the room. "And if that doesn't convince you, the open bar should."

Hunter is one of the few agents Alex works with at the Criminal Investigative Division at the FBI who doesn't make her want to punch a wall. His easy manner, slight Southern drawl, and handsome features make him popular with everyone, but Alex has always appreciated his no-nonsense approach. He's never struck her as self-serving, and they share a mutual disdain for the kiss-asses that are so common in their world you could throw a rock and hit three.

She sips her beer. "Is it really"—she makes air quotes—"open bar if we had to pay to be here?"

He chuckles. "You didn't pay a damn thing."

She leans back in her chair and does a quick sweep of the room. "No, but some donor did."

She only agreed to come to the gauche event because she wants to see who is paying to sit in a room with countless FBI agents, their department heads, and a smattering of politicians. Donations start at five thousand but can go as high as seventy-five thousand for a table of eight. Sure, it's for a good cause, but not everyone is here out of generosity. Tax write-off be damned.

He leans forward on the table and nods to the stage. "Boss man is getting ready to give his speech."

She huffs and takes a pull from her beer. "The way he tells it, you'd think he made the Fitzgerald collar all on his own."

He shrugs. "The Bureau had been chasing him for almost twenty years. It was a big deal to catch him."

Alex watches as Assistant Director Peterson steps in front of the podium. If you were to pass him on the street, you'd never know that he spent most of his career chasing down cartels or working in the Gang Unit. You definitely wouldn't be able to tell that he served as the head of SWAT or that she's known him since she was a child.

Assistant Director Peterson is how she addresses him now, but it used to be Dave—her father's best friend. She used to think of him as larger than life, a hero just like her father. But like most things, as you get older and gain more perspective, you realize there's so much more to the story. The world isn't black and white. Good guys sometimes do bad things, and bad guys occasionally have redeeming qualities. As it turns out, Dave isn't some shiny beacon of hope and fortitude she once imagined him to be. Instead, he's just like everyone else—glaringly disappointing if you get close enough to really look under the shiny surface.

She forces her eyes away from the podium and studies the people watching him. She's not interested in those pretending to laugh at his practiced jokes, and she doesn't care about the people playing on their phones. Her only interest is in the guests exuding intentional indifference—that's where the secrets lay. It doesn't take long to spot a few, and it's easy to differentiate between those full of disdain because they covet his position of power and those who are aloof because they don't want to be noticed.

Her senses tingle as her gaze drifts over one person in particular—Jeffery Fletcher. He's a vile excuse for a human being. The rumors that swirl around him are nothing short of rage-inducing.

Bribery, tax evasion, and corruption are just a few areas where he casts a long shadow of suspicion. But here he sits on a high horse she'd name Audacity if asked.

She rubs her thumbs up the sweaty neck of her beer bottle and whispers, "Check out table eight."

Hunter stretches and glances to the back of the room. "Jesus. What do you think he's doing here?"

The question is rhetorical, and she doesn't bother to answer. They both know exactly what he's doing here. It's all political theater. Spend time and make friends with people who may eventually have the opportunity to investigate you. Ingratiate yourself with political figures and make sure to get your picture taken in the event of your demise—assured mutual destruction. It pays to have friends in influential places, and events like this make it easy to collect them.

The round of applause shakes her from her contemplation, and she reluctantly joins the rest of the guests with half-hearted clapping. She's getting ready to ask Hunter to accompany her back toward table eight so she can attempt to eavesdrop when she sees his face brighten with excitement. Only one person affects him that way—his ex-wife, Cassidy Wolf.

Cassidy isn't just attractive—she's stunning. Her blond hair is swept up off her shoulders in a bun, and she's wearing a black cocktail dress that looks like it's painted on. Her blue eyes sparkle as she approaches their table, and Alex forces herself not to get transfixed by her smile. Cassidy is one of the rising stars at the FBI, and the Behavioral Analysis Unit is lucky to have her. She's worked with her on a few cases and has always found her to be intelligent, dedicated, and welcoming. The FBI often shoves her in front of the press, has her speak at colleges, and utilizes her infectious personality as a liaison between different departments. Alex has wondered more than once if she'd still be their poster child if she looked less like Margot Robbie and more like Danny DeVito.

Hunter hugs Cassidy and kisses her cheek. He pulls out her chair and waits for her to get settled. "I wondered if you were going to come say hi."

She grabs his old-fashioned and takes a sip. "They stuck me at the senator's table, and I've spent the entire night trying to get away. I don't know why I wasn't placed with the rest of the agents."

Alex knows exactly why she was put at that specific table. She watches Cassidy's facial expressions and tries to determine if she's being coy or is genuinely unaware. Cassidy seems sincere in her confusion, but that can't possibly be true. Can it?

"You remember Alex Derby, right?" Hunter nods in Alex's direction.

"Of course." Cassidy smiles brightly. "How have you been, Alex?"

Hunter laughs. "She's been planning her escape from the moment she walked through the door. She hates these things."

Alex rolls her eyes. "I don't hate them. I just find them self-indulgent and obnoxious." She raises her beer. "But I'm thrilled to be spending my evening with you." Her voice is intentionally sarcastic, and it gains her a smile from Cassidy.

Cassidy raises her eyebrow. "Hunter, it looks like you found the one woman on the planet who doesn't want to spend their Saturday night with you. Fascinating."

Hunter shrugs. "Alex doesn't count. She prefers Sarah Paulson to Chris Evans."

Alex is annoyed that her cheeks burn with embarrassment. She's never cared if people know she's a lesbian. She's been out since she was thirteen years old. There's no reason it should bother her now. It makes her uncomfortable to think it's because she's concerned about how Cassidy sees her.

To avoid any further aggravating thoughts or feelings, Alex equips herself with one of the few tools in her arsenal—biting sarcasm. "It's called culture, Hunter." She leans forward in her chair. "Sorry, culture means—"

"Fuck off, Derby." Hunter laughs and rocks back in his chair.

Cassidy smiles as she takes another sip from the lowball glass. Her eyes sparkle with amusement, and she doesn't look away. Alex forces herself to be quiet, even though she suddenly wants nothing more than to keep Cassidy's attention.

The abrupt onset of that unintended revelation forces Alex up from her seat. "I'm going to wander around for a bit. Cassidy, it was nice to see you again. Hunter, go fuck yourself."

Hunter raises his glass. "See you at the range tomorrow."

Luckily for Alex, enough is going on in the room to keep her from dwelling on any lingering unwanted effect Cassidy just had on her. She spots Jefferey Fletcher huddled in conversation by the bar and decides to head that way. She orders another beer and places her forearms on the bar top to lean over and see who is on the other side of the conversation with Jeffery. She quickly looks in the other direction when she recognizes Miles Christie, a senator from Florida.

Lately, Senator Christie has been lambasting Jeffery Fletcher all over the news. The familiar banter they're exchanging now is nothing short of dizzying. The bartender hands her a bottle, and she takes it and turns back toward the busy room. She listens to the two men and tries to pick up any words that may be of consequence. However, the longer she listens, she realizes that it's not what they're saying—it's what they're not. There doesn't seem to be any rhyme or reason to their conversation. *Are they talking in some kind of code?*

She's so engrossed in trying to memorize any phrases that stand out that she doesn't notice Assistant Director Peterson until he slaps her on the back. "How you doing, Derby?"

She chokes on the beer in an attempt to not spit it out. "Director Peterson." She turns to look at him. "Great speech."

He looks at her sideways. "You weren't listening to any of it."

She shakes her head. "No, but I'm sure it was great."

He chuckles and nods toward the room. "You should go mingle. Networking is good for your career."

She raises her bottle. "On my way."

He gives her a look that indicates he doesn't believe her. "I'm going to see your dad tomorrow."

"Another riveting day on the golf course." She can't imagine anything worse.

He laughs and smacks her on the back again. "You should join us. You used to play with us when you were a teenager."

She shakes her head. "Driving you guys to and from the course so you could drink beer all day hardly counts as playing with you."

He shrugs. "The offer still stands."

She looks over to where the senator and Fletcher were moments before, but they're gone. She curses under her breath and puts her almost full bottle back on the bar. "Sorry, I have plans." She checks her watch. "In fact, I should get going. Early day tomorrow."

"Alex," he says and puts his hand on her shoulder. "You're never going to get ahead if you don't start playing the game."

She looks down at his hand and then back at him. "What game? Golf or office politics?"

He sighs heavily. "You know what I mean." He leans closer. "There's going to be an opening in the Counterterrorism Division soon. I know you've always wanted to work there." He makes a circular motion with his hand. "It could be yours with a slight attitude adjustment."

She crosses her arms, her defenses flaring. "I've closed more cases for my division than any other agent. You know that."

"And you and I both know there's more to it than just being good at your job. You should try to be more like Cassidy Wolf. Have you met her? Delightful young girl."

Her neck flushes hot. She shouldn't say the words screaming in her mind, but she can't help herself. "Cassidy is an FBI agent and a woman—not a girl. I'm sure she'd appreciate it if you referred to her as such."

"You know what I mean."

"No, Director Peterson, I truly don't." She steps backward. "Now, if you'll excuse me, I really do have a busy day tomorrow. Enjoy the rest of your evening."

She doesn't look back to see if he's staring after her, and it doesn't matter. He's probably right. She probably should try to be more amicable. It wouldn't kill her to participate in extra-curricular activities with her peers, and it definitely wouldn't hurt her career. But the thought of pasting on a fake smile and pretending to laugh at their crude jokes is more than she can bear. It should be good enough to be the best in her division, but she knows it isn't true even as she thinks it. That's not how the world works, and certainly not the FBI.

Fuck. She was going to have to make a friend. Perfect.

The range is practically empty when she arrives at zero nine hundred the following day. Alex prefers to go when attendance is sparse. It allows for a layer of anonymity and saves her from small talk. Hunter started showing up during her favored time about six months ago. Her initial instinct was to change her schedule, but she's grown to enjoy their banter and easy camaraderie. He's the closest thing she has to a work friend, albeit they don't participate in activities outside the range. Maybe it's time to change that. She can tolerate Hunter for longer periods of time than she allows for now.

Alex checks in at the armory and signs for a hundred bullets. The young agent staffing the desk barely looks up from his tablet as he slides the roster sheet to her and hands her two ammunition boxes.

As she approaches their typical lanes, she's surprised to see he isn't alone. Cassidy is in the lane to Hunter's right—her usual spot. Her lack of immediate annoyance is startling. Her internal monologue would be grumbling if it were anyone but Cassidy. She thinks about placing her gear to Hunter's left but changes her mind. She prefers to see who's entering the range, and the only clear line of sight is next to Cassidy. *You're doing some impressive mental gymnastics to justify being next to her, Derby.* She shrugs the thought away.

Alex drops her bag on the table and secures her ear protection and safety glasses. "Morning."

Hunter peeks around Cassidy's back and flips her off. By contrast, Cassidy offers her a warm smile. "Hi, Alex. I hope you don't mind me tagging along and infringing on your and Hunter's range time. I haven't been able to make it down here lately, and I'm feeling a little rusty."

Alex pulls her service weapon from her bag and starts unloading the bullets from her magazine and replacing them with the ones she just acquired. "No worries. It's not like we're going to braid each other's hair between rounds."

Cassidy turns back to her target and begins firing off several rounds. Alex pretends not to pay any attention, but her curiosity gets the best of her. It isn't surprising that shooting seems to come as effortless as everything else Cassidy does. Five clean shots to the head, three in each shoulder, and six in center mass.

"Impressive," Alex says as she slides the magazine into the butt of her gun.

Hunter points downrange. "I told Cassidy at coffee this morning that you're the only person I know who is a better shot than her."

Alex's attention hangs on to the reference of them being together this morning. *Did that mean they also spent last night together? Why should I care? I don't.* She desperately needs to talk about something else—or not talk at all. Either works for her.

Alex configures her target for intermittent training and then presses the start button. "Pay attention, Hunter. I'm only going to show you how to do this one more time."

Alex takes her stance and exhales a deep breath. The target moves backward ten yards and then angles right another five. She squeezes the trigger five times in immediate succession. The target then moves forward eight yards and angles left six more—five more shots. The target changes direction and heads directly for her, stopping seven yards away before moving backward twenty. She fires directly into it as it retreats.

Alex ejects her empty magazine and places the gun on the table while waiting for the target to return. It takes effort not to smile at how Hunter is diligently trying to count the bullet holes in the silhouette.

He pulls the target off the board and smiles. "You missed two shots." He points to either side of the head. "Here and here."

"No, I didn't," Alex says as she reloads the magazine.

Hunter points again. "It's okay to lose sometimes, Derby."

Cassidy bumps him with her shoulder. "She didn't miss. She gave it earrings."

Hunter pulls the target closer to his face. "Fucking show-off." He puts it on the table next to Alex. "I hate playing with you."

Alex smiles. "Oh, Hunter, we're not competing."

Cassidy nods toward his target. "You two aren't even playing the same game."

"Good thing my self-esteem isn't reliant on praise from the two of you," he says as he stomps back to his lane.

As Hunter passes, Cassidy winks at her. Alex's pulse quickens, and it takes all her concentration not to smile. She spends the next thirty minutes trying to put all of her focus into firing her weapon. She's successful...mostly...a little. It's difficult to fully concentrate, knowing Cassidy is watching her between her own rounds. Difficult, but not unpleasant. In fact, it's the opposite of unpleasant, with a dash of excitement.

"Anyone interested in brunch?" Hunter slings his bag over his shoulder.

Alex has never been to brunch with anyone other than her mother. She thinks back to her musings the night before and the need to make more friends. This is the easiest possible solution. She already likes Hunter, and she's struggling to find anything to dislike about Cassidy.

"Sure, that sounds like fun," Alex says while stowing her gear.

"Really?" Hunter looks surprised. "You've never agreed to go with me before."

Alex rolls her eyes. "Don't make it weird. If you're going to make it weird, I'm not going."

Cassidy smacks Hunter playfully. "Let's go to the Secret Garden."

Hunter shakes his head. "I don't want to go all the way out there. Let's hit up The Spot."

Cassidy sighs. "They're across the street from each other. Plus, The Secret Garden has better brunch."

Hunter shrugs. "But the Spot has better Bloody Marys." He nods to Alex. "What do you prefer?"

Alex has never been to either, but she doesn't want her lack of a social life to be on full display. "If I'm going to be stuck eating with you, Hunter, I prefer a place with better drinks."

Hunter smiles. "You're kind of an asshole, but I'll take the win."

Before she walks off, Cassidy gives her a look that's a cross between confused and disappointed. Alex wonders if she's violated some kind of girl code she isn't privy to by siding with Hunter. She wants to explain that her decision wasn't meant as a slight as much as a cover for her embarrassment, but she says nothing. The only thing more humiliating than acknowledging she isn't even slightly familiar with popular brunch locations in an area she's lived in for ten years is admitting the actual humiliation.

CHAPTER TWO

It only takes Alex two Bloody Marys to understand why Cassidy and Hunter divorced. It wasn't because of a lack of chemistry—they have that in spades. But the chemistry isn't rooted in sexual desire. They treat each other like brother and sister, far more than current or even ex-lovers.

"So, Alex, tell me how you ended up in the FBI." Cassidy points in Alex's direction. "Don't you dare cop-out by telling me it's because of your father. I want the real answer."

Hunter orders another drink. "She's too mean to do anything else."

Alex throws the small wad of paper she's been working between her fingers for the last half-hour across the table at him. "I always liked the idea of keeping the bad guys away from the good guys." She pauses to make sure Hunter doesn't interject with an obnoxious comment, "I thought it'd be easy to tell the difference between the two, and my work would be fulfilling. I like purpose."

Cassidy leans forward in her chair. It feels like she's singularly focusing on Alex. "And is it? Still fulfilling?"

"Sometimes." Alex eyes Hunter and ignores the impulse to make a joke as a way to mask her vulnerability. She doesn't want to do that with Cassidy. "Some days, it feels like the good guys and the bad guys aren't all that different."

Cassidy cocks her head slightly. "I know what you mean."

Hunter scoffs. "That's lunacy. We collared one of the worst serial killers in history just four months ago. There was zero good in that guy."

Cassidy keeps her eyes on Alex but answers Hunter. "That's not what she means."

Cassidy's stare is intense and addictive. Alex forces herself to look away. "What about you? How did you end up being the poster child for the FBI?"

Hunter hisses. "She hates when people say that."

Cassidy leans back in her chair, and whatever moment they just shared is left on the small table separating them. "I really like what I do, and I happen to be good at it. As far as why they parade me out in front of cameras more frequently than my peers"—she shrugs—"I've never asked."

If Alex could take her comment back, she would. She knows what other agents say about Cassidy behind her back. She knows the assumptions and what the winks and head nods mean. She's never participated in their banter, but she's no better than any of them at this moment.

"I'm sorry. I didn't mean to—"

"It's fine," Cassidy says before she can finish. She slides on her sunglasses, and whatever she's feeling now is no longer discernable behind the opaque protection.

Hunter taps the table. Maybe he senses a little tension too. "How's your white whale coming, Derby?" He shakes his finger at her and smiles. "You don't think I notice you sometimes turning off your computer screen or stashing a folder away in your desk when you think someone isn't watching, but I do." He pushes the sweating glass closer to her. "So now that I have a few drinks in you let's hear it. Who knows? We may even be able to help." He nods to Cassidy. "She's one of the best profilers at the Bureau."

Alex's throat is suddenly a desert. "I don't know what you're talking about, Nagle. There's no white whale. You know all my cases."

He slides a toothpick into his mouth and turns it in a slow circle. "I call bullshit."

Alex stares at them. Her gut tells her to trust them, but she can't bring herself to say anything. Maybe it's because she doesn't know who is in earshot. Or maybe she doesn't want to drag either of them into the mess she's already trying to wade through. But she knows it's likely option three—she doesn't want them thinking she's bananas.

Alex desperately tries to think of a sarcastic comment to end the conversation entirely. Lucky for her, Hunter's phone rings, and he excuses himself to take the call.

"He's right, you know." Cassidy spears a piece of watermelon. "Another set of eyes never hurts."

"You'll think I've lost my mind." Alex's honesty catches her by surprise, and she shifts uncomfortably in her seat.

Cassidy smiles at her. "Try me."

There's a hint of flirtation in her statement, and Alex doesn't know what to make of it. Hunter returns to the table before she can respond, and she feels a mixture of irritation and relief toward him.

He shakes his phone. "We caught a break in that bank fraud case. I'm going into the office. You want to come?"

This shouldn't even be a question. Alex lives for her job. She'd spent the last ten years jumping from one case to the next, trying to close as many as possible to prove that she wasn't just some legacy. She wants everyone to know she's the real deal. But in the flash before she agrees, there's a smidge of regret. She doesn't know when she'll see Cassidy again, and that thought is almost enough to keep her rooted in her spot. Almost.

CHAPTER THREE

Good boy, Thor." Cassidy kisses the top of her English Labrador's block-shaped head. She refills the bowl of water he just finished lapping up and continues to rub his head. "It's such a beautiful day for a run."

Thor pauses from drinking and stares up at her to articulate his agreement. Once he's finished, she places the small collapsible bowl into her running backpack and tightens the straps around her shoulders. She checks her earbuds, and once she's sure they're secure, she starts down the trail.

When she speaks with her family back home in San Francisco, she often laments about the weather and the lack of decent local wine here in Washington, DC. Today is an exception regarding the former. The oppressive humidity common for the late spring is gloriously absent. She wants to enjoy every minute as she works through the hilly dirt trail.

Her mind wanders through her current case file, skimming through it from memory as if it were sitting in front of her. They're currently looking for a serial bomber targeting high-level Democrats. The bombs have been ineffective thus far, and the more she reads the files, the more she's convinced it was intentional. The bomber is patient, calculating, and the media attention they garnish is like a narcotic. She doesn't believe they intend to harm anyone, but instead want to stoke fear and paranoia. These facts, of course, don't absolve them from any crimes, but it does help to narrow down a profile to assist the agency in their apprehension.

Cassidy is deep in thought when she takes a corner on the trail and practically collides with a runner coming in the opposite direction. "I'm sorry." Once her bearings are back, she realizes that she recognizes the person in front of her. "Alex?"

Alex pulls her earbuds out and puts her hands on her hips, breathing heavily. "Oh, hey. What are you doing?" She rolls her eyes and says something under her breath. "I mean, obviously, you're running."

Alex is surprisingly adorable when she's flustered, and Cassidy can't help but smile. "I've never been on this trail before but thought I'd give it a try." Thor is losing his mind with the need to be rubbed by this new person. He's dancing in front of her, and Alex points to him as a way to ask for permission. "Sure, he might explode if you don't."

Alex gets down on her knees and rubs his big black head. "He's gorgeous." She turns her attention to him. "You're a gorgeous boy. Yes, you are."

Thor is smitten. He licks her and tries to crawl into her lap. Cassidy pulls on his leash. "Sorry. He has no concept of personal space."

"I have a cat, and all he wants is personal space. Well, until he doesn't."

Cassidy has never pictured Alex Derby with a pet of any kind. She just seemed too…too…what? Aloof maybe. "You have a cat?"

Alex shrugs. "Not on purpose. When he was a kitten, I saw him wandering around the parking lot at work. He kept crying and following me to my car. This went on for almost two weeks. When the weather got bad, I took him home. I was just going to get his shots done, get him fixed, and give him away." She shrugs again. "But I didn't know if the next person would know that he likes chicken flavor treats instead of fish. Then I started thinking that maybe he'd go to someone who wanted him to be just an indoor cat. Briggs would've been miserable. He needs to be able to meander. It seemed more practical to ensure his comfort myself."

Cassidy is utterly charmed by her matter-of-fact tone. "I think that's really sweet. He's lucky to have found you."

Alex stands and shifts her weight back and forth. She's clearly uncomfortable with compliments. "He's a good cat. A bit mouthy, but a solid decision. Ten out of ten. Would recommend."

Cassidy laughs. "I'll keep that in mind if I'm ever considering expanding my family." She checks her watch. "Hey, do you want to grab lunch? I'm almost done with my run. It might be fun to hang out."

Alex looks up at the sky and rolls her shoulders as if Cassidy had just asked something tremendously personal instead of making a friendly lunch invitation. "Okay. I can make that work. Do you mind coming to my house though? I had my heart set on homemade pizza, and I want to see it through." She points at Thor. "You can bring him. I like him."

Cassidy glances down at Thor, who looks thrilled by the use of the word pizza. "Sure, that sounds nice." Cassidy holds out her phone, and Alex enters her information. "I'll see you in a little over an hour then."

Alex puts her earbuds back in and rubs Thor's head again. "I'll warn Briggs."

Cassidy spends the remainder of her run considering the complexity of Alex Derby. She's notorious for being hard-headed, brash, and a bit of a hothead. But that's not what she witnessed at all. Sure, she's forward with what she wants, but that's not a character flaw. She's beginning to think the people who said those things haven't spent any real time with her. Hunter always spoke highly of Alex, but he never spoke ill of people unless he genuinely disliked them.

She glances down at Thor. "Doesn't hurt that she's beautiful too." He answers by wagging his tail and happily panting. She takes that as his agreement.

It takes a full ninety minutes for Cassidy to get home, shower, and head over to Alex's house. She hasn't spent much time picturing Alex's house before she arrives, but it doesn't involve a suburban neighborhood. Her house has a brick exterior, beautiful trees, and a large fenced-in yard. Children are playing in the street, and the smell of barbeque wafts through the air.

"Some profiler I am, huh, Thor?" She puts the car in park and heads up to the front door.

Thor sits next to her, bubbling with excitement as they wait for Alex. After a few moments, she hears a muffled call for her to come inside. Cassidy pushes the door open and looks around. The floors are all hardwood, and the walls are tastefully decorated with earth tones. The pictures on the wall are of Alex in different stages of her life, surrounded by who she assumes are her brother, sister, and parents based on their strikingly similar features. Alex's house is warm, airy, and comforting.

"I'm in the backyard," Alex calls.

Thor moves toward the back of the house, obviously eager to greet his new friend. Once Cassidy finally catches up, she finds Thor in the throes of an enthusiastic embrace with their hostess.

"Hi," Cassidy says, sounding shier than she intends.

"Hey." Alex nods toward the outdoor pizza oven. "Sorry, I was putting it in when you got here." She pets Thor again before heading to her outdoor fridge. "Want anything to drink?"

"Whatever you're having is fine."

"Perfectly mediocre beer it is." Alex pops the tops off two bottles and hands one to Cassidy as she sits down. "Thanks for agreeing to come over. I really did have my heart set on this pizza."

"I appreciate the invitation, but I'm a little disappointed Briggs isn't here to greet me."

Alex looks toward the house. "He's probably still asleep in his room. I'm sure he'll be down shortly. He needs a solid twenty to twenty-three hours a day of rest to stay handsome."

Cassidy laughs. "Your cat has his own room?"

"Of course," Alex says seriously. "He lives here. I'm not going to make him sleep on the couch."

Alex looks at her as if she's just answered an absurd question. It's clear that she's confident in all her decisions, no matter how silly they may seem to other people. Cassidy has spent enough time studying human behavior to be delighted by the anomaly. Alex is offbeat in the most delightful way possible.

"You're not really what I expected."

Alex smirks. "I assume that doesn't happen to you very often."

Cassidy nods. "Rarely."

"Well, I live to surprise people." She leans forward and pulls at the label of her beer. "I'll be honest. I don't normally hang out with people from work. I feel like it muddies the waters. Brunch last week was a first for me." She blushes slightly.

This piece of information is intriguing. It's difficult to make friends as an adult, and usually, people gravitate toward people they work with because there's an immediate and easily accessible common interest. Alex seems embarrassed by the admission, but Cassidy doesn't see it that way at all. She feels lucky and special.

"Why did you make an exception for me?" Cassidy tries to keep her tone nonchalant, but the answer matters far more than she realizes as she poses the question.

Alex seems to consider her response. "Because you asked, and you don't seem to have an agenda."

"Do you think people usually have an agenda when they ask to spend time with you?"

Alex looks at her sideways and squints. "Are you trying to profile me?"

Cassidy laughs. "No. Really, I'm genuinely curious."

Alex points to the pizza oven. "I need to rotate it."

Cassidy watches her work. She's always thought Alex was beautiful, but watching her in her element adds another layer of attraction. The cut-off jeans and tank top probably have something to do with it as well. Cassidy does her best to push down the stirring she feels in her stomach as Alex's muscles flex with the work of wielding the large wooden pizza paddle.

Alex sits back down and smiles. "So, do you?"

Cassidy wonders if she missed a large part of a conversation. Has she been so tied up staring at Alex's tan skin and green eyes that she blacked out for the last several minutes?

"Do I what?"

"Have an agenda?"

"I'd like to be friends. Do you consider that an agenda?" The friends part is partially true. Her attraction to Alex becomes more poignant with each passing minute she spends in her presence. But she won't be presumptuous, and friendship is better than nothing.

Alex studies her until a slight smile curls at the corner of her lips. "We'll see."

Cassidy raises her beer. "I guess we will." She takes a sip. "Are you seeing anyone?" *Real subtle.*

Alex shakes her head. "Most women don't like how much time I spend at work. They lose patience after a few months." She shrugs. "How about you? Any new men? I'm sure Hunter is a hard act to follow—especially since you two are still really close."

Cassidy has been questioned by the few men she dated after her divorce about why she remained such close friends with her ex. It came from a place of distrust and jealousy, but she gets the impression that isn't why Alex is mentioning it. The sincerity is refreshing.

"Hunter and I should've always just been friends. We're actually closer now than we were when we were married. I deeply value our relationship. But you're right. Men don't like it. I haven't dated a woman since him to see how they'll fare with the friendship."

A deep blush covers Alex's face, and Cassidy has to keep herself from laughing.

"I didn't know you dated women."

Cassidy smiles. "Now you do." It would be a lie to say she didn't enjoy watching the realization click in Alex's mind. Alex seems thrown by the information, and Cassidy likes being the cause of it. "But to answer your initial question, I'm not seeing anyone right now. Mostly for the same reason as you—I have no time."

"We can spend our limited time together then." Alex flushes red again. "Not like we're dating. I didn't mean it like that." She rubs the back of her neck. "I meant we can be friends since we don't have time to do anyone else…I mean, spend time with anyone else." She lets her chin fall to her chest. "Feel free to let me off the hook any time now."

Cassidy sips her beer. "I think I'm going to watch this one play out entirely. You know, see it all the way through."

Alex reaches down to pet Thor. "Your mom is ruthless." She stands and heads to the pizza oven. "Spared by the need for nourishment."

"For now," Cassidy calls back.

While Alex busies herself with getting their lunch, Cassidy tries to remember a time when she felt this at ease with someone she's only seen a few times. Sure, it was easy with Hunter, but it wasn't like this. She'd known immediately that Hunter was trying to sleep with her. It was written all over his body language and dripped from every innuendo he tossed at her. It's a stark contrast to the limited time she's spent with Alex. She's relaxed and almost giddy at the possibility of spending more time with her. That train of thought is jarring in the best possible way.

It would be real cool if you stopped being such a goddamn weirdo. But is that something you can manage? No. Obviously not. Alex doesn't typically suffer from anxiety—it just isn't how she's built. But she'd give anything to take back the last several minutes of verbal blunder she'd just spewed.

Her mind slides in dozens of different directions. It's not just because she's attracted to Cassidy. She's old enough to know that attraction can mask red flags that a person can wave off as insignificant—until it's not. Her gut tells her Cassidy is trustworthy. Well, her gut and the countless hours she's spent listening to Hunter talk about the kind of person she is, even after their divorce.

Since last week she's been considering Hunter and Cassidy's offer about her white whale. She's spent the better part of two years trying to break this case. Maybe it's time for a new set of eyes. Cassidy is somewhat of a happy accident because those beautiful blue eyes are attached to the mind of a profiler, and that may be precisely what she needs.

She pulls the pizza from the oven and rolls the cutter through it. Certainly, there's a limited amount of time one can spend cutting a pizza before it becomes apparent they're avoiding something else, and she's rapidly approaching that limit.

She puts the plate in front of Cassidy. "If you hate it, don't tell me. My heart can't take it."

Cassidy takes a bite and groans. "Oh, my God." She takes another bite and closes her eyes. "It's absolutely terrible. You should never feed this to anyone ever again."

Alex tosses her napkin at her. "Nice." She takes a bite out of her pizza. "You're a real gem. You know that?"

Cassidy smiles and shrugs. "I've definitely been called worse."

"Please, I was told just last week that I should be more like you."

Cassidy scrunches her nose. "Who told you that?"

"Assistant Director Peterson. He said you're delightful." Alex intentionally leaves the part out where he called her a girl.

Cassidy's mood seems to shift slightly. "I've never really liked him."

Alex wants nothing more than to swing the conversation in another direction. "Can I show you something without you thinking I'm an absolute head case?"

This seems to pique Cassidy's interest. She raises her eyebrow. "That depends. It may be a little soon to show me a sex dungeon."

"It's definitely not a sex dungeon." Alex stands, but then it clicks. "When *is* a good time to disclose a sex dungeon?"

"That's a third date topic, for sure." Cassidy clears her throat, but she doesn't correct the usage of the word date, which is very interesting.

Alex takes her down to the basement before she can talk herself out of it. She's never shown anyone what she is about to show Cassidy. She's not even sure why she's doing it. She hardly knows her, and hasn't had time to forge a bond of trust with her. But her decision doesn't waver, even as they get closer. Alex needs help with this project, and her gut has yet to oscillate from its initial appraisal. On the other hand, the last two years will all be for nothing if she runs out of time, and that tipping point is rapidly approaching.

Alex opens the door and turns on the light. She holds her breath while Cassidy moves to her wall-sized whiteboard and takes in the information. Cassidy walks up and down it several times, pausing only briefly to look back at Alex as if she's checking that what she's seeing is real. She tries to imagine what it would be like to be standing in Cassidy's shoes right now, and it's nothing short of shocking that she hasn't run out the door.

Alex stands beside her and takes a deep breath. There's no good place to start, so the easiest plan of attack is to simply jump in. "This is everything that I've gathered over the last two years. I've been doing it completely off book and on my own time." In her head, the justification is essential to prove the only time potentially being wasted is her own.

"Can you tell me what I'm looking at here?" Cassidy's voice is calm and even. There's no hint of anything she may be feeling. It should be reassuring, but it leaves a bitter taste of desperation in Alex's mouth.

Alex briefly flashes back to the first glimmer of this case. "A few years ago, we questioned Roger McMinn about a hit-and-run where he was the suspect. I'm not sure if you remember him, but he's a disgraced representative out of North Carolina." She glances at Cassidy and sees recognition in her eyes, so she doesn't elaborate further on his backstory. "He was in the middle of a primary fight and was throwing out all kinds of wild accusations. He was flailing. He accused sitting House members of having orgies, doing drugs—things like that. None of it interested or surprised me until he commented on fixing the next election. He said we should watch our backs because we'd be the ones behind bars if everything worked out the way they'd planned. He said it was all but guaranteed." She presses her thumb between her eyes to release some of the pressure that's been building since she started her explanation. "Everyone else thought he'd lost it. The GOP turned on him, and he lost his primary by a few points. It was nothing outlandish, but I couldn't get what he said out of my head." She points to the board. "So I started digging. I lifted small stones at first, shook a few trees, nothing to put me on anyone's radar."

She takes a deep breath and ignores the sweat accumulating on her palms. "Then I was sitting behind two guys in a café popular with politicians. They kept discussing Ascendancy. The word stood out because I'd heard the company name discussed on the news. They're responsible for Canada's voting machines and had recently won the bid for large swaths of America. One of the men discussed how their auditing process worked, different encryption protections, and physical locks and seals." Alex points to a picture of one of the machines taped to her board. "To anyone listening, it could just be an average conversation about voting machine protection, and I thought it might be—until I heard the last sentence. Before they left, one guy told the other that the remainder of the funding had been secured by America First." Alex pulls a picture of Jeffery Fletcher down from the board. "I recognized the phrase but didn't think it was an actual organization, so I did a little digging. America First is registered as a shipping company, but it's nothing more than a shell. That in and of itself isn't illegal, but the previous owner was listed as Fletcher Industries. People establish shell companies to transfer assets of a previous company without inheriting their liabilities. America First was previously known under Fletcher as American Stands. Now it's operated by an anonymous LLC out of New Mexico. Sketchy as hell, but again—not illegal." Alex shrugs. "Someone has gone to extraordinary lengths to create a company that could hold copious amounts of money and ship large products without being tied to any one person."

Cassidy taps the picture against her hand. "What exactly are you trying to say?"

Alex takes a deep breath and doesn't allow herself a moment to consider the implications of what she's going to say. "I think there's a high-level plot to steal the next presidential election. The corruption runs deep and reaches the highest levels of elected officials." Cassidy's eyes are fixed on her, and it's slightly distracting, but she keeps going. "I don't think the plan is as unsophisticated as they made it out to be this last time. No one is stealing mail-in ballots or committing voter fraud. I think they're having duplicate voter machines made that have already been manipulated. They'll

PROFILE

use them in a few swing districts to push the election toward the Republican nominee."

"Won't they audit the machines?"

Alex shakes her head. "I think they're going to write a code that will self-destruct. It will be untraceable. I believe the code is going to change every other Democratic vote to Republican. That system makes it impossible to figure out who will be picked."

"But they can audit those too. They can check the rolls against the votes and prove it's fraud. Surely someone will question why so many registered Democrats suddenly voted for a Republican, especially if there's any pattern. Not to mention, something like this involves a lot of people. Someone will talk. Someone always talks."

Alex nods. "I think they want people to talk. The intent isn't to actually win. It's to sow chaos and fear. They want another civil war. You saw how it went last time, and there was no actual evidence of voter fraud. The country is like a powder keg, and all it needs is a small spark. No one will know who to trust, and everything will fall apart. Democracy works because we believe it does. If that belief goes away—"

"Jesus Christ. We'll fall into autocracy before anyone can prove what happened. Then, even if there's proof, it won't matter. Elections will hold no value."

"Exactly." The validation of someone not only listening but understanding what's at stake and agreeing makes her skin tingle.

Cassidy turns to face her. Her eyes look desperate. It's like she's searching for something. "Why are you telling me? Why are you trusting me?"

Alex rubs the back of her neck and takes a deep breath. "I need help. I'm running out of time to prove all of this." She waves at the board. "And for whatever reason, I feel like I can trust you. I know it's asking a lot, but I don't know what else to do. I can't sit back and do nothing."

Cassidy looks down at Thor, dutifully sitting between them, looking back and forth. "I'll help you."

"Really?"

• 41 •

"Yeah, I mean, what kind of agent would I be if I didn't? What kind of person?" She rubs Thor's head and gives him a sad smile. "Who else have you told?"

"No one at the Bureau. I have a few contacts in the tech world who've been helping me. I also have a friend at the CIA who tipped me off and gets me info when she can, but that's it."

Cassidy nods and moves closer to the board. "We should get started."

Alex takes a deep breath and sends a silent thanks out into the universe for bringing her to that trail this morning.

CHAPTER FOUR

It's edging close to midnight when Cassidy finally tosses the last of the files onto the desk. It's all still a bit surreal. As a child raised in America, you're taught to believe certain truths. Some of those ideals crumble under the weight of reality as you get older. Thanksgiving wasn't a harmonious exchange between the Natives and the European colonizers—it was genocide. Our white ancestors traded, purchased, and treated human beings like they were less valuable than livestock and then made those same people fight for even a scrap of the rights white men were handed at birth. Women weren't *given* the right to vote—they fought, were beaten, spit on, and in some cases, murdered in order to gain it.

Cassidy is under no illusions. She knows politics is a dirty game. But finding out an elite portion of our politicians are willing to burn the whole thing to the ground and watch their fellow citizens die in the streets in order to steal and maintain power...it's like discovering Santa isn't real. You always knew it was a possibility but weren't quite ready to give up that last bit of naivete. They were no longer cloaking their plans or intentions in the shadows of some extremist group. They were infecting people with real power and means. The consequences could be dire.

She rolls her shoulders to loosen some of the tension that's been building at the base of her neck. She finishes gulping down the last of her water when she hears Alex coming down the stairs.

Alex hands her a purring orange cat. "This is Briggs. He may or may not make you feel better. It depends on his mood."

Cassidy stares at the orange tabby. One eye is focused on her, and the other has more colors than Cassidy has the vocabulary to identify. "Has his eye always been like this?"

"He's blind in the one. He got into a fight a while back, and it's never been the same." Briggs lets out a weird chirp to weigh in on Alex's summation. "He's got quite the mouth on him."

Cassidy scratches his head and smiles at the way he leans into her. "He's so sweet." Thor walks over to investigate, and Briggs seems completely unbothered. "Does he like dogs?"

"He knows they exist in the world. He just doesn't care."

Briggs jumps off Cassidy's lap and lets Thor smell him. Thor seems to think he's found his long-lost best friend and starts spinning in circles. He gets down into his play position and practically falls over with excitement when Briggs drags his tail across his face.

Alex pulls up a chair and leans forward with her elbows on her knees. "Now that you've read everything I have, what do you think?"

"I think we're fucked."

Alex nods slowly. "I was hoping for a more formal assessment, but we can start there."

Cassidy sighs. "I can't give you a profile on any one person because this is obviously in the hands of several, possibly dozens. I think we need some hard evidence before we take this anywhere else. If we swing and miss on this one, we're the only people who will lose." She grabs one of the file folders off the table. "Tell me more about the tech guy you've been working with. Do you trust him?"

Alex nods. "I got his name from my contact over at the CIA. They'd gone to MIT together, and she vouched for him. She set up our first conversation, and I've been working with him ever since."

"And this contact at the CIA, how do you know her? They've been known to set people up just to watch them fall. Why isn't she working on this? It seems like we all have a vested interest in democracy not crumbling around us."

"I've known Brooke since she was a kid. I used to babysit her. Her dad was career Navy, and my dad worked with him pretty frequently once he took a position at the Pentagon. She's now a computer analyst for the CIA, and her wife, Tyler, works for Homeland Security. She sends me pieces here and there, but CIA workstations are closely monitored, and they undergo polygraphs pretty frequently. She works with a team, and they'll assist us, but only when we get our ducks in a row. We can't take the chance of showing our hand any sooner. If Brooke elevates this with the CIA before we have any hard evidence, we may get shut out and lose our chance to bring these people down. But, as I said, I'm not sure how high this goes, and we can't risk it."

Cassidy sits up straighter, immediately knowing who she's referencing. "Brooke Hart and Tyler Monroe?"

Alex nods. "You know them?"

"I don't live under a rock. They circumvented the last attempt at a government coup. I read Carol O'Brien's interview after she was arrested. They're responsible for bringing her down." She blows out a long breath. "They're very impressive."

Alex walks over to the whiteboard and writes the number eight. "We have eight weeks to break this case. Voting machines go out to their designated districts in nine weeks. We have to stop them before they're sent out for delivery. I'm meeting with my tech guy tomorrow. Will you come with me?"

Cassidy doesn't hesitate. "Absolutely."

Alex walks over to a safe, pulls out a cell phone, and hands it to Cassidy. "Only use this phone when discussing or texting about any of this."

Cassidy takes the phone. "What time tomorrow?"

"Meet me at the parking lot of the trail we were at today at zero nine hundred."

"How very James Bond." Cassidy slides the phone into her pocket. "Is there anything else I need to know before we meet with this guy tomorrow?"

Alex chews on her bottom lip. "He's a bit awkward. It can be off-putting if you aren't expecting it." She shifts her weight back and forth. "I appreciate you agreeing to help me. I know you don't really have a reason to trust me. So thank you."

Cassidy finds herself unable to pull her attention away from Alex's lips. She mentally scolds herself for wondering what they'd feel like against her neck when they have such a monumental task in front of them. She has no business thinking about Alex in any way other than as a friend and a colleague. Yet she feels a pull to Alex she can't quite explain.

"You're welcome. Thanks for trusting me." She turns her attention to Thor before her thoughts transform into action. "Let's go, buddy. Big day tomorrow." Thor gets up from the puddle of fur he's created with Briggs and walks beside her. "The pizza was fantastic, by the way."

Alex smirks. "I know."

Cassidy heads up the basement stairs before her attraction gets the best of her. She shakes her arms out in the cool breeze of the night air. She's out of sorts, and the loss of control is unnerving, no matter how minuscule. She sets her thoughts on tomorrow and tries her best not to think about Alex at all. Although, the likelihood of her being successful at the intended task is minimal at best.

Cassidy drums her fingers against the steering wheel as she waits for Alex to arrive. She's listening to an audiobook, but none of the words are infiltrating her mind. It's all background noise to the racing thoughts in her head. She'd been so caught off guard by the enormity of the situation and her unfortunate attraction to Alex that the gravity of it wasn't tangible. It wasn't until she'd tried to find sleep in the silence that the weight of the situation took up residence on her chest.

People are a kaleidoscope of thoughts, feelings, motives, traumas, and experiences. No two ever turn out the same. There are countless examples of people with normal childhoods who went on to do terrible and unspeakable things: Dennis Rader, Richard Cottingham, Ted Bundy, and Randy Kraft. Their siblings, friends, and family all noted the absence of family trauma. Some would even go as far as to say they were popular and well-liked. Yet, they went on to be some of the most prolific serial killers ever to live. What made them different? It was that question that had drawn Cassidy to the BAU.

That question is behind every major professional decision Cassidy has ever made. It's part of what brought her here today. The serial killers she's interviewed impact not only the victims and their families but the way people perceive the world. They were the thieves of innocence and cautionary tales for vigilance. This situation isn't any of those things. This tableau is shrouded in narcissism, power, and greed. The excitement prickles her skin, and she wonders, not for the first time, how much darkness lives inside her too.

Alex pulls up alongside her and motions for her to get in the car. She's pleasantly surprised by the coffee Alex hands her and can't help but smile when she points to a bag with about twenty creams and sugars.

"I don't know how you like your coffee. Just covering my bases," Alex says as she pulls out of the parking lot and gets on the highway.

"I know it's cool to say you like it black, but I don't." Cassidy opens several coffee creamers and pours them into her cup. "In fact, the less like coffee it tastes, the better."

"Then why drink coffee at all?"

"I don't think the Bureau wants me doing lines of cocaine to stay awake."

Without missing a beat, Alex answers, "I remember seeing that memo."

It doesn't take long to reach their destination. St. Elizabeth's Hospital has been abandoned for almost twenty years, but it's an intimidating presence, nonetheless. It's one of the country's first psychiatric hospitals, and the decaying brick shows the one-hundred and sixty-something years of age.

"This is the guy's hideout? Seems a little too on the nose," Cassidy whispers.

Alex shakes her head and looks confused. "What? No." She points to a van in the parking lot.

Alex knocks twice and waits for someone to answer. The van door cracks open, and a single eye looks Cassidy up and down before closing.

Alex knocks again. "Leo, open the door."

"I didn't approve an additional party, Alex. You can come in when you get rid of her." His voice is muffled behind the door.

Alex rolls her eyes and crosses her arms. "She's a profiler. She's here to help."

It takes several seconds for him to open the door again. "Full name."

Cassidy points to herself. "Me?"

"Obviously."

"Cassidy Wolf." When he doesn't answer, she continues. "I've been with the Bureau for—"

"Parents are Marjorie and Scott Wolf. You graduated from UC Berkeley with a master's in political science and a second one in psychology. You've been with the Bureau for ten years. Four of them with the BAU. You graduated at the top of your class and were recruited by the CIA and NSA, but you chose the FBI." He opens the door and sticks out his head. "Why waste your time at the FBI? You could've been so much more."

Cassidy doesn't bother asking how he knows what he does. She read his file too, and his hacking skills are unmatched. "Probably the same reason you turned them down when they asked you to join."

He squints. "Issues with authority?"

She smiles. "To piss off my parents."

He slides the door open and waves them inside. Monitors of all different sizes line the inside of the van. There are four different keyboards set up and a large bank of drives under a small flimsy table. He points to Alex's pocket, and she pulls out her phone. Cassidy mimics her actions and hands her phone to Leo. He places two small silver dots on both and hands them back.

"He disabled our microphones and location," Alex whispers to her.

"This is quite the setup you have in here. When we first pulled up, I thought you'd set up shop inside the hospital," Cassidy says as she puts her phone back in her pocket.

He opens a Red Bull and pulls a cupholder down from the side of the van. "That's absurd."

"Because you need to be able to move quickly?" Cassidy adjusts herself on top of a small milk crate.

He looks at her as if she's just asked the most ridiculous question in the history of conversation. "Because it's haunted." He points at her and looks at Alex. "You couldn't find a better profiler?"

"Did you run those names I gave you?" Alex ignores his question.

He blows out a long breath and swivels in his chair toward a computer. "These guys are terrible." He pounds away on his keyboard. "Jeffery Fletcher is into some shady shenanigans. He has his fingers in everything." After a few more keystrokes, another picture fills the screen. "Senator Miles Christie is no better. They're both involved in several overseas black market deals. They've done a really good job of trying to cover their tracks, but nothing is anonymous anymore. Not for people like me anyway."

"Anything that ties them to voting machines?" Alex pinches the bridge of her nose, and Cassidy has to stop herself from asking if she has a headache.

Leo smiles. "Both Fletcher and Christie have purchased four hundred mattresses each from Mattress Lounge. They've been donated to various shelters from New Orleans to DC."

Cassidy feels like she's missing something. "Donating to the homeless doesn't seem all that nefarious."

Leo rolls his eyes and turns back to his computer. "I guess it's a good thing you're a profiler and not a detective."

Alex sighs. "Don't be a dick." She turns her attention to Cassidy. "We've thought for quite a while that the company, Mattress Lounge, is a way to launder money and hide black market purchases."

Cassidy's cheeks flush with embarrassment. She can vividly remember having conversations with people about the odd number of these stores in close proximity to each other. She never considered they were a front—and she absolutely should have. She's been exposed to the inner workings of the worst of humanity but never thought to give such an obvious anomaly a second thought.

Alex gives her a sympathetic smile as if she knows what she's thinking. "It works because it's obvious. People tend to assume the sleight of hand happening in front of them is a misconception on their part."

"I don't," Leo says as he continues to type. "Here." He points to his screen. "I have all the transactions. It looks like they paid one thousand five hundred and fifty dollars for each mattress and frame. These usually run about three hundred for the full setup." He looks up at the ceiling for a brief moment. "That's a four hundred and sixteen percent markup—a total payout of one million dollars when considering purchases from both parties."

"Does a million dollars buy coding to take down an entire government?" Cassidy looks at Alex, a small part of her hoping it will cost more to incite a coup.

Alex sighs. "No, but it's a good down payment."

Leo nods. "Assuming the American dollar will be worth almost nothing after this comes to fruition, I'll keep an eye out for other anomalies. If it were me, I'd be looking for purchases that can be tied to the euro, yen, pound, yuan, and franc. I'd consolidate them in an account in the Cayman Islands and laugh all the way to Laos."

"Do we have any leads on who is writing the code or where the money eventually came together?"

Leo eyes Cassidy. His mouth twists before he answers. "Brooke sent me a name for the coder, but I haven't found the end of the funnel of money yet." He pulls a small piece of paper from his pocket and hands it to Alex. "Before you go chasing this guy down, I think you should know something." He chews on his thumb cuticle. "He's not like you and me. He's volatile, manipulative, and sometimes violent. Serious bad guy vibes."

"How do you know him?" Alex puts the piece of paper in her pocket.

"He was at MIT with Brooke and me."

"Do you think he'd be willing to see Brooke again? Maybe she could get close enough to get us some information."

Leo waves dismissively. "Have you seen Brooke? Of course he'd be willing to see her." He hands her a small black box. "I need you to get within three feet of him with this in your pocket. As soon as you're close enough, text me, and I'll use this to clone his phone. Even if he's encrypted his device, and I'm sure he has, I can hack it if I know it's happening. Once I can do that, I can clone his computer when he gets near it."

Alex flips the device over in her hand. "It's illegal to clone a phone without a warrant."

He makes a face and mocks her. "It's illegal to clone a phone without a warrant. Do you want to get these guys or not?"

Without thinking, Cassidy puts her hand on Alex's leg. "I know a judge who will help us out with a warrant. I trust her."

Alex nods and shifts in her seat when Cassidy pulls her hand away. "How long do we need to be near him to ensure it takes?"

Leo tilts his head back and forth like he's thinking. "Five minutes, but ten would be ideal. I'll text you when it's done." He glares at Cassidy. "I assume you understand what's at stake here?"

"I do."

He chugs the rest of the Red Bull and slams the can in the wastebasket at his feet. "This is my only lead. Don't blow it. We're running out of time." He grabs Alex's arm when she goes to stand. "Be careful. I know you think I'm sometimes prone to the dramatic, but he's dangerous."

Alex nods once and opens the door to the van. "I'll text you when we're close to him."

Once they're in the car, Alex tucks the device Leo gave her into a small bag in the back seat. "So that was Leo."

"He's an interesting character."

"Interesting is one way to describe him." She slides on her sunglasses and exhales deeply.

Cassidy isn't familiar enough with her facial expressions to pinpoint her feelings, but it doesn't take an expert to sense Alex's stress. Cassidy thinks about the burden she's been essentially carrying on her own. Alex seems like the kind of person who carries the world's weight on her shoulders because she either doesn't want to admit it's too heavy, or she doesn't know any other way. Cassidy wants nothing more than to make her feel better, but she gets the feeling that addressing it outright will make her defensive.

"Want me to get a hold of the judge to see about the warrant?"

Alex rests her head against the steering wheel and closes her eyes. "If I say no, will you still help me?"

Cassidy reaches for her. She pulls Alex's shoulder back, forcing her to make eye contact. "That depends on why you don't want the warrant."

Alex sighs and shakes her head. "You saw the list of people who could be involved. Their reach is vast. I know you trust this judge, but what if that's misplaced? What if they're connected? I don't know if we can risk it."

Cassidy's fingers still rest on Alex's shoulder, and she makes no move to place them elsewhere. Every voice that has ever lived in her head is screaming to follow protocol. But her gut tells her to follow Alex's lead in this instance. Will protocol matter if they can't stop this from happening? Hell, there may not even be an FBI to answer to if they can't stop this.

Cassidy fights the urge to rub Alex's knotted shoulder. "Okay, but we have to tell Hunter what's happening."

Alex closes her eyes again. "I don't want to drag anyone else into this."

Cassidy gives in to the thrumming in her chest and rubs Alex's cheek with her thumb. "Hunter isn't just anyone. He's one of the best at the FBI, and you know that. You said yourself that we're running out of time. If you're going to start pressing people, and it sounds like you are, it's essential to have more knowing eyes and ears on our side. The implications of what this could mean if we can't stop it could have a global reach. You need a team. Even Brooke and Tyler have a team. Plus, he'll have a million questions when he finds out I'm going with you to wherever"—she points to Alex's pocket—"is written on that little piece of paper."

"San Francisco," Alex says quietly. Her sight drifts from Cassidy's eyes down to her lips. "You're right about Hunter. I should've told him a long time ago."

The silence isn't awkward or uncomfortable. It's crackling with whatever is happening between them. Cassidy would've already kissed her if this were the end of a date. The realization forces her to remove her hand from where it rests against the delicate skin of Alex's neck. This certainly isn't the time to treat their situation like anything other than work. There's too much at stake.

"Let's go talk to Hunter."

Cassidy nods because she doesn't trust her voice. The severity of the situation itself could have her feeling out of sorts, and maybe it has nothing to do with Alex at all. It may even be the speed and intensity of what is at stake as they navigate territory never covered in any coursework she's been exposed to during her time leading up to and since the FBI. She's craving the familiar and comfortable, and Hunter fills that bill.

CHAPTER FIVE

"What the fuck, Derby?" Hunter runs his hands through his hair and begins to pace. He stops at the wall-sized window and stares out at the street below. "How long have you been chasing this down?" There's no venom in his voice. On the contrary, he sounds hurt.

"Almost two years." She glances over at Cassidy, who gives her a half-hearted smile. "Don't take it personally. I haven't told anyone."

Hunter turns his attention to her. "You told Cassidy." He puts his hands on his hips. "How did you think you'd pull this off on your own? Are you really that desperate to get out of the unit?"

The accusation stings. "I didn't keep you out to collect the glory for myself. I kept it to myself because of the probability of it blowing up in my face. And I didn't know if I was chasing ghosts, imagining the connections." She stands. "I'm not some arrogant prick despite what the others say of me. You should know better." She's fully aware of what the agents think and say about her, but she expects more from Hunter. He's spent time with her, and he should know what does and doesn't motivate her.

He stares at her for several beats, and then his face softens. "I know you're not. I'm sorry. This just wasn't what I was expecting to hear when you called and asked if you could come over." He puts his hand on her shoulder. "What do you need from me?"

There's lulling anger still simmering at his explanation, but she forces herself to let it go. She doesn't have time for unnecessary emotions. "Cassidy, Brooke, and I are heading to San Francisco for a few days. I need you to test the waters with a few bosses while we're gone. See if there's anyone we may be able to trust if we come back with any information."

"You haven't done that yet?"

She sighs, annoyed that she has to spell it out for him. "People don't like me the way they like you. You have the ability to work it into a conversation—I don't."

He doesn't argue her assessment. "How long are you going to be gone?"

"A few days. I don't know how long it will take to convince this guy to meet with us."

He nods. "I know this goes without saying, but be careful. We have no way of knowing what could happen if this guy gets spooked." He puts his hands up before she can respond. "I know you're capable, but I'd say the same to anyone."

"We will." She turns to walk to the door. "Hey, Hunter?" She shifts her weight back and forth, trying to put the words she wants to say together in her head. "Thanks for believing me." The statement only scratches the surface of what she's feeling, but it's all she can muster.

He grabs her and hugs her. "I'll even check on your cat if you give me a key to your house."

"Really?" She steps back and looks at him.

He laughs. "Yeah. We're friends, Alex." He pats her on the shoulder. "That's what friends do for each other."

Cassidy hugs him. "I'm glad you said that because I'm going to need Thor to stay here while I'm gone."

He chuckles and shakes his head. "So you two get to go off and save the world, and I'm stuck here pet sitting."

Cassidy shrugs. "Fuck the patriarchy, right?"

He smiles. "Right." He kisses her cheek. "Be careful. I love you."

She rubs his arms. "Love you too."

Alex waits until they're in the silence of the car to ask the question that's been bouncing around her head for the last several minutes. "Are you sure you want to go with us? I know you want to help, but Brooke and I can do this, and we can meet up when I get back."

Alex knows she sprung this situation on Cassidy. Sure, Cassidy said she wants to help, but Alex wants to make sure before she gets in too far. She needs to give her one last opportunity to get out before there's no turning back. Alex wants an honest answer, but even as she says it, she knows it will hurt her in a way it shouldn't if Cassidy wants out now.

Cassidy's expression is serious. "Of course, I'm going with you." She puts her hand over Alex's. "I'm in this now, no matter what happens."

As if realizing she's touching her, Cassidy quickly removes her hand. Alex almost reaches for her, wanting nothing more than to feel the tangible connection. But she doesn't. Cassidy pulled away for a reason, and Alex has no intention of pushing those boundaries—not now.

Alex starts the car. "I better get you home so you can pack." She turns onto the main road. "Brooke texted. I'm going to book us on the zero eight hundred flight for tomorrow morning."

Cassidy nods. "I'll drop Thor off with Hunter on my way to the airport." She pulls out her phone. "I'll make the hotel reservations in San Francisco."

"That's not necessary. I can manage."

Cassidy lifts an eyebrow. "Do I need to remind you that I'm from there?"

"I have Google."

Cassidy scoffs. "I'm better than Google when it comes to this. I have a friend who works at one of the big hotels. He'll check us in under false names. It will help us be undercover. Just trust me."

Alex nods her consent. Cassidy has no way of knowing that she already trusts her with far more than what she's typically comfortable allowing. It goes beyond her skills as a profiler, although Alex is sure those will come in handy. It's also not because of the undeniable attraction she feels toward Cassidy. That would usually cause her to keep her distance in a professional setting. Cassidy says what she's thinking, asks thoughtful questions, and if she has an agenda, Alex hasn't seen it yet. Alex trusts her because Cassidy is unmistakably herself.

❖

"You look like hammered dog shit." Brooke smiles and hugs her.

"Here I was worried about being embarrassed by your endless compliments." Alex kisses her cheek. "I don't think I slept more than an hour last night."

Brooke raises an eyebrow. "I hope it was in the name of extravagant sex."

Alex laughs. "More like excessive anxiety about what we're getting ourselves into."

Brooke slaps her arm. "You're no fun." She looks behind Alex. "Where's Cassidy?"

Alex nods toward the endless row of overpriced shops and restaurants. "She said something about it not being legal to fly without gummy worms."

Brooke smiles. "Woman after my own heart." She sits and pats the seat next to her. "I noticed when looking through her file—"

"Of course you looked through her file." Alex shakes her head.

"Obviously." She squints at her. "As I was saying, I noticed that she's your type."

"I don't have a type." Alex intentionally doesn't look at her. Brooke has always been able to see right through her bullshit.

"Umm, yes, you do, and she's it."

Alex notices Cassidy walking back over and gives Brooke a look that states the conversation needs to end. "Don't embarrass me."

Brooke puts a hand against her chest. "I'm not twelve anymore. I would never."

"Yes, you absolutely would."

Brooke sticks her tongue out and extends her hand to shake Cassidy's. "Cassidy Wolf, it's so nice to meet you. I'm Brooke Hart."

Cassidy smiles warmly. "I'm so happy to meet you, Brooke. Alex speaks very highly of you."

Brooke smacks Alex's leg. "That's only because she doesn't want me telling all the torrid details of her teenage rebellion." Brooke doesn't wait for anyone to ask her to elaborate. "Did she tell you about when she was supposed to be babysitting me and snuck her girlfriend over to watch movies with us?"

Alex sighs. "I didn't sneak anyone. I asked your parents for permission. I swear they think it's my fault you're gay."

Brooke nods. "I make sure always to blame you, so that makes sense."

Cassidy laughs. "It's hard for me to picture Alex as a teenager. I know intellectually that she was, but it's difficult to imagine. You know what I mean?"

Brooke nods. "I do. It's because she's such a Rule Book Randy."

Alex scoffs. "You married a Rule Book Randy."

Brooke looks as if she's going to respond, but their boarding announcement cuts off her thought. Alex sends a silent thanks to whatever entity has just saved her from Brooke's teasing.

"I like her," Cassidy whispers against her.

"She gets that a lot."

"Don't worry. I like you too." The way Cassidy smiles at her sends a jolt of electricity through her body.

Alex is so caught off guard by the comment that she doesn't have a chance to respond before the line starts moving. She's left alone to ponder the push and pull they both seem to be playing. She knows there's something between them. Alex is acutely aware of Cassidy's proximity to her at all times, and when they aren't together, she can't help but think about her. Cassidy isn't like anyone she's ever dated, despite what Brooke says. Alex tends to draw the damaged, the needy, and the broken. Cassidy isn't any of those things, which is far more terrifying than anything she's feeling.

CHAPTER SIX

The flight had gone by much faster than any other cross-country journey Cassidy had made since moving to the East Coast. She'd sat between Brooke and Alex, and after the chatting subsided and Brooke and Cassidy had settled into their books, Alex had fallen asleep. It only took about twenty minutes before her head ended up on Cassidy's shoulder. Cassidy couldn't concentrate on anything she was reading. Her thoughts kept tripping over the feeling of Alex so close to her. The smell of her hair, the cadence of her breathing, and the soft noises that escaped her throat. Cassidy didn't want it to end.

Now here she stood, in the bathroom of her hotel room, staring at herself in the mirror. There are two choices in front of her. She can either continue to push the feelings away and remain professional or jump in headfirst. She should push them away. She's been telling herself that since she started spending time with Alex, but it's becoming increasingly more difficult.

A knock on the door pulls her from her internal reflection. She splashes some water on her face and gives herself one more glance in the mirror before opening the door.

Brooke walks in with Alex on her heels. Brooke pulls a small black box from her back pocket. She pushes a switch on the side and places the box on the desk. Cassidy doesn't need to ask what it is. She knows the device keeps people from listening in. It emits a low frequency to prohibit people from hearing what they're saying.

Brooke claps her hands together. "Okay, bring me up to speed on everything."

Cassidy listens as Alex fills Brooke in on the last few days. Their interaction is anchored in the familiar, and she finds herself grateful that the aloof Alex has had someone like Brooke in her life for so long. Brooke is strikingly beautiful. There's no other way to put it. Her confidence only accentuates that fact. When people talk about magnetism, they mean Brooke. But Brooke isn't who has her attention. Alex possesses an androgynous appeal that most can't pull off—even when they're trying. It's effortless for Alex. Her confidence matches Brooke's, but its foundation doesn't come from her awareness of her looks. Instead, it's rooted in her intelligence and zero tolerance for bullshit. Cassidy's skin prickles as she traces the lines of Alex's bare arms and strong back with her eyes.

She shakes herself when she hears her name. "I'm sorry. What was that?"

Brooke smiles knowingly. "How do you feel about a stakeout?"

Cassidy leans forward, giving Brooke her full attention. "I love a stakeout. What are you thinking?" The first part isn't true. Cassidy's never been on a stakeout, but that isn't important. She doesn't want anyone to think she's letting her mind wander to anything other than the case, especially when her focus was entirely on how Alex looks.

"I had the unfortunate experience of going to MIT with Hugh Bradley for two years and between Leo and I, we figured out he's at least one link in the chain of this clusterfuck. I don't know if he's the final code creator or just someone working alongside someone smarter. He works for Goldstone, a cybersecurity firm. His primary role is encryption software, and I have to admit that he's good at what he does. He's also obnoxious, mean, and vicious. He's also a creature of habit through and through." Brooke shakes her head as if she's thinking about a specific memory. "There's a coffee shop inside his building, but he's not going to go to it. He'll use the craft coffee shop across the street. He's a snob about his coffee, and he won't want to associate with anyone he works with."

Cassidy nods her understanding. "Sounds like he's a narcissist. He thinks he's special. He's arrogant, entitled, and lacks empathy.

He gets hyper-focused on fantasies of great success and needs high levels of admiration to function."

"That's him exactly," Brooke says and sits at the desk. "If we keep an eye on the coffee shop, we'll be able to run into him, so to speak."

"All we need is five to ten minutes near him, and that should be that," Alex says. "It seems too easy." She looks between Cassidy and Brooke. "Will he be paranoid? Is this something Brooke should do on her own, or should we go with her?"

Cassidy contemplates the question. "Did he have a thing for you in college, and does he know you're gay?"

Brooke nods. "He was borderline obsessive. It got to the point where I took a different route to several of my classes to avoid him. But, yes, he's aware that I'm a lesbian."

"What's the rest of his job history? Do you know if he worked directly for any women?"

Brooke pulls a file from her bag and flips through the pages. "He left MIT six years ago and has had seven jobs." She flips over a few more pages. "If he had a female supervisor, he'd stay at his position for no more than five months."

Cassidy sighs. "Our best course of action would be to convince him that you're dating one of us and that we have a job in tech. He won't be able to pass up the chance to try to prove that he's smarter and better than either me or Alex. It will buy us the most time with him. Even if he wanted to, he wouldn't be able to blow you off. He'll want to prove that you're missing out and that you should've been with him."

"I'll do it," Alex says.

Brooke scrunches her nose. "No offense. You know I love you, but you're not his type. I think it would work better if Cassidy went with me."

Alex looks at Cassidy. "Do you agree?"

Cassidy shrugs. "It will make him less upset if Brooke is with a more feminine presenting woman. He won't see it as direct competition, and the likelihood of violence will decrease. I'm not a direct threat to his masculine identity. You would be."

Alex's face softens, and Cassidy is instantly relieved. "Whatever will keep everyone the safest."

Brooke opens her computer and cracks her knuckles. "I'm going to give you a surface level identity in case he looks you up after we leave. It won't hold up under extensive scrutiny, but it will pass a cursory check."

"Make sure you base her out of the area." Alex's leg bounces rapidly. "It's probably best to give her a small start-up somewhere on the East Coast, and it shouldn't be in anything he's worked in before."

Brooke stares at Alex's leg until it stops moving. "This isn't my first rodeo."

Cassidy has been sitting on her hands to avoid soothing Alex, but she gives in now and reaches for her knee. "Everything will be fine. Everyone here is good at their job."

Brooke grunts. "I'm amazing at my job."

Cassidy smiles. "I promise it will be okay."

Alex nods. "Yeah, I know." She lets out a long breath. "I trust you both."

Cassidy watches Alex as Brooke types away. She seems uncomfortable with relinquishing control, or it could be that she's nervous about not having Brooke and Cassidy under her perceived protection during the exchange. She's a protector, a hero type, and that type likes to make sure the people she considers her responsibility aren't in the line of fire. Cassidy doesn't reassure her further. It's sometimes best to let people sit with their unease and let them work through it. It's how people learn to cope, and if they're going to be friends or more, Alex needs to be comfortable with Cassidy taking risks.

"I emailed your backstory to you in an encrypted file." Brooke shuts her computer and stands. "Let's go out and practice your identity. It'll ease the worrywart's mind and is a perfect excuse to do something fun." She points at Cassidy. "I trust you know where we can get some decent food and go have some drinks?"

Cassidy nods. "Absolutely."

Brooke grabs Alex by the shoulder and steers her toward the door. "Everyone meet downstairs in thirty minutes?"

Alex glances over her shoulder. "When did you become so bossy?"

"I prefer the term assertive."

Alex rolls her eyes. "How about annoying?"

Cassidy can't hear Brooke's retort as the door shuts behind them, but that doesn't prevent her from smiling. The more time she spends with Alex, the more she's convinced she wants to know everything about her. She enjoys the layers and complexity of her personality. She can quickly move between earnestness and playfulness. So many people get stuck in their feelings and tend to dwell. Alex doesn't seem to suffer from it, and it makes Cassidy want to be better at it.

CHAPTER SEVEN

When Cassidy said she was taking them to the Sausage Factory, Alex had convinced herself it was a strip club in the heart of the Castro. She had the location correct, but the ambiance was utterly off base.

The old Italian restaurant has floor-to-ceiling wood paneling, and every nook and cranny seems to be covered with old photographs of San Francisco and Italy. Their old table wobbles slightly, reminding Alex of the table that sat for years in her grandma's kitchen. Her grandpa never got around to fixing it before he died, and her grandma refused to after he was gone. She said it reminded her of him, and Alex thought it was both the weirdest and sweetest sentiment.

There's only one reason that memory crosses her mind now, and it's because of the proximity of Cassidy's fingers to her own. Their hands rested on the table next to each other, drawn together like magnets. The quick brush of skin is consistently electric. Cassidy must notice too. There's no other reason for her cheeks and neck to flush red the way they are now.

"Okay, so your name is Cassidy Warren, and you run a small media start-up in Virginia called Ace Prime. It focuses on providing interactive apps for smart TVs and media companies." Brooke takes a bite from her salad. "If he followed me at all, and I'm sure he has, my CIA cover is that I'm an independent tech contractor. I work primarily on the East Coast. If he asks, we can say we met at a conference."

Alex reluctantly pulls her hand away from Cassidy's and picks up her napkin. She needs to concentrate. "This isn't overkill? You may be able to sit near him and accomplish the same thing without even talking to him. We only need a few minutes." The idea of Cassidy and Brooke being in any danger is making her chest ache.

Cassidy looks at Brooke and then back at Alex. "There's no way he doesn't notice Brooke. Look at her." She waves at her as if to prove her point. "We won't approach him, but we need to be prepared when he sees her."

"Fine." Alex takes a bite from her pepperoni pizza and drops it back on the plate. "Bring your gun." She points at Brooke.

Brooke rolls her eyes. "I'm not bringing my gun." She laughs. "You're as bad as Tyler."

Alex shrugs. "I think that's a compliment."

Brooke dabs her mouth. "I know you do." She smiles. "I didn't intend it as one." She pulls a vibrating phone from her pocket. "Speak of the devil." She stands and pushes her seat back under the table. "I'll be right back. I'm going to take this outside."

Alex takes Brooke's absence as an opportunity to find out a little more about Cassidy. "Did you come here a lot when you lived here?"

Cassidy shakes her head and takes a sip of water. "It's kind of a touristy thing to do, but I figured you'd enjoy it. Plus, the likelihood of running into Hugh Bradley in the Castro is absolutely zero. I liked our odds better here."

"Do you miss San Francisco?"

Cassidy sighs. "Every single day. I like the East Coast, and I love my job, but this is home. For all its flaws, I've never loved a place more."

"It's too bad we're here for work. I'd love for you to show me around. I've never been here before," Alex says and hopes she doesn't sound as desperate as she feels.

Cassidy's mouth turns into a half-smile. "I would love that." She stares at Alex's lips. "There's a lot of things I'd like to show you."

It's hard to breathe. Alex feels her heart beating in her stomach—or maybe it's the proverbial butterflies. It's been so long since she's felt like this. Being near Cassidy is like bearing witness to the moment the seasons change. It's magical, and Alex doesn't care that she feels childish thinking it.

Alex traces the back of Cassidy's hand with her fingertips. "Maybe after—"

Brooke flops down in her seat. "Sorry about that." She looks down at their hands but pushes on without acknowledgment. "Where were we?"

Cassidy turns her attention back to Brooke. "We need to keep him occupied for five to ten minutes. I'll text Alex once we're close enough to him for Leo to make the connection. She'll text me once Leo has what he needs."

"Sounds foolproof. This will be a walk in the park compared to my last mission. I had to wait in a hallway with hired killers from the Russian mob wandering around a hundred feet away." Brooke grabs the check off the table and opens her purse. "Dinner is on me." She points to Alex. "But drinks are on you."

Alex snorts. "I have a feeling I'm getting the short end of that stick."

Brooke winks at her. "Smart woman." She wiggles her eyebrows at Cassidy. "Take us someplace gay and fun."

Cassidy nods. "Done and done."

Typically, Alex would protest. They have a big day ahead of them tomorrow, and going out drinking is the last thing that should be occupying their time. They need clear heads and to be able to think quickly if necessary. But the prospect of spending a few more hours with Cassidy was a proposition she couldn't let pass.

It's been ten years, a move to the East Coast, and a marriage since Cassidy has walked through the door of Toad Hall. It's nice to see that almost nothing is different except an upgrade in television sets. The small bar may not be much to look at, but she spent some of her best nights here prior to her career with the FBI.

The nostalgia hits quick, and she makes herself busy by pointing to the bar. "I'll grab us some drinks if you guys want to find a place to sit."

Alex bumps her shoulder. "I thought I had to buy drinks all night."

She shrugs. "It's only right that I buy the first round. I brought you two here."

Brooke claps her hands together. "As long as it isn't me."

It doesn't take long to collect the three vodka sodas, and she's grateful it's a Wednesday night and not a weekend. She places the drinks in front of Brooke and Alex and waits for their reaction after the first sip.

Alex's eyes bulge. "Jesus, this is strong."

Cassidy laughs. "They pour heavy here."

Brooke wiggles her eyebrows. "I knew I liked you."

"So is Tyler as impressive as she reads on paper?" It doesn't matter to Cassidy who answers her question. She just needs to think about anything but Alex's knee resting against hers.

Brooke closes her eyes and sighs. "She's even more than whatever you've read." She looks down at the wedding band on her finger. "I never thought I was the marrying type. But I knew after our first kiss that she was it for me."

Alex rolls her eyes. "I remember when you first called to tell me about her. You were absolutely smitten."

Brooke shakes her head. "You told me to stay away from her."

Alex nods. "You're damn right I did. She was your instructor at the Farm. You had no business getting involved with her."

Brooke shoos away her comment. "I couldn't help it. There's no way I could've stayed away from Tyler. Even if I'd wanted to— and I didn't—it wouldn't have been possible. When I met her, it felt like everything in my life had led to her. Every decision, every heartbreak, everything made sense."

Alex stares into her drink, looking contemplative. "You were right to ignore me. Tyler's your perfect match."

Brooke listens with her chin resting on her hand. "We're very lucky." She sighs and turns her attention to Cassidy. "What about you, Cassidy? Any great loves?"

Cassidy's cheeks burn hot, and she shakes her head. "I should probably say Hunter, but it was nothing like you described. We'd dated for a while, and marriage seemed like the next logical step." She can't bring herself to look at Alex. "We're better as friends. I love him, but I'm not sure I was ever in love with him." She sips her drink and remembers the last night she was in this very bar. "I fell hard for a woman in college, but it didn't work out." She points to the table in the corner of the room. "We ended things right there the night before I left for Quantico."

Alex squeezes her knee. "She was a fool to leave you." She grabs the glasses. "I'm going to get us another round."

Brooke leans forward on the table when Alex walks away. "Alex is wrong, isn't she? You broke it off with her."

Cassidy nods and is impressed with Brooke's instincts. "It would've ended eventually. I needed to concentrate on Quantico, and she was starting her medical residency. Our lives had been moving in different directions for a while, but neither of us wanted to admit it. I did us both a favor." She smiles at her. "If you're ever considering a career change, you'd be a hell of a profiler."

Brooke's stare is heavy. "I see the way she looks at you."

Cassidy considers the platitudes available to her. She could blow off the comment, tell her they're just friends or say she no longer mixes business and pleasure. But none of that would be true. The truth is, even if she never saw Alex after this was over, she'd always wonder, "what if." There's an intensity when she's with Alex. It feels like a third presence—demanding her to discover more.

She watches as Alex leans on the bar to order their drinks. An attractive woman is standing a few feet away, watching her. Cassidy can't pull her eyes away. She's not a person inclined to jealousy. That's not what this is. It feels more like fear. Fear that she'll miss her chance or that maybe she'll never get one. It doesn't matter—it's making her uncomfortable either way.

The woman looks as if she's going to make her move, but Alex grabs the drinks and heads back to the table before the woman is out of her seat. Cassidy shouldn't be surprised by the relief that simmers through her body, but she is.

"As promised." Alex hands both Brooke and Cassidy their drinks.

"Looks like you have a fan club." Brooke nods in the direction of the woman at the bar. "Can't take you anywhere."

Alex looks confused as she scans the area. The woman gives her a little wave, and Alex looks away quickly. "I don't have time for that right now. We're here to do a job. You know—save democracy and all that. I can't afford to be distracted."

Cassidy's skin prickles at Alex's words. Alex isn't wrong, but the truth is rarely a numbing agent against the sting of rejection. Was this all in her head? Surely, she hadn't misread all the signals she thought she was receiving from Alex.

Brooke raises her eyebrow. "There's never a perfect time in our line of work. Someone always needs saving. A case always needs to be solved. The country is always on the brink of disaster. Blah, blah, blah." She pulls the hairband off her wrist and ties her hair up in a ponytail. "If you'll excuse me, I'm going to go dance before your cynicism contaminates me." She grabs Cassidy by the hand. "You're coming with me."

Brooke moves to the beat thumping out of the speakers. Cassidy does her best to keep up with her, but her gaze always finds Alex. Alex sits perched on the barstool watching them. She's the picture of control and aloofness with her elbows back on the high tabletop and one booted foot resting on her knee. Her shoulders pull against the tight fabric of her black buttoned shirt, and Cassidy wonders when she last found someone so effortlessly attractive. The answer may be—never.

It only takes Cassidy another drink and four songs before she retrieves Alex from her spot at the table. Cassidy mentally prepares herself for another rejection—perceived or otherwise, but is pleasantly surprised as Alex slides off her stool with no cajoling.

Brooke promptly makes an excuse to leave the dance floor after one song, feigning exhaustion. Cassidy would've called her on her bullshit had she not been so utterly enchanted by how Alex slid her hand around her waist. Alex's fingertips whisper along the exposed skin of her back as she pulls her closer. Her body shivers as Alex's cool cheek bushes against her flushed skin.

Cassidy slides her hands up Alex's triceps and around her neck. "I thought you weren't interested in distractions?"

Alex's breath is warm against her ear. "Is that what this is?"

Cassidy leans slightly back to look at her. She expects to find flirtation in her eyes, but sincerity is all that's staring back. "I'm not sure."

Alex stares at her lips. She wets them, and Cassidy's heart starts hammering in a cadence she's never felt before. Alex is going to kiss her. The excitement and anticipation spreads like wildfire to all her nerve endings. She leans forward slightly, and Cassidy moves to meet her halfway. Her brow furrows, and she pulls her phone from her pocket.

She looks apologetic as she holds it up and nods to the door. "I have to take this. It's my mother, and she never calls unless it's important."

Cassidy nods because she's unable to trust her voice. Her feet won't move until Alex is out the door. She finds Brooke sitting at their table with a devilish smile.

Brooke shakes an ice cube out of the glass and into her mouth. "That looked intense."

Cassidy pokes the cubes in her glass with the straw. "I don't know if coming here was a great or terrible idea. I can never tell if Alex is coming or going."

Brooke shrugs. "I've always found it's better to be as straightforward with Alex as possible. Picking up on subtleties isn't her strong suit."

"Is that what you had to do with Tyler?"

Brooke laughs and intertwines her fingers around the sweating glass. "I practically had to beat Tyler over the head to get her to take a chance on me."

Cassidy snorts. "I doubt that."

Brooke ignores that halfhearted accusation. "Listen, all Alex has ever cared about is her career. She's been obsessed with not being in her father's shadow since I've known her. She won't blindly make a move on a woman she works with and risk whatever the perception may be if there's fallout. Her bravado doesn't extend into her personal life. It starts and ends with her job."

Alex walks back into the bar and slides her hands into the back pockets of her jeans. "Sorry about that."

She looks worried, and Cassidy puts her hand on her arm. "Everything okay?"

Alex shrugs. "My dad had a heart attack. He's okay, but my mom wanted to let me know."

Cassidy stands, feeling much more concerned than Alex looks. "Do you need to go? Brooke and I can cover tomorrow if you need to be with your family."

Alex shakes her head. "No. there's nothing I can do there. I've been working on this case for years. I want to be here." Alex shifts uncomfortably. "I'm going to go. You guys should stay."

Cassidy grabs her purse. "We're going with you."

"It's really okay. I'll just grab a Lyft."

Brooke waves her off and hops off the stool. "I don't care how tough you are; we aren't letting you wander around in a city you don't know." She holds up a hand before Alex can protest. "Don't waste your breath."

The car ride back to the hotel is quiet except for the low sounds of the radio. Alex stares out the window as if she has the weight of the world on her shoulders. Cassidy would be losing her mind to get to her father if she were in Alex's position, and it makes her sad that Alex feels she's not in a position to do so.

Brooke says good night once they reach their rooms, and Cassidy lingers at Alex's door. "Do you want to talk about it?"

Alex taps her electric key against the door lock. "No. I want to focus on tomorrow."

Cassidy leans against the wall and studies her face. "It may be easier to focus on tomorrow if you get whatever you're feeling off your chest."

Alex holds the door open and looks like she wants nothing more than to escape inside. "Have a good night, Cassidy." She hesitates, but only for a second, before she shuts the door.

Cassidy holds her fist up to the door, ready to knock, but stops herself. She learned a long time ago that you have to meet people where they are. Forcing Alex to talk to her wasn't going to do anyone any good. She tells herself that Alex knows where to find her if she wants to talk, but she knows she won't see Alex again until the morning.

CHAPTER EIGHT

A lex blinks, trying to push the dry irritation that's been present in her eyes since the moment she begrudgingly turned off her alarm this morning. Her sleep had been fitful at best, and it was taking its toll on her. Of course, it doesn't help that they've been staring out the same window, at the same coffee shop, for the last four hours. There are only so many cups of coffee a person can drink and stay in one place—she reached that limit two cups ago.

Hearing her father had suffered a heart attack had affected her in ways she wasn't ready to examine. All of the things unsaid between them had flashed before her eyes and pulled at her heart. Still, it hadn't been enough to get her to abandon her mission, and he hadn't asked. For the entirety of her life, her father had been a steady and unwavering presence. He's a man of few words, but the ones he chooses always seem to hold so much significance. One of the many attributes she's inherited from him is his ability to compartmentalize. She calls on that trait now as she shoves all her worry and regret into a small box and tosses it to the back of her subconscious. She'll open it later when concerned expressions aren't searching hers for answers and vulnerability she isn't ready to give.

She's stolen as many glances at Cassidy as she can muster without seeming creepy. Her desire to explain away her unwillingness to talk last night had nothing to do with Cassidy and everything to do with her needing to process what happened. Cassidy has been sweet and caring. Alex met her with indifference and avoidance. *You'd think you'd learn a new trick or two by now.*

"There he is." Brooke leans toward the window and pulls her phone out. She dials Alex's number and waits for her to tap her earbud before putting it back in her pocket. "Make sure you record everything."

Alex rolls her eyes. "I'm not going to remind you that I'm an FBI agent."

Brooke stands. "Yet here you are...reminding me." She smiles and squeezes her shoulder. "Sorry. Sometimes I say things aloud to make sure I did them."

Cassidy stands and runs her hands down her jeans. "Do I look like I could date Brooke?"

Alex answers before thinking. "You look like you could date whoever you wanted."

Cassidy blushes slightly, and Alex swallows any regret her words may have triggered.

"Wish us luck." She glances at Brooke, who is waiting in the doorway. "I'll text you when we're close enough."

Alex nods and watches them walk out the door. She can't do anything now but listen, wait, and hope. Wait to see if they can get what they need, and hope everyone comes back unscathed.

Cassidy and Brooke make it across the street to the other coffee shop, and Cassidy holds the door open for Brooke. Brooke smiles and slides her hand down Cassidy's arm and intertwines their fingers. They stand in line for coffee and make idle chitchat. Neither looks in the direction of Hugh Bradley, who sits alone at a table, watching the other customers. Brooke speaks loud enough not to draw attention but to be heard. It works. Hugh approaches their table just as they've finished splitting the muffin they purchased.

"Brooke Hart?" He stands much closer than necessary.

Cassidy would usually find the invasion of personal space obnoxious, but she uses his lack of peripheral vision to text Alex and let her know they've made contact. Her phone with the device Leo placed on it is on the table, innocuous looking.

He stretches his arms out for a hug like they're long-lost friends. "I knew that was you as soon as I heard your voice. I swear I could pick you out of a crowd of thousands."

Brooke stands to hug him, and if you weren't paying attention, you wouldn't notice the slight cringe on her face when she lets him wrap his arms around her. "Hugh Bradley. I'd heard you were working in San Francisco."

They'd spoken at length the night before about using phrasings such as these to stroke his ego. If he believed Brooke was keeping up with him in any way, it would help them obtain their goal.

She steps away from him, but he keeps one hand on her shoulder as Brooke points to Cassidy. "This is my girlfriend, Cassidy Warren."

Cassidy extends her hand to shake his, and she can see the hesitation and annoyance on his face. "It's nice to meet you. Brooke speaks so fondly of you."

A spark of triumph crosses his face as he takes her hand. "We're an elite group. MIT only accepts seven percent of applicants."

Cassidy plasters a warm smile over the immediate annoyance. "Wow, that's very impressive."

He's just as obnoxious as she expected him to be.

He pulls up a chair and places it between them. "Are you still consulting?" He reaches for Brooke's hand, and she makes a show of going through her purse.

She holds up her lip gloss as if she needs proof she isn't avoiding his touch. "I am. That's actually how I met Cassidy."

He glances over at Cassidy. "You work in tech? I've never heard of you."

Cassidy doesn't bother to point out that he's probably never bothered to look up a single female tech CEO. "Nothing as impressive as you, I'm sure. I run a small start-up." She's about to add the firm's name as they'd practiced, but he doesn't give her a chance. He's turned away again, focusing on Brooke.

He leans forward in his seat. "How long are you in town for? I'd love to take you to dinner."

"I'm afraid we're on our way to the airport now," Brooke says.

He leans back in his chair, looking angry. "You can't extend your trip a few hours? I haven't seen you in years."

Cassidy glances down at her phone. There still isn't a text from Alex saying they could go. They need to drag this out for a few more minutes. She shakes her head subtly when Brooke makes eye contact with her.

"Tell me about your new job. I hear you just switched firms." Brooke leans in slightly, ignoring his invite to dinner and playing to his ego instead.

"I did, but it's just to pay the bills." He glances around the small shop. "I have something much bigger in the works, though. Much bigger."

Cassidy practically chokes on the piece of muffin she's just put in her mouth. Is this asshole really going to do their job for them? He can't possibly be that stupid.

Brooke's eyebrows raise. "Oh, really? What's the job?"

He traces the seam in the table with his thumbnail. "It's classified." He scoots his chair closer. "But it's not like anything that's ever been done before." He looks at Cassidy again. "Where did you say you worked?" His brow furrows, and Cassidy figures his paranoia may be setting in.

Cassidy waves her hand dismissively. "A company called Ace Prime. We work on media apps for Smart TVs and other—"

He rolls his eyes. "Sounds utterly boring." He looks at Brooke. "You're too intelligent to be with someone who works on apps."

Cassidy's phone vibrates in her lap, and she glances down at the screen. *All set.*

Cassidy reaches across the table and puts her hand on top of Brooke's. "We need to get going if we're going to make our flight."

Brooke stands, and he grabs her by the wrist. "Stay."

Cassidy watches Brooke's face. She doesn't know Brooke well, but she's seen enough to know she's considering it. Hugh has tossed them a nugget, and Brooke is probably considering if she can get any more information from him. But it's Cassidy's job to read people, and she can tell by the way his fingers are wrapped around Brooke's wrist that whatever she may be able to glean from him isn't worth the potential danger she'd be putting herself in. Cassidy doesn't doubt that Brooke is capable of taking care of herself, but any man this plainly forceful in public is capable of so much more behind closed doors.

Cassidy stands and slips her hand into Brooke's. "It was nice meeting you, Hugh."

This seems to shake Brooke out of whatever mental calculus she's been making and she pulls her wrist from his grip. "Take care of yourself, Hugh." She grabs her purse off the back of the chair. "Good luck on your new project."

He opens and closes his fist but doesn't make a move to stand. "Sure."

Cassidy pulls her out the door and around the corner into the alley where Alex is waiting.

There's concern etched on Alex's expression. "Are you okay?" She puts her hands on Brooke's shoulders. "He sounded awful."

Brooke shivers and then shakes out her arms. "I've been around worse." She straightens her hair. "I'd forgotten how intense he is." She glances down the other side of the alley. "Let's call a Lyft and go back to the hotel. We can debrief there."

Alex grabs Cassidy's hand, and she swallows against the jolt she now associates with Alex's touch. "You guys did a great job. Leo said he got exactly what he needed. He'll be in touch."

Cassidy squeezes her fingers. "Good. I'm glad it was worth it."

Alex lets go of her hand and follows Brooke down the other side of the alley. Cassidy watches her go and wonders—not for the first time—if she's strong enough to break down the walls Alex seems to have erected around herself, and if she could, if that's what Alex would want.

CHAPTER NINE

A lex pinches the bridge of her nose as she listens to Leo bark at her on speakerphone. "Just tell me if we got what we need, Leo. I don't need to hear about how it works."

"That's your problem, Alex. You don't appreciate art." He continues to tap away on his keyboard.

Alex flops down on the bed and silently curses and thanks the gods for brains like Leo's. She's been chipping away at this case for two years, and now it all hinged on ethically questionable technology. Everything they've been doing lived somewhere in the shadows of legality. She doesn't even know if it will hold up in court if it comes down to it. But those were problems to sort out for people much smarter than her.

"It will take me some time to decipher it into terms you can easily present, but I've been able to pinpoint the algorithm."

Alex sits up, a rush of excitement surging through her body. "You found it? You got what we need?"

"I got what you need to prove it *exists*. Convincing people of the consequences and who's responsible is your problem. He's done enough to keep it from being clearly him behind it, and there's another code that has a kind of signature I can't pinpoint. So there's someone else, not just this guy." He slurps into the phone, and Alex hears him crush a can.

Tears of relief unexpectedly well in the corners of Alex's eyes. Her breath shudders with relief. It isn't a lot, but it's something, a small bit of proof they can build on. "Thank you, Leo. Truly."

"I'll send you everything I have. But, Alex, this was never going to be the hard part. Maybe you, me, and Brooke can have coffee when you come home. If you have to bring Cassidy, that's fine too."

Alex looks over at Cassidy, who has a single eyebrow raised and stifles a laugh. "Will do, Leo. Thanks again."

Alex hits the end button and throws the phone onto the bed. "I can't believe we actually got the algorithm."

"He's right," Brooke says from where she's standing at the window, looking at the city below. "That was the easy part."

"Is there anything you can do from your end?"

Brooke rubs the base of her neck and stares out the window. "Not without drawing suspicion as to what we know and bringing in people who will do nothing but slow down the investigation and possibly tip off others. If I highlight exactly what we're doing, the case will be taken from my team and moved up the chain of command. I can talk to my boss and see if I can get clearance to listen in on Senator Christie, but I doubt the senator is dumb enough to do anything that flagrant."

"Never underestimate the sloppiness of people who've gotten comfortable," Cassidy says.

This has Alex's full attention. "Elaborate, please."

Cassidy nods. "We often build people like this up in our heads. We think they're playing chess, but it's usually just checkers. People like Fletcher and Christie have gone untouched for an obscene amount of time. They're comfortable in their perceived invisibility. They understand the stakes of what accusing them would be, and they operate accordingly."

"So, what do you suggest?" Alex wants to hear any and all possible scenarios.

"You have an element of proof now, a thread that can be tugged on and followed to its source. I suggest you notify your supervisor of what you've found and see how the information trickles down from here and how people react. We'll be able to tell a lot by how the situation is handled and by their reactions." Cassidy looks definite in her appraisal.

Alex almost commits to the plan without further question. Almost. "We'll lose the element of surprise if we reveal our information too soon," she counters.

Cassidy shrugs. "If you hang on to it too long, you could lose the ability to stop it altogether and you also run the risk of doing too much outside the rule book, which could work against all the work you've done. Time isn't on your side. You need to start throwing a few things against the wall and see what sticks." She puts her hands out as if to stop any objection from Alex. "It's not ideal, but the second you start questioning people, you'll tip your hand. At least if you approach it this way, you aren't accusing anyone. You're keeping that aspect close to the chest."

Alex rolls her shoulders and winces at the sound of her neck creaking. "Okay." She takes a deep breath. "It's not ideal, but it's all we have. It's like finding a smoking gun in an empty room and no fingerprints. We have to start setting traps."

Cassidy looks at her phone for the fourth time in the last several minutes. "Sorry." She nods to the door. "I need to take this."

Alex pushes away the curiosity that bubbles up as to who is on the other end of the phone. It's none of her business. That's what she keeps telling herself. She glances at Brooke, who is staring at her with a knowing grin.

Brooke crosses her arms. "Playing it real cool, Derby."

"Shut up." Alex shifts in her seat.

Brooke puts her hands up in surrender. "Sure thing. You clearly have it all under control."

"I do."

Brooke stares at her looking amused. "I didn't say anything."

"You didn't have to. I know what you're thinking."

Brooke shakes her head and smiles. "Nice to see you've never outgrown your stubbornness."

Alex is about to bite back when Cassidy walks back into the room. "Sorry about that. It was my mom confirming dinner for tonight. I don't suppose I could tempt you guys with an invite?"

"Definitely. We'd love to," Brooke says before Alex has an opportunity to say otherwise.

Cassidy looks relieved. "Great." She points to the door. "I'm going to hop on the treadmill in the hotel gym and then shower. Can you guys be ready in two hours?"

Brooke stands. "I'll go with you. We'll leave this one to make her calls back to Quantico."

Alex stares at her phone for several minutes after they leave. She needs to make another call before she talks to her supervisor. She dials the number, and it takes much longer than normal for the person on the other end to answer.

"Hello?"

"Hey, Dad."

"Hey, kiddo." Her dad sounds much better than she anticipated. "How you doing?"

"Me?" She chuckles. "You're the one who just had a heart attack. How are you feeling?"

He sighs. "I feel fine. They keep fussing over me, and I can't get your mother to leave me alone." He's pretending to be annoyed, but Alex can hear the love in his voice.

"We're worried about you. I'm out of town for work, but I'll come see you as soon as I get home tomorrow."

"They'll keep me here for one more day, and then I'll be home. You can see me then. I don't want any of your memories of me to be in some hospital bed."

She sighs. "Dad, I don't care where you are. I just want to see you."

It's like she's twelve years old all over again, asking to visit him at the hospital after he'd been stabbed on the job. The fear had been all-consuming after they'd gotten the knock on the door. He'd refused to see her then too, and she wonders if all parents suffer from this same affliction. Do children ever really become real adults in their eyes, or is it that a parent's love is so pure that they'll always love you with the fierceness of a small being that needs their protection?

"Something on your mind, kiddo?" His voice is full of concern.

The desire to get his advice on the decision in front of her is gripping. She pushes it away. She can handle this. "No, everything is fine. I'm just worried about you."

His silence indicates that he's deciding if he believes her. She can't bear the thought of lying to him. As much as she wants to make a name for herself, surpass his success, and stand on her own—she's never been anything but honest with him.

"I love you, Dad."

"I love you too, sweetheart. I'll see you in a few days." There's a rustling sound that she assumes is sheets. "Do your old man a favor and sneak me a Snickers bar. The warden runs a tight ship around here."

She smiles. "Let Mom take care of you. It makes her feel better."

He chuckles. "Anything for you. Bye, honey."

"Bye, Dad." She hits the end button and opens her contacts list.

She lets her thumb hover over her boss's name for several seconds. After she makes this call, this will no longer be her little theory. It will be out there, with real consequences—good or bad. Depending on how this plays out, it could be career making or ending. Cassidy's words play through her mind. She's out of time.

Fuck it.

CHAPTER TEN

Cassidy rolls the ring on her pointer finger in circles while waiting for Alex and Brooke in the lobby. Unfortunately, the treadmill hadn't served its intended purpose of working out her stress. The hot shower hadn't added any reprieve, so now she's reduced to rudimentary fidgeting. Perfect.

The elevator dings, and she holds her breath, waiting to see who is on the other side. Alex looks phenomenal in her black jeans, Nirvana T-shirt, and black blazer rolled to her elbows. Her black, pixie hair is still wet from the shower, and when she pushes her long bangs out of her eyes by running her fingers through them, Cassidy has to remind herself to breathe.

"Hey," Alex says. She slides her hands into her back pockets. "Were you waiting long?"

Cassidy shakes her head and reminds herself that words exist. "Nope. Just got down here." She holds up her phone. "The Lyft should be here any minute." She racks her brain longer to find her excessive and normally accessible vocabulary. "How did everything go with Quantico?"

Alex blows out a long breath. "I told Gregory about the algorithm and that I think it's linked to a voting scam, but asked him not to say anything until I could get back and explain everything in detail. I told him that it potentially involved some people from different government agencies and a few elected officials. I didn't give him enough to tip our hands fully, but we'll know soon if he can be trusted. If he's in on it at all, they'll be all over me when I get back. So now we wait and see."

Brooke clips her small clutch and slings it over her shoulder. "As you can see, she's totally made peace with it and is completely chill."

"I am chill," Alex says.

"Uh-huh." Brooke looks down at Alex rubbing her thumb into her palm. "That's what I said."

Cassidy closes the back door to the small back seat. "How did Gregory seem? He strikes me as pretty open-minded."

Alex snorts. "I swear people are completely different around you than me."

"What does that mean?"

Alex shrugs. "I think people just like you more than they like me. Gregory will vet the information, but he wasn't happy about it. He seemed irritated that I bothered him with it. He said I blindsided him. The good news is that I think I blindsided him with it. That's how it felt anyway."

Cassidy only hesitates for a brief moment before taking Alex's hand and squeezing it. "Once they're able to vet the information and we can put the pieces together, anyone who doubts you will feel foolish. Don't worry about it right now." She bumps her shoulder into Alex. "And not everyone likes me. Stapleton down at Cybercrimes rolls his eyes every time he has to talk to me."

Alex turns her head and gives Cassidy her full attention. Her eyes glimmer in the passing streetlights. "Stapleton is an asshole." She smiles. "If he's your only evidence of people not liking you, I'm afraid that's circumstantial and doesn't count." Alex leans around her and looks out the window. "Holy shit. This is your parents' house? I didn't think anyone in San Francisco owned anything this big, much less on property. I thought your parents were professors?"

Cassidy turns to look at the house. Her chest warms like it always does when she comes home. "They are." She opens the door and waits for Alex and Brooke to get out of the car. "This house has been in my family since 1903. My parents have done a gazillion upgrades and improvements, but they never had to buy it. When I was born, my grandparents gave it to them."

"It's beautiful," Alex says and looks a bit awkward. "I didn't mean to insult you or anything. It just wasn't what I was expecting."

"You didn't insult me." Cassidy turns to go up the brick walkway. "I'm not as delicate as you think I am."

"I'll remember that."

Cassidy's mom is out the door to greet them before she can say anything else. "Hi, honey." She wraps Cassidy in a hug.

Cassidy breathes in the familiar smell of old books and Chanel perfume. "Hi, Mom." She turns to make introductions. "This is Alex Derby and Brooke Hart." She gestures to her mom. "This is Marjorie Wolf."

Alex sticks her hand out, and her mom waves her off, wrapping her in a hug. "It's so nice to meet you." She moves on to Brooke and does the same. "Your father will be back with dinner soon. He wanted to cook, but we don't need the fire department here tonight." She walks toward the house and motions for them to follow. "I wish you would've given me more notice that you were coming. We would've had the whole family over."

"It was a last-minute work thing, Mom. I only knew I was coming two days ago when I called." Cassidy is telling the truth and is also glad she isn't going to subject Brooke and Alex to all the flavorful colors of her sometimes very intense family.

"You have a beautiful home, Mrs. Wolf." Alex points to her dad's prized possession on the far wall. "Is that a Cate Turner painting?"

"You know Cate Turner?" Her mom takes a step closer. "I didn't take you FBI types for art aficionados. I'm impressed."

Alex blushes slightly. "Believe it or not, if the whole FBI thing didn't pan out, I wanted to be an art curator."

"You did?" Brooke and Cassidy ask at the same time.

Alex ignores them and steps closer to the painting. "I've never seen this one before. It doesn't look like her other work. It's not quite as clean or concise."

"That's because it was never for sale," her father says, handing the bag of food over to Cassidy's mother. He kisses Cassidy on the top of her head and moves toward Alex. "She painted this when she was fifteen years old." He smiles fondly at it and traces lines in the air to mimic the brush strokes. "She did the whole thing in the bed of my truck. She hated it so much that she told me to toss it when she was done." He crosses his arms. "I obviously didn't. I always knew she'd be someone one day." He turns and looks at Alex. "I'm Scott Wolf."

Alex shakes his hand. "You know Cate Turner?"

He laughs. "We grew up together. She lived two doors down from me." He nods toward Cassidy. "She's her godmother."

Alex stares at Cassidy. "Buried the lede, huh?"

Cassidy pretends to be offended and puts her hand over her heart. "She's just Aunt Cate to me. How was I supposed to know you were some art geek?"

"I got Italian." He looks at Alex. "Have Cassidy show you the library after dinner. I think you'll get a kick out of it."

Cassidy listens fondly as her father regales Alex and Brooke with his fabulous stories and contagious wit. Her mom is always quick to pop into the conversation with corrections and a dash of realism. She's constantly aware of how much she misses her family, but moments like these remind her how lucky she is to have them.

Having the chance to sit back and observe Alex away from any work scenario is a bonus. She's one of those people who laughs with their whole body. She loves the way her shoulders bounce when something is particularly funny. Cassidy waits with anticipation for every sip of wine, knowing she'll lick her bottom lip when she finishes. Her pulse quickens with every sometimes accidental and sometimes intentional brush of their fingers. She's caught up watching Alex trace the top of her wine glass with her fingertip when her father pulls her back into the conversation.

"How's Hunter?" Her dad hands Brooke the wine bottle. "We were going to play golf last time I was in DC, but he couldn't get away from work." He leans back in his chair. "You all work too much if you ask me."

Cassidy blinks, focusing on answering her father and not that Alex gently squeezes her knee under the table. "He's good. He's watching Thor for me while we're gone."

He nods. "I always liked him. Not with you, but I like him."

"I know, Dad. He's a good guy." Cassidy traces her fingertips across the back of Alex's hand. She's giving her a lazy smirk that makes Cassidy want to put her mouth on hers. "Want to see the library?" she asks before she talks herself out of it.

Alex nods. "Sure."

Cassidy leads her up the stairs and into the library. There are several paintings from her aunt Cate on the walls. Her parents' extensive book collection drenches every square inch of shelf space. She takes Alex's hand and pulls her over to the far side of the room.

She stands slightly in front of Alex and points to the painting on the wall. "Aunt Cate painted that for my eighteenth birthday."

Alex steps closer, and she can feel her breath on her neck. "It's beautiful. You're beautiful in it."

Cassidy tries to keep her breathing measured. "How do you know it's me? The person's back is to us."

Alex reaches around her and points. "The way the shape of the person becomes one with the sunset. The lines of the neck and hips are so delicate—she wanted to protect your youth while showing your evolution into adulthood. You can tell she was painting someone she truly loves. It's exquisite."

Cassidy's skin flushes hot. "You should've kissed me last night."

Alex brushes her lips across Cassidy's neck and stops at her ear. "Do you want me to kiss you?"

Cassidy turns to face her and runs her hands through her short hair. She leans closer and brushes her nose against Alex's. Alex's grip around her waist tightens, and she pulls her tighter against her body. Alex smells like wine and sandalwood, and it's intoxicating.

"I want you to devour me." Cassidy kisses her cheek and lets her lips linger on her skin.

Alex doesn't hesitate after that. She crushes Cassidy's lips with her own. There's nothing timid or restrained about Alex's intentions. If Cassidy ever wondered if Alex wanted her, that thought is extinguished now. This was the kind of kiss that was capable of parting seas. She knows the heat she feels building is matched by

Alex's. Their hands explore and press and pull. She slides her hands under Alex's shirt and up her back. Alex's soft skin and hard muscles make her dizzy. She wants more of her. She wants all of her.

Alex's hands move without apprehension. She feels her way across the landscape of Cassidy's body, and each movement leaves goose bumps in its wake. Cassidy's desire is growing rapidly, persistent and demanding. She loves the feel of Alex's skin against her own and how her strong and steady hands feel as they travel up her stomach. Cassidy pulls at Alex's shirt, and her knees almost buckle from the surge of desire that spreads through her when Alex whimpers at the movement.

Alex pulls away. "We have to stop." She bites her bottom lip and kisses her again. "We're in your parents' house."

Cassidy shivers at the broken contact. "I'm not sure I care."

Alex's eyes say she wants to do anything but stop. "I care." She runs her thumbs along her cheeks and then kisses each one. "We have plenty of time." She steps back.

Cassidy only lets her get a step away before pulling her back and kissing her again. She allows herself a moment to believe they'll have more than this night—more than this moment. It's the only reason she finally lets her go.

Alex makes it through the rest of the evening on autopilot. She knows people are talking around her, but the laughter and stories are ambient noise against her acute awareness of Cassidy's proximity to her. It's like she's plugged into something intangible. It's an electrical current without a name or source. Her body hums with need, and it's exhilarating.

The ride back to the hotel is filled with subtle touches and glances in the dark back seat of the car as Brooke makes comments about the passing city structures and the hospitality of Cassidy's parents. She watches Cassidy take long breaths as she traces the seam of Alex's jeans and keeps her eyes focused on the road in front of them. Cassidy lightly touches her back as they exit the vehicle, and all Alex can focus on is five minutes from now when she can pull Cassidy into her room and show her everything she wanted to do in the library.

She hears him before she sees him. Heavy breaths and grunting noises are the only warnings. The poor lighting in the alley next to the hotel gives him the few seconds he needs before anyone can stop him. Once her eyes finally adjust, her mind catches up to what is happening. Her heart lodges itself in her throat, and her hand tingles with a surge of adrenaline. He has Brooke by the neck, her body pressed against him with a knife to her throat.

Alex grabs the gun from her ankle holster once she realizes what's happening and immediately trains it on him. "Let her go, Hugh."

"Why would you do this to me, Brooke? I used to love you." His eyes are wild, and spit clings to the side of Brooke's face as he talks. "Did you really think I wouldn't figure out that you cloned my phone? Do you think I'm stupid?" Beads of sweat accumulate along his forearms.

Brooke says nothing, but Alex knows she's waiting for her opening. She's always been fearless. Hugh may be smart enough to figure out that his phone was cloned, but he has no idea who he's dealing with. Brooke has the ability to take him apart piece by piece if the opportunity arises.

Alex's hands are steady as she calculates whether she has a clear shot. "Let her go and tell us who you're working for. Do that, and we can work out a deal."

"A deal?" He has tears in his eyes, but based on his mannerisms, it's not clear if it's from hurt or pure rage. "You have no idea what you've done. We're all as good as dead."

Alex doesn't want to shoot him. They need him and all the information he can provide. Brooke is eerily still. She glances to the right, and Alex understands that's the direction she'll go when she makes her move.

"You want to do something big. You want your life to matter," Cassidy says from beside her. "You're tired of working for people who aren't as smart as you. You deserve better. This was your chance. No one faults you for that. Let us help you."

He pushes the knife into Brook's neck. "Who do you work for, the FBI?" He snorts. "You're all as corrupt as they come. I'm done dealing with your kind. You can't help me."

"Who *can* help you then, Hugh?" Cassidy steps closer. "Tell me, and I'll get them for you. There must be someone."

"No one." He draws the knife up to Brooke's ear. "I know you got the algorithm. I'm not going to let them come for me. I'm not going to end up in some ditch. I'm going out on my own terms, and she's coming to hell with me."

Alex has seen it before. He's hell-bent on killing someone because he intends to die here tonight. Brooke takes the slight opening from his movement and slams her elbow into his stomach. She rolls to the right when his grip loosens.

He spits and sputters. "You fucking bitch."

"Drop the knife and put your hands on your head." Alex prays he listens. Arresting him could break this open.

He glares at Alex. The fury in his eyes is heart-stopping. She tightens her grip on the gun as he charges toward her with the knife above his head. Brooke lands a kick flat into his back, and he stumbles forward. He turns toward Brooke, and she punches him square in the face. He seethes as he wipes the blood away from his mouth. He uses his free hand to reach into the back of his waistband and pulls out a gun. He points it at Brooke and laughs.

Alex slides her finger onto the trigger and squeezes. One shot rings through the narrow alley. His body falls back against the brick wall and slides down to the pavement. Hugh had been vibrating with rage a moment ago, and now there is nothing. The adrenaline that courses through her body exits in heavy breaths. It's all she hears— her breathing, her rapid heartbeat.

Alex looks at Cassidy. "Call the San Francisco FBI office." She holsters her weapon and grabs Brooke. "Are you okay?"

Brooke nods and shakes out the hand she used to punch Hugh. "Yeah." She hugs Alex. "Thank you."

Alex hugs her and rubs her back. "It's going to be okay."

She's saying it to herself as much as she is to Brooke. The problem is, it's a lie. Nothing is going to be okay. This is just the beginning, and they all know it. Hugh's fear had been very, very real. He believed that they were all dead people now that the algorithm has been exposed. She doesn't want to call this in, but there's no time. Her supervisors will be notified as soon as the local FBI agents arrive on the scene, and it's better that it comes from her.

Alex pulls her phone from her pocket and is surprised her hands aren't shaking as she calls the deputy special agent in charge. It takes four rings for him to pick up. "Gregory." He sounds more alert than he should be for three in the morning.

"Sorry to bother you, DSAC. I've just been involved in a shooting and need to report."

"What the fuck, Derby?"

Alex explains the situation and winces when she divulges Brooke's presence. Of course, this was an off-book operation for all of them, but knowing a member of the CIA was with her will tip her hand more than she wants. She didn't mention Brooke when she briefed him last, and he's sure to remember that.

Gregory is quiet for longer than Alex is comfortable. "Get your ass back here ASAP, Derby. I want to see you in my office by sixteen hundred tomorrow." He hangs up the phone.

Shit.

The coroner is on the scene with three San Francisco police units. She sees Brooke and Cassidy talking to a woman in an FBI jacket. There hadn't been time to decide what they'd say. She's going to have to trust them not to divulge too much. It's stupid even to think that. She trusts them. They aren't rookies, but it's hard for her to let go of the control, all the same.

Alex pulls her credentials from her pocket and hands them to the agent. "Special Agent Alex Derby."

The woman scribbles her badge number down and hands it back to her. "Special Agent Iris McCoy." She holds the clipboard against her chest. "Why do you think Hugh Bradley attacked Analyst Hart?"

Alex lets out a long breath and shoves her hands in her pockets. "I assume after he ran into her today, he decided that he wanted her. Hart has told me about their time in college together and how he stalked her. I assume seeing her again dredged up some old memories and some old anger."

Iris nods and studies her. "You only fired once."

"It's a narrow alley. I couldn't take the chance of hitting someone else or hurting someone with a ricochet."

"Do you want to tell me why two agents are here with a CIA analyst? We don't have anything on the books." She looks at the three of them—waiting for someone to answer.

Cassidy clears her throat. "Would you believe me if I told you we were here for the wine?"

Iris cocks her head. "No."

"It's classified," Alex says.

"You know I'll have to confirm that with Quantico, right?" Iris clicks her pen and puts it in her pocket.

"I know."

Iris checks her watch. "When are you three leaving San Francisco?"

"Tomorrow morning. I have a debriefing with my DSAC at sixteen hundred."

Iris pulls business cards out of her pocket and hands them each one. "I'll be in contact if I need anything else from you, and feel free to call me if you think of anything I need to know."

Alex taps the card against her hand and makes a split-second decision to ask a question she's been turning over in her head since the moment she pulled the trigger. "What's the news coverage like here? How long until this is covered?"

Iris looks up and down the block. "There are no news vans, but a police involved shooting?" She shrugs. "Two days tops. He works at a pretty big tech firm, and his family will be notified within the hour."

Alex rubs her pounding head. "Okay."

Brooke pulls a card from her purse and hands it to Iris. "They're going to want the name of the assault victim. Under no circumstances will you provide them with mine. I gave you that as a professional courtesy. If there are no other options, you can use the name on the card. Use that name in your report as well. When you turn the report over to Quantico, they'll know it's me."

Iris nods, clearly unfazed by Brooke's commanding tone. "Got it." She slips the card into her pocket. "I'd say it was nice meeting you, but it's not nice meeting anyone at this time of the night."

As soon as Iris walks away, Alex grabs Brooke's hand. "Are you okay?" She touches the bloody red line on her neck she hadn't noticed in the dark of the alley. "We need to get that cleaned out."

Brooke squeezes her hand. "I'll take care of it." She checks her watch. "I need to call Tyler before she hears about this from anyone else."

"We need to be on the first flight out of here in the morning. I'll text you with the information as soon as I confirm it." Alex hugs her.

Brooke kisses her cheek. "Thanks for not letting me die."

"Always."

Brooke gives her a half-smile. "I know."

Cassidy slides her hand into hers as she watches Brooke pull out her phone as she walks toward the hotel. "She'll be okay."

Alex reluctantly pulls her hand away and shoves it in her pocket. "Brooke? I know. She's as tough as they come." Alex starts walking back toward the hotel. "Listen, things just became infinitely more complicated. Now that we have a dead coder on our hands there are going to be a lot more questions from Quantico. Our time line of people finding out just sped up to warp speed."

"I can handle it." Cassidy crosses her arms across her chest as she walks next to her.

They spend the elevator ride in silence. Alex hates how quickly things shifted. She wants to rewind time. She wants to fast-forward time. She doesn't know what she wants. All she knows is that she doesn't like the look on Cassidy's face. It's a mixture of hurt, confusion, and annoyance. She hates putting it there, but it's for the best. She needs to get through this meeting with Gregory and see if she still has a job. Alex is practically radioactive at this point, and she has no intention of dragging Cassidy down with her any further.

They reach Alex's door, and Cassidy stops. "I need you to stop trying to warn me that things will be hard. I'm an intelligent woman. I don't need you to be some knight in shining armor. I chose to be here."

Alex unlocks the door. "I'm not trying to save you. I'm trying to protect you."

Cassidy rolls her eyes. "I don't need that either."

"Then what do you need?"

Cassidy places her hands on Alex's cheeks, and for a second, Alex is sure Cassidy is going to kiss her. "I need you to trust me."

Alex searches her eyes, looking for a hint of regret for putting her in this position, but all she finds is sincerity. "I do trust you." But the distraction she'd been worried about has had consequences. Brooke could have been killed, and all because Alex wasn't paying attention.

Cassidy's eyes travel over Alex's lips. She takes a deep breath and lets her go. "Then act like it. I'll see you in a few hours." She walks down the hall and into her room.

Alex falls onto her bed and stares at the ceiling. Tonight definitely didn't go as planned. Her whole world is about to blow up, along with the most significant case of her career, and all she can do is think about whether or not Cassidy is okay. *Fuck my life. What is wrong with you?* The good news is that if she can't come up with the answer on her own, Gregory will be sure to point it all out in a few short hours.

CHAPTER ELEVEN

Cassidy smiles at the sound of Thor dancing behind Hunter's door when he hears her voice. When Hunter finally opens it, she gets on her knees and hugs him, kissing his giant head repeatedly.

She rubs his face and scratches his belly until his paw scratches at the air. "I missed you too, buddy. Who's the best boy?" She kisses him again.

"You know, if you'd greeted me like that when we were married, we might still be together."

Cassidy walks into the apartment, still rubbing Thor's back. "If you were as sweet as him, you may have gotten that kind of greeting."

"Touché," Hunter says as he heads into the kitchen. He pulls a glass out of the cabinet and fills it with water before handing it to Cassidy. "So?"

Cassidy takes the glass and flops down on the couch. "How much do you know?"

Hunter shakes his head. "Nothing. I haven't spoken to Alex, but I know Gregory was pissed as hell all day."

The fact that Gregory was angry is interesting, and a fact she'll ponder later. Now, Cassidy considers where to start, and she figures the beginning is the best place. She fills Hunter in with all the details, minus the part where she practically tore Alex's clothes off in her parents' library. And the part where they almost kissed at the bar. Or when she thought about shoving her into her hotel room after the shooting. Okay, she fills him in on everything pertinent to the case.

Cassidy hadn't been able to sleep after leaving Alex at her door. The adrenaline from the shooting, the remnants of arousal, and the swirling confusion regarding Alex kept her staring at the ceiling until it was time to head to the airport. Alex is equal parts infuriating and captivating, and she feels a constant pull to her—which is also infuriating and captivating.

"Jesus, Cassidy." He slides down next to her on the couch. "Where is Alex now?"

"Meeting with Gregory. I'm going to have to talk to my boss in the morning and tell him everything. I'm actually surprised I wasn't called in today." She scratches Thor's head. "Actually, it's weird that I wasn't called in today, isn't it?"

Hunter shrugs. "Alex was the one who pulled the trigger."

Cassidy continues to pet Thor's head. "Yeah, but Gregory knows most of the story now. Wouldn't he have told Sykes by now? And if he hasn't, why hasn't he?"

Hunter's brow furrows. "Do you think Gregory is in on it?"

"I don't know what I think anymore. I mean, we're talking about people who want to send our republic into freefall. Even if Fletcher and Christie are pulling the strings, there have to be puppets at the other end." Her head starts to pound behind her eyes—a reminder that she hasn't gotten any decent sleep. "Gregory doesn't fit the profile, though. He's not the 'burn it all down' type."

"What if they had something on him?"

"It would have to be something pretty big. And maybe he has nothing to do with it. Maybe we're jumping at shadows." Cassidy stands. The exhaustion is rapidly sucking up the last of her energy. "I appreciate you watching Thor for me, but I need to get home and get some sleep."

He stands and hugs her. "Be safe, and call if you need anything."

Cassidy loads Thor in the car and walks around to the driver's side. She notices a car parked down the street with two people sitting inside, but she can't make out their faces at this distance. She gets in her car and moves her gun from the middle console safe to her front seat. Even if she's being paranoid, it doesn't hurt to be cautious.

It only takes her two stoplights and a series of turns to confidently determine that they're following her. She mentally runs through the options available to her. She can go home as she planned, go to a neutral location and see if they confront her, or drive directly to the FBI and wait for Alex to get out of her meeting. She asks Thor for his opinion, but he just licks the side of her face and pants happily next to her.

She's sitting in her driveway seven minutes later as they drive past. She manages to catch a partial plate and feels the bile rise in her throat when she realizes it's government-issued. *Shit.* She pulls the burner phone from her pocket and texts Alex to tell her what just happened. The response is almost instant. *Be there in 45.*

Cassidy makes herself busy by feeding Thor and taking a shower. Unfortunately, the hot spray does nothing to wash away the lingering feeling of being watched. It sticks to her like honey, making her uncomfortable and irritated. Almost forty-five minutes on the dot, she hears a tap on her sliding glass door. Alex puts a finger to her lips as she approaches, indicating she shouldn't say anything.

She unlocks the door, and Alex comes in with Leo right behind her. He's carrying a large duffel bag that he sets quietly on the floor while Alex closes the blinds and checks the windows. He points to the stereo in the corner of the room. Cassidy hurries over and turns it on.

Leo starts pulling out a variety of equipment and then raises an eyebrow at her and whispers, "Taylor Swift? Seriously?"

Cassidy crosses her arms. "She's the best lyricist of our generation."

Alex waves angrily. "Can you two not?"

Leo slides a small metal disc onto the coffee table and waits to speak until a small green light starts blinking.

Leo puts his hands on his hips. "Bob Dylan is the best songwriter of all time."

"I said of our generation, not ever."

He puts his hand on his chin and stares at her. "Eminem? Jay Z?"

Cassidy shrugs. "Their vibe is very different."

Alex is gripping the chair and staring at the floor. "Are you two done?" She grips the chair until it creaks. "Because we're in the middle of a shit storm. Think you can have this debate later?"

Leo pulls a handheld device and laptop from his bag. "I checked before we came inside, and there's no video feed coming from your house, but you're bugged." He points to the metal disc. "Right now, all they can hear is Taylor Swift. That disc is synced to your stereo through Bluetooth. It will amplify whatever is coming from your speakers to a frequency the bugs will hone in on and drown out other sounds. So, make sure you turn your stereo or TV on whenever you're talking to anyone."

Cassidy goes to touch the device, and Leo slaps her hand. "I didn't even know these things existed."

Leo straightens the device. "They don't. I made it. This is just the prototype."

"It's very impressive." Cassidy straightens. "You're a whole other level of smart."

"You have no idea." He turns his attention away from her and to his computer.

Cassidy almost laughs at his unbridled arrogance, but she's grateful he's on their side. She turns her attention to Alex, who is looking through a file she pulled from Leo's bag. Her face is etched with stress, and she has to force herself not to hug her.

Cassidy pulls a chair out and sits next to Alex. "How did things go with Gregory?"

"I've been suspended." She flips a page of the file. "The official story is because of the shooting, but he told me to keep him in the loop before I left. I had to turn over my gun and badge."

Her nonchalance momentarily catches Cassidy off guard. "What?" She stills Alex's hand with hers. "Tell me what happened."

Alex stares at her hand and looks reluctant as she pulls it away. "I gave him a little more detail this time. I explained that I was chasing down a lead that implicated voting machine fraud aimed at the next election. I explained that Hugh Bradley was the individual responsible for writing the algorithm. We were trying to get more information from him to see who else was involved. He asked if I had any names yet, and I told him no. He cussed a lot, threw a paperweight against the wall, and told me that I was suspended pending the investigation results from the shooting. Then he told me to keep him in the loop and that he'd keep it under wraps for as long as he could. He said the most he could give me was two weeks before people started asking questions."

It's then that Cassidy sees the file Alex is flipping through. "How did you get a copy of Gregory's personnel file?"

Alex nods toward Leo. "He pulled it for me. He also got a few scraps from Hugh's phone."

"I was also able to grab a few encrypted chats off Hugh's phone before he realized I'd cloned it and cut me off. Fletcher had funneled the down payment to him through cryptocurrency. Christie wasn't named explicitly, but he did mention a partner by the name of C. It's circumstantial at best, but from everything else we know, I think we're safe to make assumptions." Leo grabs a roll of electrical tape from his bag and starts walking around the room with his handheld device. He places small pieces in different areas. "I'm marking the bug locations. You should avoid these areas even with the device on, so you don't wash out the frequency with your voice."

Cassidy leans closer to Alex. "You need to be careful how you're using Leo. I'd hate for you to go to jail at the end of all this."

There's anger in Alex's eyes when she turns to look at her. "That is the least of my concerns. All I care about is stopping these guys. The consequences are secondary."

"Okay, I'd also prefer that you not get yourself killed," Cassidy says.

"I don't care about that either." Alex pulls another file from the duffel bag and slides it in front of Cassidy.

Cassidy looks at the name and feels her face heat. "Assistant Director Peterson? Dave Peterson?" She runs her hands over her face. "Alex, are you sure you want to go down this road?"

Alex flips the file open. "Hugh said we're corrupt, and he's done dealing with us. He spoke as if he had firsthand knowledge of dealing with someone at the FBI. If you were going to try to pull off something like this, you'd need someone close to the top, but not someone as visible as the director. You'd need someone with unfettered access to our files and who everyone would be afraid to question if their name ever popped in your head. And you'd need access to them. They'd have to be in your orbit. Peterson fits every category and Leo recovered selfies of the two of them from his cell. Peterson did a keynote speech about cybersecurity at a convention Hugh was at a year ago. According to the geotag from the pictures, the two went to a bar after the speech. That's too much of a coincidence for me." Alex sighs heavily. "I don't need your opinion, Cassidy. I need your expertise."

Cassidy searches her face, trying not to let the flippant comment sting. Alex's eyes are rimmed red, she's clenching and releasing her jaw, and there are dark circles under her eyes. She can feel the stress and frustration coming off her in waves. Cassidy picks up the file and scans the information. She reads the first few lines six times, unable to bring the words into focus.

She closes the file and hands it back to Alex. "I don't need the file to tell you if he fits the profile." She rubs the back of her neck and considers her words. She doesn't want to amp Alex up and get her fixated, but it may already be too late for that. "Of course he does. He's been at the top of the food chain for almost twelve years. He's nearing retirement. It's pretty clear that he harbors resentment for not reaching the position of director. He thinks it's owed to him. He believes he's the best in any room, the smartest, best looking, most charismatic." She looks away at the excitement building on Alex's face. "I would bet that if you look through that file, you'll see that he was passed up for either a promotion or significant award in the last year. I'd also bet that would coincide with some major life change—a spouse leaving, parent or child getting sick, something."

Alex taps the pen against her chin. "You're good." She flips open the file and starts poring over the pages.

Leo sits down with Cassidy's last soda and pops open the top. "Let's see what Dave Peterson is hiding." He cracks his knuckles and puts his fingers on the keyboard. "I took your last soda, by the way. You should go shopping. There's nothing to eat here."

"You're a real charmer."

Alex continues to read. "I don't need him for his people skills."

Leo snorts. "Thank God." He taps away for several more minutes with a pained expression. "This guy isn't going to be easy to nail down. He doesn't do any online banking, and he's not on any dark web chat groups. Even his emails are few and far between. He's like a ghost."

Alex stands, and her irritation is palpable. "I know he's involved. I can feel it. I've known him since I was a kid. He was always kind and funny. He was a staple at all our family events and holidays. A few years ago, that all changed. He missed my dad's sixtieth birthday, and he stopped going to all our family events. The few times I've seen him and my father together, it usually devolves into arguments about politics and our government. They used to be completely aligned, and now they're on opposite sides of the spectrum." She shrugs. "I know it doesn't sound like much, but I'm good at what I do, and I'm telling you, the arrows lead to him."

Leo shrugs. "None of that matters if I can't prove it."

Cassidy traces the grain in her wood table with her thumb. She mentally replays all her interactions with Dave Peterson. "His suits are always impeccable. I've never seen him without a fresh haircut, and his nails are always perfectly trimmed. I've even seen him remove scuff marks from his briefcase."

Leo sighs. "So? Are you writing a dating profile for him or something?"

Cassidy picks up the pen to throw at him but changes her mind, refusing to give in to his goading. "No. He's meticulous and craves control. He wouldn't trust online banking or cloud servers with his emails. He'd keep everything nearby. He'd want to be able to get rid of it if need be, and he'd want to know exactly who had access. It will be in his home office. If there's anything to find on him, it will be there."

Leo blows on his fingers and rubs them against his chest. "I'm always down for a little breaking and entering."

Alex nods. "Agreed, it's the only way."

Cassidy shakes her head. "You can't just break into his house."

Alex leans her forearms on the top of the chair. "You're right. You, Hunter, and Leo are going to do it."

Cassidy stares at her. She's waiting for the punchline, a laugh, anything to indicate that she's joking, but she just stares at her with determined eyes.

Alex continues. "He's going to go visit my dad after work tomorrow. That's a perfect time. I'll be there already. I'll have eyes on him and will be able to tell you when he's leaving."

Cassidy's chest tightens, and a resounding "abso-fucking-lutely not" rests on her tongue. It's what she wants to say, but a nagging agreement pulls the words back down into her throat. If he really is the key to this group's law enforcement protection, they need to know before getting any further along. Hell, for all she knows, he's directly involved with the plan and not just acting as a shield. Either way, they couldn't go after Fletcher and Christie without removing this obstacle.

"Okay," Cassidy says to Alex, but she stares at Thor. She's ashamed of her decision, and even though it was born in Alex's mind, it's hard to look at her.

"Well, fuck me, that was easier than I thought." Leo shakes his head and goes back to typing.

Alex sits down next to her and takes her hands. "Are you sure about this?"

Cassidy sighs and gives a half-shrug. "I'll talk to Hunter."

Alex rubs her thumbs back and forth over the back of Cassidy's hands. "I know I don't always seem appreciative of everything you're doing and everything you've done, but I am. Thank you."

Cassidy studies the blatant sincerity etched across her face. For a moment, she lets herself imagine what it would've been like had they connected under different circumstances. Where would they be if whatever was happening between them wasn't weighed down and colored by evil people, possible traitors, and perhaps even a crooked FBI assistant director? Would the chemistry still be there, or did it exist because it had been infused with chaos? In the best of circumstances it's difficult to wade through evolving emotions—this feels almost impossible; impossible yet thrilling in a way Cassidy has never experienced. The intense draw to Alex in these circumstances eclipses logic and some may even say common sense, but the need to be near her is hypnotic.

"Can I show you something real quick?" She stands and pulls Alex with her. She holds Alex's hand as she leads her into her bedroom.

Alex shuts the door. "Is everything okay?"

Of course, it's a ridiculous question because, logically, nothing is okay. Alex killed someone, she's been suspended from her job, Cassidy's house is bugged, and they're planning to break into Assistant Director Peterson's house. But the rapid drumming of her heart with Alex this close to her drowns out all the other noise.

Cassidy puts her hands on Alex's shoulders and pushes her slowly until her back hits the wall. She slides her hands up her neck and into her hair. She lets her body rest against hers. She brings her mouth to Alex's and waits for Alex to give in by closing the last of the distance between them.

They only share a single breath of anticipation before Alex captures her mouth with her lips. One of the most enthralling aspects of Alex is that she kisses with her entire body. Her hands are in Cassidy's hair, her chest rises and falls rapidly against her own, and she pushes slightly into her hips. The fuse Alex is always able to ignite is short. It burns hot and golden and hypersonic. Cassidy's hands roam down her body until they find Alex's belt. She tugs on it, prompting a soft growl from somewhere low in Alex's throat.

There's a tap on the door. "I umm...I haven't checked that room. Just putting it out there."

Cassidy pulls away from Alex, panting. "You've got to be kidding me," she mumbles against Alex's neck.

Alex kisses her forehead and adjusts her belt. Cassidy reluctantly pulls away and straightens her hair with her hands. Alex looks at her reassuringly before she opens the door. Leo is standing on the other side looking apologetic. Cassidy can't bear to make eye contact with him as she passes.

The few minutes they spend at the kitchen table waiting for him to finish his bedroom sweep are spent in silence. Alex drags her hand lazily back and forth along Cassidy's leg. Cassidy meticulously tracks her movements and mentally berates herself for glancing around her kitchen, considering all possibilities.

Leo walks out a few minutes later. "I checked all the bedrooms. Only the family room and kitchen are bugged." He awkwardly puts his devices into his duffel bag and turns to Alex. "I hate to do this, but you're my ride." He points to Cassidy. "I'll meet you at the gas station three miles east from the target tomorrow night at six."

Alex smirks and turns to Cassidy, kissing the top of her head. "I'll see you tomorrow night."

The desire to grab Alex's hand and ask her to come back after she drops Leo off is strong, but the sudden and overwhelming exhaustion that pierces her is sharp. Thor follows them to the back door and watches them leave as Cassidy moves around the space turning off the lights. She ignores the little specks of black tape marking different pockets of her house. An hour ago, the initial surge of intrusion was replaced by annoyance and anger. Her mind springs between the memory of Alex touching her and her desire to neutralize the people threatening her and three hundred million unknowing citizens. She crawls into bed and lets the exhaustion take her before her brain can offer a counterargument.

CHAPTER TWELVE

It feels like the clock is screaming the passing seconds at her as Alex waits in the driveway in front of her parents' house. She's always felt safe here. Her parents have always accepted her exactly as she is. She's never taken that fact for granted. She knows how lucky she is and how things could've been very different for her. Yet, here she sits. The unknown of what waits for her on the other side is so painfully acute that it's rendered her motionless. She's been telling herself it's the unease of Dave Peterson's arrival, but the truth is, she's scared to see any remnants of pain on her father's face—proof that he isn't going to live forever and how close she'd come to losing him.

In the front window, her mother's face pulls her from her internal reflection. *Shit.* She pulls her phone from the car charger and taps the front pocket of her jeans, checking for the burner phone. She hasn't quite reached the front door when her mom opens it and grabs her, wrapping her in a forceful, almost desperate hug.

"Hi, Mom."

"I'm so glad you're here." Her mom squeezes her a little tighter. "Maybe you can talk some sense into him. He thinks he's going fishing next week."

Alex nods, but they both know that will never happen. No one talks her father into or out of anything. Her mom used to lob her likeness to her father at her like small grenades—stubborn, willful, bull-headed. The teenage version of Alex would roll her eyes and swear they were nothing alike. She'd make deals with invisible entities to ensure she never resembled anything close to her father. Now she'll proudly accept that label.

He's sitting in his recliner, idly pushing buttons on the remote. "Hey, kiddo." His smile is bright and full of life.

The frustration, fear, stress, and uncertainty she's been feeling the last few weeks spill from her body as tears. "Hey, Dad." She swipes at her eyes forcefully, not wanting him to see her cry. "Please don't tell me the situation is so dire that you've taken to watching soaps."

He turns off the television and tosses the remote on the couch next to him. "Never." He smiles. "It's so good to see you."

"Sorry I didn't come sooner." She sits next to him on the couch her parents have owned for the better part of her life.

He waves her off and leans closer. "You didn't happen to bring me any contraband, did you?"

She pulls a Snickers bar from her pocket. "Don't tell Mom."

He winks at her and quickly unwraps the candy. "Clark and Elizabeth came by earlier today. They both said they've been trying to get a hold of you the last few weeks."

The mention of her siblings makes her chest burn. She hasn't necessarily been avoiding them, but she also wasn't eager to talk to them. The three of them are close, and it's difficult to lie to them. She's thought several times about picking up the phone to tell them about Cassidy, but that would inevitably lead to conversations about life and work—she couldn't take the chance.

"Yeah, I need to call them. I've just been really busy with work."

He stares at her. "I heard a rumor about that." He takes a bite of the candy bar. "Do you want to talk about it?"

"Not really."

Her dad is one of the few people who won't require a further explanation. It's not surprising he's already heard about the shooting—she'd expected that. He'd been involved in two throughout his long career, and he understands the desire not to want to rehash the events. But had he heard about her suspension and the fears she'd shared with Gregory?

He smacks her leg. "I'm here if you want to talk about anything."

She grabs his hand. "I know. Thank you." She squeezes a little tighter. "How are you feeling? Mom says you're planning on going fishing next week. Do you think that's a good idea?"

He waves in the direction of the kitchen. "She worries too much. I can't stay cooped up for the next ten years."

Alex chuckles. "Of course not, but would a few weeks be the worst thing?"

"Yes." He winks at her. "It will make you both feel better to know your brother is coming with me. It's about time he puts that expensive doctor degree to use."

"Pretty sure he does that every day."

He shrugs. "Now he can take his show on the road."

Her mom comes in with a glass of water for her dad and wine for herself and Alex. Alex checks the clock on her phone. Cassidy, Leo, and Hunter should be meeting at the gas station now. They won't go to Peterson's house until she lets them know it's safe to do so. Her leg starts to bounce with nervous energy, and she forces herself to stop. She's been involved in many missions over the years, but this was the first with the kind of consequences that would be catastrophic if she didn't succeed.

"Did you talk him out of fishing?" Her mom perches on the side of her dad's recliner and runs her fingers through his hair.

"A fishing trip I wasn't invited on?" Dave Peterson says from the entryway. He kisses her mom on the cheek. "Gloria, you look as beautiful as ever." He shakes her father's hand vigorously. "Tom, you look terrible."

Her father laughs. "Still better looking than you, Dave."

Dave looks Alex up and down. "You doing okay? I heard what happened."

"As good as can be expected." She stands, wondering how much he knows. "If you'll excuse me for a minute, I need to use the restroom."

He grabs her by the shoulder as she walks past. "From what I hear, you didn't have a choice. It will work itself out."

"Thanks." She concentrates on not shrinking away from his touch.

She opens her burner phone to text once she's away from prying eyes inside the bathroom. *He's here. Be safe.* She splashes cold water on her face and takes several deep breaths. The internal conflict squeezing her lungs and doing flutter kicks in her stomach is jarring. Part of her hopes they find something tonight that brings them a step closer to stopping these assholes. But the part of her that just witnessed the familial exchange with her parents hopes the worst they find is porn and some old scotch.

She dries her face on the towel and heads back into the living room. She takes her seat on the couch and picks up her wine. She's only half-listening to Dave and her father joke about anything and everything. An uncomfortable feeling of guilt and worry pinches at her temples. If they did find something, this would have consequences that reached far beyond work. Her father would feel betrayed and angry—he'd also do the exact same thing in her situation.

"So you ended up taking my advice?" Dave sips the glass of scotch her mother had brought him.

She knows he's referring to Cassidy, but she wants him to say it. Perhaps she can get a read on him if they continue down this conversation path. "What do you mean?"

He winks at her. "You took Cassidy Wolf to San Francisco." His expression doesn't give any hint as to what he's thinking, and she can't tell if he's playing games or is genuinely curious.

Based on what she's disclosed to Gregory, he should've kept the bulk of her report and the situation surrounding the shooting confidential. That wasn't standard practice, but Gregory said he'd do what he could until either more evidence was presented or if she was found negligent. He'd given her two weeks and then suspended her. He knew full well that any investigation she was going to do would be off-book.

"I did. We had a nice time."

"Until the shooting." He leans forward, and his stare is intense. "What happened with that anyway? I asked Gregory for the report, but he said he was still putting it together." He lifts his glass in her direction. "If I'm going to protect you, I need the facts."

Her dad clears his throat. "I don't think this is the time or place. Plus, when you came in, you said you heard it wasn't her fault. I'm sure the report will reflect that."

Dave doesn't look at her father. He continues to stare at her.

She sits still, keeping eye contact. "A guy pulled a knife and then a gun on my friend. He was a direct threat, and I fully believed he'd kill her or one of us. I don't need you to protect me from a justified shooting."

"Someone pulled a knife on Cassidy?" He squints at her, and it's the first time since the conversation began that she can sense his anger.

"It wasn't Cassidy. It was another friend of mine."

His composure has returned. He sits back in his seat and rests his glass on the arm of the chair. "I'm surprised they let you go a few hours later."

She shrugs. "I cleared it with the local field office and immediately reported to Gregory. I'll go back if need be."

She only has about another twenty-four hours before this story is likely to hit the press. Once that happens, all involved parties will be suspicious. The likelihood of them destroying evidence increases exponentially. She needs every minute available to her.

Her mom finally fills the silence that is sucking all the oxygen out of the room. "Tell me about Cassidy." She smiles. "Are you two dating?"

The answer to this question is much more important than it seems on the surface. If she lies and says there's no romantic interest, it will pique Dave's curiosity. He'll have more questions than answers about why they took off across the country together on such short notice. But it also makes Cassidy a target as someone important to her. If she says no, then that only leaves work as a reason they would've been together.

She smiles warmly at her mother. "We're exploring the possibility of being more than friends." For all her mental fumbling over what to say, she accidentally told the truth.

"I think that's lovely. No reason to rush into anything. Even if you are the only one of my children who isn't married." She hides her raised eyebrows behind her glass of wine.

Her dad is looking between her and his best friend. He seems uneasy and almost agitated. "Alex, honey, can you help me get something out of my office for Dave?"

Alex quickly stands. "I can get it for you, Dad."

He waves her off and stands. "It's under a bunch of papers. It's easier just to show you." He points to Dave. "Don't go anywhere. You're going to want this."

Dave nods and checks his watch. "Sure thing. I have a few more minutes."

Once inside the office, her dad peeks out one more time before shutting the door. He pulls her over to the far corner. "I don't know exactly what was going on in San Francisco, and I don't care. Dave is fishing for information. I worked with him for a long time, and he was interrogating you."

Alex crosses her arms feeling more vulnerable than she'd like. "The shooting was solid. I have nothing to hide."

He grabs her arm and whispers, "I'm not talking about that. Dave has been acting off since his wife left. I've tried to keep him focused and even told him to retire with me, but he refused. Based on his behavior and your shitty poker face, I'm assuming you think he's involved in something, and that's why you were out in San Francisco. Chasing down a lead?"

Alex takes a deep breath and says nothing, hoping her silence speaks volumes.

He scratches at the scruff of his few-day-old beard. "If you're going to take a shot at him, make sure it lands." He squeezes her shoulder. "Missing would sink your career and everyone involved."

"I know," Alex says softly, seeing only concern, not judgment, in his expression. "I don't plan on missing." The knowledge that her dad already had concerns about Peterson only serves to underscore her distrust of him, and knowing her dad supports her, even without knowing what was going on, gives her spine the steel it needs.

He pats the side of her face. "Good girl."

He shuffles a few papers around and grabs a small envelope from the bottom of the pile. He motions for her to follow him back out into the living room.

Her dad hands Dave the envelope. "Here are my Washington Nationals tickets for the next month. I promised my bride I'd take it easy." He kisses the side of her mom's head. "See? I listen."

Dave puts the envelope into his breast pocket. "Thank you. I'll put these to good use." He stands. "I should get going. I still have a lot of work to do." He kisses her mom and shakes her dad's hand. "If you need anything, don't hesitate to call." He turns his attention to Alex. "If you feel like talking, you know where to find me."

Alex nods. "Thank you."

Alex sits on the couch where she can watch him get into his car. As soon as he's out of the driveway, she texts Cassidy. *You have twenty minutes left until he arrives. Meet me at my house immediately after.*

Her dad stares at her intently. "Good?"

She stands and kisses her mom. "I need to get going."

Her mom points to the kitchen. "But I made us dinner. I want to hear about Cassidy."

Her dad stands. "I would love a romantic dinner with just the two of us, my love." He hugs Alex. "Remember who you are." He kisses her forehead. "There's nothing I won't do to help you."

"Thanks, Dad. I love you too." She kisses her mom again. "As soon as things slow down at work, we'll have lunch, and I'll tell you all about Cassidy. I promise."

Her mom squeezes Alex's hands. She's had a lifetime of these interrupted meals and knows better than to ask anything further. "I'm going to hold you to that."

Alex heads back to her house, hoping the entirety of the short drive that she'll be seeing Cassidy a few minutes later. It's alarming to realize that her longing isn't entirely because of the case but also because being near Cassidy brings her more peace than she's felt in a long time.

CHAPTER THIRTEEN

L eo gives Hunter the thumbs-up, meaning he's looped the surveillance cameras to hide their presence inside the house. Hunter pulls out his lockpick and moves them around until there's a quiet tick, and he opens the door.

"Told you I was handy," he whispers as he walks through the door.

"I never said you weren't handy." Cassidy uses her redlight flashlight to look for the office door. "I said you are a poor communicator who spent more time at the gym than with me."

Hunter points to a pair of doors about twenty feet from them. "Well, looking like this doesn't happen on accident."

Leo scoots up between them and opens the twin doors that lead to the office. "Does he know you're sleeping with Derby?"

Cassidy smacks him as he walks past. "I haven't slept with Derby." She pauses. "Not yet anyway."

Hunter doesn't seem fazed in the slightest. "I wouldn't have to be an investigator to have guessed that. I'm honestly not surprised."

"You're not?" Cassidy pulls back several books from the shelf to see if there's anything hidden behind them.

Hunter pulls the redlight flashlight from his mouth. "No. You're both hot. It makes sense."

Cassidy rolls her eyes, even though he can't see her. "It's not just about that."

Hunter picks the lock on the desk. "I know, but that's more fun to say. You're both intelligent, successful, and driven." He pulls the desk drawer open. "Is that better?"

Leo plugs his computer into the one on the desk. "And people say I'm bad with women."

Hunter flops several ledgers on the desk. "I'm not bad with women. Cassidy and Alex don't count."

Cassidy stands behind him. "In case anyone was wondering why we're now divorced, I think you just cleared that up."

Hunter takes pictures of several pages. "Not that you need my permission, but I think you and Alex are a great idea. I hope it works out for you guys. All I ever wanted was for you to be happy."

Their divorce hadn't been messy, but it had still been painful like all endings. Admitting that you failed at something—even for the right reasons, is always hard. She values the friendship they've built since then, and it touches her to know that Hunter feels the same.

She bumps his shoulder with hers. "I want you to be happy too."

Leo sighs. "I'm sure there are a quadrillion better places to have this conversation."

Hunter points to the page he just flipped over. "Three transactions made exactly two weeks apart totaling three million dollars. I'll bet if we run these account numbers they trace back to Fletcher, Christie, and Bradley." He takes pictures of different pages of the logbook. "Fuck. I was really hoping he wasn't involved."

Leo's fingers fly across the keyboard. "You're right about Fletcher and Christie, but the third one doesn't belong to Hugh Bradley." He shakes his head. "Whoever it is, they're very well hidden." He tosses his phone down and turns back to the computer on the desk. "I'll see if I can crack it later."

"It's unfortunate, but it's not surprising," Cassidy says and moves over to the corner of the room, where she sees several pictures.

Leo scoffs. "People never surprise me. I just assume everyone is shitty."

Cassidy picks up a framed photo of Dave Peterson and Tom Derby holding a large fish. "Living like that isn't healthy either." Her burner phone vibrates, and she opens the message. "We need to get out of here. We only have twenty minutes until he's back."

Leo taps the desk impatiently. "I need three more minutes."

Cassidy acts on a hunch and opens the back of the picture frame she's still holding. There's a small ultra-thin flash drive taped to the back. Adrenaline starts to burn the back of her throat.

She taps Leo and holds it up for him to inspect. "We're going to want to see what's on this."

Leo grabs it and slides it into a small port attached to his phone. "Shit. I've never seen encryption like this. It's going to take me a while to crack it."

"Take it," Hunter says. Before anyone can protest, he continues. "Fuck this guy. What's he going to do? Have us arrested? We need to stop this before it happens."

Cassidy nods, and Leo slides it into his pocket. They're outside the house a few minutes later and heading toward the gas station to pick up the car. They may have just decided to put the whole ring of conspirators on alert, but the decision could buy them the opportunity to be a step ahead. Whatever the outcome, they are in this together. She just hopes that Alex feels the same way.

Alex paces in her basement, waiting for her hodgepodge team to arrive. Briggs tracks her movements with indifference. "What if they find something? What if they don't find anything?"

He stares at her blankly and then dismisses her by licking his paw.

She runs her hand through her hair. "My thoughts exactly. There are no ideal outcomes." She stares at him. "But something is better than nothing." He hops off the back of the sofa, and she flops onto it. "I've lost my fucking mind. There's no other way around it."

Hunter enters through her side door with Cassidy and Leo close behind. The instant reprieve of seeing them unharmed flashes hot. Her relief forces her off the couch and directly to Cassidy. She instinctually wraps her in a hug and lets out the breath she hadn't been able to release since they arrived.

Her cheek is cool against Alex's hot skin. "I'm glad you're okay."

Cassidy pulls back and searches her face. "Are you okay?"

Alex ignores the other eyes on them and kisses Cassidy's cheek. "I am now." She rests her forehead against Cassidy's. "I needed you to be okay."

Leo clears his throat. "You know how I hate to break up... whatever this adorable thing is, but we need to talk."

Alex listens as they tell her what they found at Dave Peterson's house. "How long do you think it will take you to crack that encryption?"

Leo smiles. "It should take about six hours, but I'll have it done in two."

Hunter prints the photos from his phone and hangs them on the wall next to the rest of the evidence. "Peterson is clearly involved with Fletcher and Christie. People don't exchange millions of dollars to settle bar tabs. But the third person is a wild card. We don't have anything pointing to a third. Not in the texts that Leo was able to get, and there's nothing solid in any of the information you've gathered."

Alex stands next to him and looks at all the information she's gathered over the last two years. "How can we be missing such a big piece of the puzzle?"

Hunter scratches his chin with his thumb and moves closer to the board. "Cassidy, who has the most to gain if this election is compromised?"

Cassidy moves over to the section of the board where dozens of pictures are stuck with small magnets. "It's going to be someone who doesn't necessarily care about the outcome—that's secondary in their mind." She moves several high-profile politicians off to the side. "This person will crave chaos and disorder while wanting to be in charge of it. They'll have grand ideas about installing a shadow government, and they'll have their cronies in line to take up the mantel."

Alex pinches the bridge of her nose. "Dave Peterson. He'd be easy to install and has the credentials to warrant a high-profile position."

Cassidy nods and continues to stare at the board. "Not just him, the others too. Christie and Fletcher are expecting positions as well. This person will want to break our alliances and isolate the country completely. They'll want to cut us off from the global economy and any diplomacy. Messing with the election this way isn't about gaining a presidency or more seats in congress. This is about a deeper anarchy, something so volatile that only the group who set it in motion will be able to corral it into something they can then use for control." She moves four individuals associated with far-right extremists to the top of the board. "According to your tracking, these four have been the most vocal. They've been saturating the far-right media with appearances on podcasts, YouTube channels, writing in fringe newsletters, and popping into events. The answer is somewhere in there, and I believe it's one of these four people. I don't think the person at the top will necessarily believe all that nonsense, but they'll have been planting seeds for a long time. They've been building an army for a while."

"We should talk to Carol O'Brien. She'll know who we should be looking for," Hunter says to no one in particular. "She was ready for a takeover before, and she's moved in these shady circles for a long time."

Alex doesn't bother to stifle her laugh. "She's in a black hole somewhere. It's not like we can just sign in on a visitor's sheet or make an appointment."

"Brooke can get Cassidy in for a BAU interview." Hunter shrugs. "Doesn't hurt to ask."

Alex shakes her head. "Brooke won't have access, but her wife, Tyler, will."

"Set it up. I'll go as soon as she can get me in," Cassidy says. "We're running out of time."

Alex manages to get Brooke on the phone within a few minutes, and they agree that talking to Carol O'Brien is the most efficient path forward. It's easy to negotiate with people who have nothing to lose—you can offer them very little in return for information.

Alex tosses her phone on the table. "We're going to meet Tyler tomorrow at zero seven hundred."

Hunter shakes his head. "Cassidy should go alone. You're suspended, and I'd have no reason to be there. I know that's not what you want to hear, but she's more than likely being kept at a black ops facility, and they're going to scan everyone's badge. Not only that, from everything I've read about Carol O'Brien, she treats every encounter like a game. She'll be more likely to play if she thinks the odds are in her favor."

"You're right. I didn't even think of that," Alex says. The idea of Cassidy being in a room with Carol O'Brien should make her uneasy, but in reality, there's no one better suited. "Tyler will meet you in the lobby of DHS."

Cassidy twirls a pen between her fingers. "The likelihood of my interview with her tomorrow being recorded is incredibly high. They'll know what we're after, and that will be it. They may try to shut us down."

Alex shrugs. "They're going to know by tomorrow that I killed Hugh Bradley, if they don't already know." She points to Leo. "Not to mention the little device you lifted from Peterson. The outcome will be the same if he finds out it's missing."

Leo smacks the table. "One hour and eighteen minutes. I cracked this bitch in one hour and eighteen minutes." He stands and claps several times.

"Well? What did you find?" Alex moves to look at the computer.

"Oh yeah, sorry." He sits back down and points at the screen. "There are hundreds of files on here, but these look like building plans. Not just for houses or businesses but entire cities." He opens a few more files. "Holy shit." Lines and lines of garbled letters and numbers fill the screen. "This is the algorithm for the voting machines. Or, more accurately, the virus. This is definitely a copy, but here it is. It connects him to Hugh, no question."

"Why in the world would Peterson be keeping that on a disk in his house?" Hunter moves his face closer to the screen. "Why keep evidence like this on hand?"

Cassidy moves Peterson's picture up closer to the top of the board. "Leverage. He wants to be able to blackmail whoever he's working for if things don't go his way. He wouldn't trust it anywhere else but in his home."

Leo smiles widely. "I know this is bad, but can we all take a minute to appreciate my brilliance? I mean, I'm fucking impressive."

Alex claps him on the back. "Great job, Leo."

Leo continues to type. "I was hoping for a little more excitement, but I guess I'll take your scraps. So unappreciative."

Alex's nerves are fried. Nervous energy trickles down her spine, simultaneously bringing on overwhelming feelings of exhaustion and energy. Finding compartments to place all these crushing feelings in is becoming more difficult as time transforms from hours to days to weeks. The only compartment she's getting better at accepting contains her feelings for Cassidy.

Alex heads up to the kitchen. She grabs several bottles of water and places them on the counter. She intends to bring them downstairs, but she feels hands on her back before she can head in that direction.

"Are you okay?" Cassidy's tone is tentative.

Alex doesn't turn to face her. She wants to concentrate on the next few days and the possibility of Cassidy derailing that—if even for a night, is too high. "Yeah, I just needed to move around a little bit."

Cassidy drags her fingertips down her back. "You know I'm here if you want to talk. I know this is all overwhelming, especially considering your family's connection to Peterson."

Alex rarely talks about her feelings. She knows it's not actually a sign of weakness, but it feels that way sometimes. But wanting to share things with Cassidy is starting to become as instinctual as breathing. "I'm trying to shove all these feelings into different boxes, but I don't know how to label them."

Cassidy forces her to turn around. She rests her hands on Alex's shoulders and puts her thumbs gently on her cheekbones. "I need you to really hear what I'm about to say." She waits for Alex to nod her agreement. "These boxes you're so desperately trying to organize in your head aren't real. You can't compartmentalize your feelings because you're a fully functioning person. Fears, hopes, dreams, love, hate—it's all glitter. You can't escape any of it. Every experience, every interaction sticks to you. It clings to you and colors every decision you make. Over time the colors become more expansive and either aid or hinder you." She pushes a piece of hair out of Alex's eyes. "People only ever pretend to compartmentalize. When really, the glitter is in every crevice of our minds."

Alex swallows back the lump in her throat. "How did you become so smart?"

Cassidy smiles and presses her forehead to Alex's. "I embrace the glitter," she whispers. She kisses her softly on the lips. "Come down when you're ready."

Ready. It is such a definitive word. Ready implies that you're either prepared or you aren't. A month ago, if you had asked her if she was ready for Cassidy Wolf, she would've answered unequivocally no. But no one is ever ready to be affected the way Cassidy stirs her. Now, all she can say with certainty is that she can't stay away.

CHAPTER FOURTEEN

Cassidy wakes to a cold paw tapping her cheek. She opens one eye to see Briggs standing on her side and aggressively investigating her face. Her neck and back are kinked in a way she hasn't experienced since college. It's not surprising. Alex's basement couch seems to be older than her. She gingerly pushes herself up and realizes the reason for her body aches. She quite literally fell asleep on Alex.

Alex looks peaceful and unperturbed by the movement. Alex is always beautiful, but she looks ten years younger without worry and stress etching her features. Cassidy carefully reaches out and moves a strand of hair away from her eyes. Alex's lips curl into a smile, and the delicate unconscious action warms Cassidy's chest.

Briggs enthusiastically jumps from Cassidy's leg to Alex's shoulder. In the process, he slips and slides behind Alex, meowing loudly.

"I'll rehome you if you don't let me sleep for five more minutes," Alex says without opening her eyes. Briggs meows again. "Fine." She sits up and notices Cassidy. "Hey."

"Hey," Cassidy says and moves back to give her room to move. "That's not how I thought our first night sleeping together would go."

Alex chuckles. "There are definitely better reasons to have only gotten," she checks her phone, "three hours of sleep."

Hunter and Leo come down the stairs with cups of coffee. "Oh good, you two are finally awake. I was coming down to wake you."

Cassidy glares at them. "Why do you two look so rested?"

Hunter points up the stairs with his thumbs. "I slept in Alex's bed, and Leo took the guest room."

"You didn't think to wake us up?"

Leo scoffs. "I wasn't ending up on that fifty-year-old couch."

"It's IKEA." Alex takes the cup of coffee Hunter offers her.

Leo rolls his eyes. "Same thing."

Cassidy takes the other cup from Hunter. "Don't you sleep in a van half the time?"

"With very expensive pillows." Leo's tone is incorrigible.

Hunter hands Cassidy her phone. "I went by your house, fed and walked Thor, grabbed you some clothes, and charged your phone."

Leo grunts. "You after a five-star Yelp review or something?"

Hunter smacks him in the back. "She needs a clear head, and we're friends. You know what those are, don't you?"

Leo continues to tap away on the keyboard. "I had a pet rat for a while." He stops typing and turns. "Well, I guess technically he wasn't a pet. He just started living in my van, and I let him stay."

The room is quiet until Cassidy finally breaks the silence. "Okay, on that note...I'm going to take a shower. I don't need any rats following me around."

Cassidy showers quickly and gets ready while turning over the best way to approach Carol O'Brien. She's read her one and only interview with the BAU, which turned up very little. Carol is brilliant and driven by vanity and perception. She'll use a solid approach of astonishment and curiosity to get as much information as possible.

Will it work? Maybe. Do they have a better option? No.

Alex stops her before she heads out the door. She looks unsure of herself, and the idea that Cassidy has this effect on her causes her stomach to flip. "I just wanted to tell you good luck." She rocks back on her feet and slides her hands into the back pockets of her jeans. "So, good luck."

Cassidy grabs her shirt and pulls her closer. She kisses her until she feels Alex relax. "For the record, that's how I prefer to be seen off," she whispers against her lips.

"I'll keep that in mind." Alex kisses her again.

"I'm going to the office after the interview. I want to get a read on what's going on there. They haven't called me in yet, so either Gregory really has kept this buried or I've been fired and no one has bothered to tell me." Cassidy kisses her cheek. "I'll call you later."

"Drive safe."

Cassidy makes it to the DHS lobby at exactly zero seven hundred to find Tyler Monroe already waiting. "I hope you weren't waiting long." She extends her hand, and Tyler takes it. "Cassidy Wolf, BAU."

Tyler's smile is genuine and welcoming. "Tyler Monroe, but I guess you already knew that."

Tyler starts moving toward the parking garage, and Cassidy follows quickly behind. "I'm a big fan of your wife." She rolls her eyes at herself for sounding like some kind of fangirl.

Tyler laughs. "Me too."

Cassidy knew Tyler was attractive from her pictures, but they had nothing on the real thing. Tyler oozes confidence and strength. It was easy to see why someone like Brooke had fallen for her.

Cassidy rolls down the window once they pull out of the garage. The spring air feels wonderful against her face. "How is Brooke holding up after San Francisco?"

Tyler glances over at her and gives her a partial smile. "She's good. I know she was more scared than she'd admit to me, though."

"Yeah, it was a very intense few minutes."

"How is Alex holding up?" Tyler turns onto an unmarked private road.

"Holding up the weight of the world on her shoulders." Cassidy pulls her badge from her purse in anticipation.

"Sounds like Alex." She shakes her head. "I used to be just like that."

"What changed?"

Tyler looks thoughtful as they approach the heavy steel gate. "Brooke."

Jesus. These two are like something straight out of a romance novel. Cassidy has never subscribed to the idea that a single person could elicit such profound feelings. The premise of discovering that home isn't necessarily a place, but a person has never been something she thought was true. Some people would refer to such a concept as soul mates, but that has always seemed silly. *Seemed? When did I start thinking about this topic in the past tense?* Even if she isn't ready to admit it aloud, she knew when. The first time she'd kissed Alex.

She pushes the distracting thoughts away. Concentration is key, and she needs to be ultra focused. Anything less isn't acceptable.

The guard takes their badges and scans them with his tablet. After a few seconds, he motions for them to go through. Cassidy's shoulders relax, and she lets out a long breath.

Tyler turns into a gravel lot. "You didn't think they'd let you in, huh?"

"I honestly wasn't sure. We have a lot of balls up in the air right now and no control over how and when they land." Cassidy shoves the badge back into her purse.

"Want some unsolicited advice?" Tyler takes her sunglasses off and tucks them into the opening of her button-down shirt. Cassidy nods, so she continues. "It's going to sound cliché, but it's worked for me a thousand times over. Follow your gut and do the right thing. These people you're after, they're all the same. Believe me. I've seen my fair share. But they have no moral compass—no guiding principles. It makes them unpredictable and dangerous, but if you stay the course by following yours, you'll more than likely end up the victor."

"The right thing, huh?"

Tyler shrugs. "Is there an alternative you could actually live with?"

"No," Cassidy says without hesitation.

Tyler smiles and opens the door. "If shit really hits the fan, call me. This old cat still has a few lives left."

Tyler uses her badge to open a heavy metal door that leads directly into an elevator. She pushes the button for sublevel six. "I'm not going to tell you how to do your job, but protocol dictates that I have to be in the room with you. I should also warn you that the walls have ears, and they're always listening."

"I understand. Thank you for doing this." The elevator screeches and wobbles, but Cassidy makes an effort not to look around in terror. "When they say she's in a black hole somewhere, they mean that literally, huh?"

Tyler nods. "I'll have them get a cell ready for your perp too."

The elevator door opens to a long gray hallway equipped with the kind of harsh fluorescent lighting your eyes have to endure when there's no natural light to offset their brutality.

One guard is sitting at an immaculate desk. He's wearing fatigues, but there's no branch identification anywhere on his uniform. "Who are you here to see?"

Tyler hands him her badge. "Carol O'Brien."

He pounds away on the keyboard and stares at Cassidy with his hand out. She hands him her badge. "Leave all weapons, phones, and keys here." He slides two metal boxes in front of them.

They unload their items and wait for him to lock the top of the boxes. He takes off down the hallway, and they dutifully follow behind. They stop in front of a heavy steel door, and he peers through the small, barred window. He punches a sequence of numbers into the keypad next to the door and waits for a series of locks to disengage.

"Hit the emergency button if there's an issue," he says before slamming the door behind them.

Carol O'Brien lounges on her metal cot like she's on a beach in the Bahamas instead of a maximum security black ops facility, wearing an orange jumpsuit. "Tyler Monroe, I wondered when you'd come to visit me again." She lays her book down and saunters toward them. "And you brought a friend. How sweet." She drags her finger down Cassidy's arm. "Beautiful too." She turns and sits down, crossing her legs. "I hope everything with you and Brooke is okay." Her rhetorical sentiment doesn't so much as garner a second glance from Tyler.

Carol is elegant, arrogant, and clearly a sociopath. Cassidy's skin prickles with excitement. The profiler in her has imagined the day when she'd get this opportunity. Granted, she thought it would be under different circumstances, but it was thrilling all the same.

Cassidy pulls out her notebook and sits across from her at the small metal table. "My name is Cassidy Wolf. I'm a profiler with the BAU." She extends her hand and smiles.

Carol stares at the hand for longer than what's socially acceptable before taking it, but Cassidy knows it's a power move. Carol is setting the pace and letting Cassidy know she's in charge. "What brings you here today, Agent Wolf?" She glances at Tyler. "And don't bother telling me it's for the BAU database. If that were the case, she wouldn't be with you."

Cassidy immediately starts with her plan to stroke Carol's ego. She smiles at her. "I wouldn't have even tried to lie to you. There'd be no point. I'm here because you may know something—"

Carol cuts her off and turns her attention to Tyler. "I want new books weekly. I want to shower at least four times a week, and I want to pick the hour a day I go outside."

Tyler nods once. "I'll see what I can do."

She looks at Cassidy. "That's just for the privilege of picking my brain. Information will cost you more." She motions for Cassidy to continue.

Cassidy runs through a high-level synopsis of the situation. Carol listens with one arm draped over the back of her chair and her leg rocking up and down through Cassidy's whole spiel. She checks her nails several times and even plays with the ends of her hair. She seems bored, but Cassidy knows better. Carol is absorbing everything.

"What part of California are you from?" Carol taps the desk with her nail. "Your speech pattern and cadence scream the Bay Area."

Cassidy nods. "San Francisco." She smiles. "That's very impressive."

"Are you close with your parents?"

Cassidy hates the idea of divulging anything personal, but if she lies and gets caught, Carol may dismiss her entirely. So she'll play her game for now. "I am, yes."

"Married?"

Cassidy shakes her head. "Divorced."

Carol raises an eyebrow. "Why? Pretty thing like you—I can't imagine he cheated on you."

Cassidy smirks. "We just grew into different people. We're still very good friends."

This piques Carol's attention. She leans forward on the table. "You're so pleasant. So controlled. So drab." She draws circles on the table with her finger. "Do you ever lose control, Agent Wolf? Does staying in the little box they've built for you ever splinter against your skin? Does your rage ever bubble to the surface and burn whoever is in the vicinity?"

"Knock it off, Carol." Tyler's tone is a warning.

Carol's smile is slow and a bit sadistic. "If she wants information from me, she'll answer. That's all I want. I want her to tell me the truth about who she really is under all this," she waves her hand at Cassidy, "bullshit good girl facade."

Cassidy calmly puts the notepad and pen down. "You want the truth, Carol?" She waits for Carol to make eye contact with her before she continues. "I could sit here and tell you about the times I've gotten angry. I could divulge anecdotes of instances where I let rage get the best of me. We all have them, but that's not what you're really looking for. You want me to remember those times when I lost control to help you understand how you ended up here." Carol flinches, but she's come too far to stop now. "You want me to believe you got yourself into this situation because of a lapse in judgment." Cassidy folds her hands in front of her and steadies her voice. "But we both know that's not true. You're always the most intelligent person in the room. You have more control in your little finger than most people have when they focus all their energy. Your sophisticated brand of manipulation opened doors that other women had only ever dreamed about." She taps the desk. "You're not sitting here because of rage. You're sitting here because you trusted the wrong people. It turns out that you're a human like the rest of us."

Carol raises an eyebrow and a slow smirk tugs at her lips. "I never trusted them. I believed we had mutually assured destruction. I was wrong."

Cassidy cocks her head. "Are we looking for the same people who failed you, Carol? Wouldn't it be nice to know they were rotting away in a cell too? Why should it just be you?"

Carol's eye twitches so slightly that you wouldn't notice it unless you were studying every movement. "The person you're after won't serve a single day in jail. He's too big to fail. His wealth eclipses the GDP of two hundred countries. We don't have adequate words to describe the kind of power and protection that gives you. He's the closest thing to a God the world has ever seen."

"No one is above the law," Cassidy says.

Carol's laughter starts softly and then erupts into full belly whooping. She wipes a tear away. "Your innocence is refreshing."

Cassidy isn't amused. She puts her agitation in place and pushes on. "Think of the headlines. You could be the reason we break this case. Who knows what kind of favors that will get you."

Carol rolls her eyes and shakes her head. "I'd be dead before I could reap any of those benefits."

Cassidy grabs her hand. "We'll protect you. No one will touch you."

Carol puts her other hand over their clasped hands. "His reach is transcendental." She pulls her hands away. "We're done here." She looks at Tyler. "If you're unable to stop this wonderful inevitable clusterfuck, please know that I'll be coming for you first, the moment they let me out of here." She walks back to her bunk and retrieves her book. "You can see yourselves out."

Cassidy grabs her notebook and follows Tyler out the door. For her unwillingness to help outright, Carol gave them plenty. Only a handful of people fit the description, and Cassidy is confident their little team can nail it down from here.

CHAPTER FIFTEEN

Alex's leg violently bounces as she watches the news anchor describe the shooting in San Francisco. Images of Hugh Bradley flash on the screen, along with brief snippets from his family and friends. The words they use to describe him don't reflect the person she dealt with. She stares at her cell phone on the table, waiting for it to light up with notifications. Her heart practically jumps out of her chest when there's a knock at her door.

She looks through the peephole and is relieved to see Larry Edwards, her coworker, on the other side. She pulls the door open. "Hey, Larry. What are you doing here?"

He smiles and points inside. "I just needed to go over a few cases with you. We sure miss having you around, and I could use your advice."

She opens the door wider. "Sure, no problem."

He looks around the house. "Is Hunter here?"

Alex grabs two sodas from the fridge. "No. I haven't seen him in days."

He shifts his weight back and forth and throws his jacket back, resting his hand on his gun. "Anyone here with you?"

Alex examines his movements. He seems nervous, almost agitated. He's looking around purposefully. His finger taps the side of his gun in an unnatural rhythm. She becomes acutely aware of the low hum of her refrigerator and the muffled voices from the television in the other room. The switch in her head wired for an adrenaline dump flips.

She moves around to the other side of the counter, putting her garage door in her line of sight. "What are you doing here, Larry?"

His hand moves to the grip of his gun, and he slides the hood forward. "I don't want to do this, Alex. I really don't, but you went poking around in places you don't belong."

Alex calculates the probability of getting to the garage door and into her car without him shooting her. The truth is, the odds aren't great, but there are no other options—no good ones anyway.

She takes two steps. "What are you going to do, Edwards? Are you really going to shoot me? We came up together. What are you mixed up in?" The fact that they work for the same people doesn't escape her. This is coming from inside the bureau. It's a damn good clue, if she can live to use it.

He doesn't move. Sweat trickles down the side of his face. "No, I'm not going to shoot you. But I do need you to come with me."

She takes another step. "We both know I can't do that."

She intentionally looks behind him as if she just noticed something. The slight distraction works, and he diverts his attention to the corner of the room. She makes her move immediately. She pulls the bookcase forward as she runs down the hall, blocking his path. She makes it to the garage. Briggs is sitting on the roof of the car. She grabs him and ignores the way he claws at her arm. She tosses him into the back seat and pushes the ignition button on her car while hitting the button to open the large metal garage door.

She makes it out of her driveway just as Larry gets to his car. The speed at which she drives through her neighborhood will undoubtedly cause people to take notice. She makes several consecutive turns in an effort to lose Larry, but nothing works. He weaves in and out of traffic, matching each of her maneuvers. Heading toward the busy shopping complex will be her last chance to shake him. She knows he's called for reinforcements at this point because it's what she would do.

Her chance is the approaching yellow light. She stays in the through lane and makes a hard left at the last second. He misses it and continues straight. It won't work for long, there are only so many places this street leads, and he'll be able to cut her off when he makes it to the next intersection.

She makes a U-turn, ignores the barrage of horns and screams it elicits from the other motorists. She hits the highway at a speed that would get her license revoked. She pulls out her burner phone and calls her father, the one person she knows she can trust and who probably isn't being watched.

"Hello?"

He must be the only person alive that still answers numbers he doesn't recognize. Thank God.

"Dad, I've pissed off the wrong people with that investigation. One just came to my house. I've managed to lose them, but I need a safe place to go that won't keep me on the road too long."

Her dad doesn't waste any time asking for specifics. "I'm going to text you the address of your uncle's cabin. It's off the grid, but we all know that doesn't hold up forever. It'll buy you some time so you can figure out your next move." He shuffles several papers. "Do you need me to call anyone? I'd recommend divulging as little as possible to as few people as possible."

"I need to let Cassidy and Hunter know what's happening. I don't want her showing up at my house. She'll be able to get in contact with the others. I'll text her burner."

"No. You're going to drop your burner and your regular phone into the closest water you can find after getting the address. I'll take care of Cassidy and Hunter."

"No," she says emphatically. "I don't want you involved with any of this."

"I appreciate the sentiment, kiddo, but I'm your father and you know as well as I do how family can be used as leverage, so I'm in no matter what. Stay safe, and don't call me again. If these people are unhinged enough to come to your house, it won't be long before they monitor my calls." He makes noise as he moves around, papers shuffling, zippers zipping. "I love you."

"Love you too, Dad." She waits for the information to be sent.

She memorizes the address and grabs her water bottle from the back seat. She empties the liquid contents into a grocery bag. She pulls the sim card from under the battery of her burner phone and tosses it into the water. Next, she takes her personal phone and pushes it against the steering wheel until it snaps open. She pulls the sim card from under the battery and tosses it into the bag.

She heads south on the highway. It will take her about three hours to reach her destination. It's both too far and too close for her liking. It won't be long until these people tear her house apart. Luckily, she had the foresight to pack up her files and put them in her car if she needed to get out quickly.

The adrenaline dissipates the farther away she gets, and her thoughts morph from survival to concern. Concern for the safety of Hunter, Leo, and Cassidy and concern that she isn't going to be able to stop what's happening. If she can't piece together who is ultimately responsible and stop them, the republic isn't going to be the only thing hanging in the balance. Everyone she knows and loves will be in the crosshairs.

This is the first time since starting down this path that regret and what-ifs flutter through her mind. Can she live with herself if someone she cares about ends up paying the ultimate price? A glimpse of Cassidy reaching for her flashes in her mind. *What have I done?*

Cassidy waits for the elevator to take her to her office when she receives a text message from an unknown number. *Go to the coffee shop across the street and sit at the table in the back left corner. There will be a woman in a striped shirt waiting for you.*

Cassidy slides the phone back into her pocket. It could be a setup, but at least it's a public place, which gives her some comfort. She follows her gut and walks across the street to the coffee shop. Her unease immediately rests when she spots the woman she's supposed to meet. She's never met her, but the resemblance to Alex is uncanny, and she's seen the photos of her on Alex's walls.

Cassidy sits and stares at familiar blue eyes. "Gloria?"

Gloria smiles. "I'd wondered if you'd recognize me." She pulls a paper from her pocket and slides it across the table. "I'm not sure what's going on, but my husband asked me to give this to you." She frowns. "I know my Tom, and this paper must be important."

Cassidy picks up on the fact that they aren't mentioning Alex. She unfolds the paper. The first line is an address in Disputanta, Virginia. The second line says to get rid of all mobile communication. The last line assures her that Hunter will be notified and not to contact anyone. A surge of panic takes her over like a tidal wave. The thought of Alex being in danger is enough to make her want to vomit. The need to get to her is enough to propel her out of her seat, but she doesn't make a move. The last thing she wants to do is draw attention to herself, or worse, cause Gloria to panic.

"I appreciate you getting this to me." The calmness in her voice is forced.

Gloria smiles. "I wanted to meet you as soon as I heard about you, but I was hoping it would be under different circumstances."

A small crack of warmth works its way through her concern. Alex has been speaking to her mother about Cassidy. She closes her eyes and sends protective thoughts into the universe, hoping for any listening entity to grab them and do her bidding.

"I hope we'll get to meet again under better circumstances." Her face flushes when Gloria reaches across the table and squeezes her hand.

"Please be careful." Gloria picks up her purse and heads for the door.

Cassidy sits for as long as her body will allow. She considers her next move carefully. She knows she's being watched, and the last thing she wants to do is tip off her surveyors to anything out of the ordinary. She casually rummages through her purse and idly scrolls through her phone. Once she thinks enough time has passed, she goes into the bathroom, destroys both sim cards, and tosses both phones into the wastebasket.

There are only three things left to do, pick up Thor from doggy daycare, make sure she loses her tail, and get to Alex. Then, they can figure out the rest together.

The sun is setting when Cassidy reaches the small cabin. The dwelling backs up to a dense forest and faces the James River. The protection offered on either side lets her breathe a little easier. It had taken her longer than she would've like to get out of the city, but she had to be sure no one was following her. Thor practically ejects himself from the car as soon as she opens the door. He makes a beeline for a clearing near the river's edge. When she finally catches up, Alex is on her knees, scratching Thor's head.

"I hope you weren't counting on Thor for any kind of security."

Alex holds up a tablet. "You passed three different cameras on your way in." She kisses Thor on the head. "We don't want to overwork you. It's hard work being so handsome."

All of the fear and worry and panic Cassidy has been trying to control for the last several hours breaks loose. She grabs Alex and hugs her with as much force as she can muster without inflicting any pain.

"I'm okay," Alex says against her neck.

It's not until Cassidy tastes the tears on her lips that she realizes she's crying. "What happened?"

Alex tosses several pieces of wood into a wheelbarrow and starts toward the house. She explains the series of events that unfolded earlier in the day to lead her here. Cassidy listens without interrupting, despite the surge of anger that spears through her when she hears about Larry Edwards.

Briggs is sitting on top of the couch when they come in, and Thor greets him like the long-lost friends he believes they are. Alex throws several logs into the fireplace and pulls food from the freezer. The normalcy Alex is portraying is comforting and unnerving.

Cassidy walks across the kitchen and takes the food from Alex. "Tell me how you're really doing." She sets the food on the counter.

Alex puts her hands on her hips. "Well, I'm in one piece."

Cassidy runs her hands up Alex's arms and rests her forearms on her shoulders. "I don't want the cop answer. I want the real one."

Alex's face softens, and she takes a deep breath. "I'm mad."

Cassidy nods. "What else?"

"I was scared."

Cassidy kisses her forehead. "It's okay to be scared."

Alex relaxes against her. "Being scared can get you killed. It can cause hesitation."

"It also helps tether you to reality. It can assist in making more calculated and pragmatic decisions." Cassidy smiles against Alex's cheek. "It also means that you're human."

Alex's grip around her waist tightens. "Nothing makes me feel more alive than you."

Cassidy has always been a person who's prided herself on self-control and restraint. Those two attributes seem entirely absent when it comes to Alex. If she had a crystal ball and could foresee how this would play out, she'd still willingly give in to Alex, even if it ends in a broken heart. She knows the look in Alex's eyes. The desire, the need, the craving—it scorches Cassidy's skin as Alex drags her eyes over her. Every nerve ending in her body screams in vivid color to take this plunge.

Cassidy's lips whisper against the corner of Alex's mouth. The shudder of breath that escapes from Alex inflames Cassidy's already growing ardor. Alex slides her hands under the bottom of Cassidy's shirt. She gently kneads her thumbs against her hips. She pauses and waits for Cassidy's consent. Cassidy's words are mired in her throat—snagging on need and anticipation. Instead of trying to croak out an answer, she pulls off her shirt and puts Alex's hands back on her exposed skin.

Alex's mouth is on her neck instantly. Her mouth moves along the column of her neck and under her jaw. She bites slightly when she reaches her pulse point, and the jolt of need causes Cassidy to push her back against the counter. Cassidy pulls Alex's shirt over her head and tosses it beside them. Cassidy kisses Alex with an impetuosity she's never felt until now.

Another wave of arousal floods her senses when Alex picks her up and puts her on the counter. Alex's mouth blazes a path down her chest and stomach until it reaches the button of her jeans. Alex pauses briefly and looks up at her.

Cassidy puts her hands on Alex's face and leans down to kiss her. "Don't stop." She bites down on Alex's lip.

Alex smirks as she pulls Cassidy's pants off her legs. "I like this side of you."

Cassidy wraps her legs around Alex's waist. "Which side is that exactly?"

Alex pulls Cassidy against her. "All of it."

Cassidy's tenuous grasp on control slips further away with each hot breath between her thighs. Alex's soft moans and practiced attention push Cassidy right to the precipice before pulling her back into the rhythmic exhilaration. The urge to tell Alex to slow down because she's so close is eclipsed by the fierce need building in every nerve ending in her body. She's waited for this moment with Alex since they first kissed, and now that it is here, it is even better than she ever imagined.

The avalanche builds in her belly and rapidly crashes through her body. It spreads through her chest and limbs before spilling out in loud gasps and moans that she has no ability or desire to control.

Her shaking legs collapse at her sides, and she pulls Alex up on top of her. Alex kisses her and wipes the sweaty edges of her hair away from her face. She looks beautiful, and Cassidy lets the contentment and awe trickle into every part of her.

Alex smiles. "Think we can go to bed before one of us slips a disc?"

Cassidy laughs into Alex's shoulder. "I thought you were in better shape than that."

Alex pulls her up. "To run a few miles, not balance on a counter for prolonged periods. I think this wood is older than me."

There's no guarantee that the world won't crumble around them in the coming days or weeks. That's true for everyone, at any point in their lives. Still, it feels especially acute when you see the proverbial storm brewing before your eyes. It's enough to shake anyone to their core. But Cassidy ignores that nagging feeling of uncertainty and fear and allows herself to be in this moment with Alex. However fleeting they may be, these small reprieves will keep her going when all else seems lost.

CHAPTER SIXTEEN

The early morning sun spills through the window and drenches Cassidy's bare back. Alex draws lazy circles along her skin and marvels at the goose bumps that follow in the wake of her touch. This is undoubtedly the worst time in her life to be falling for someone, but there was never a choice. Falling for Cassidy was compulsory. She could no sooner stop it than stop the world from turning. It was entirely out of her control.

Cassidy turns over on her side to face her. "Morning." She pulls Alex against her.

Cassidy's skin is warm and welcoming. A thought of this being the only morning they may spend like this cut through her consciousness like a hot blade. She kisses her shoulder and tries to incise the moment into her mind to revisit later when she inevitably does something to fuck this up.

Thor whimpers and Cassidy turns to look at him. "I need to take him outside."

Alex sits up. For some reason, it's easier for her to get out of bed than to watch Cassidy go. "I'll take him." She kisses the top of her head. "I'll start the coffee."

"My hero." Cassidy stretches and pulls the covers back over her.

Thor takes his time smelling every inch of ground available to him. He's diligent in the task he's clearly given to himself, but Alex doesn't mind. The morning air is crisp and dewy. The smells of damp earth and river almost let her believe they're on a weekend getaway and not hiding out from people who'd like to remove her from existence. The thought pops her momentary euphoria like a pin to a balloon.

She walks along the path leading to the road and looks for any sign of disturbance. When she's confident there isn't any, she briefly berates herself for getting caught up and letting her guard down. She didn't only put herself in jeopardy. She put Cassidy there as well.

Thor trots up alongside her carrying what seems to be the largest stick he could find. "I don't think that will fit through the door, buddy."

He ignores her, as he should, and happily prances back toward the house. Briggs watches Thor from his sunny spot on the wooden railing, unaffected by the oblivious bliss his new friend exudes. Cassidy is standing on the porch with two cups of coffee. She looks gorgeous with her messy hair and lines from the pillow scarring her face. She sits in one of the chairs and holds out the second cup of coffee.

Alex takes it and sits next to her. "Listen, I—"

Cassidy holds up a hand to stop her. "Don't. I know what you're going to say, and don't. I have no regrets about last night, and I know you don't either. We should've taken more precautions, but we didn't. But we both survived, and we'll do better next time."

Alex leans back and sips her coffee. "That's not what I was going to say."

Cassidy raises her eyebrow. "Yes, it was."

Alex takes the tablet from Cassidy and starts flipping through the footage from the night before. "I wouldn't be wrong, though. We weren't paying attention. What if someone had come in here?"

Cassidy shrugs. "Then I assume we wouldn't be here sipping coffee." She grabs Alex's hand and squeezes. "Regret not taking more precautions, but don't regret us. Please."

Alex nods, and she means it. "Okay, you're right."

Cassidy smiles into her coffee mug. "You better get used to saying that."

Alex laughs, but she considers the implications of that simple statement. Cassidy is alluding to a real future together. A connection that wasn't all knotted up in this chaos they're enduring or the emotions that spark when adrenaline is pumping. A future where there are quiet mornings and coffee better than this. She could see it too. She liked seeing it.

Cassidy stretches. "I'm going to take a shower. I'm sure your dad has gotten a hold of Hunter by now." She kisses her. "I'd invite you to come with me, but I don't want to make you combust with concern over being caught."

"I'm not some insane rule follower that can't have any fun."

Cassidy kisses her again. "Then prove me wrong and come with me."

Alex sighs. "I can't. They may actually be here soon."

Cassidy kisses her forehead. "Told you so." She walks into the house before Alex can offer a rebuttal.

Thor watches Cassidy go inside but decides to flop down next to Alex with a heavy sigh. She pats his head. "I knew I liked you."

Her review of the cameras from the night before reveals no disruptions or anything to cause concern. She chews on her thumb and stares out at the river for several minutes before finally opening the browser on her tablet. She searches for any news reports on Hugh Bradley.

Surprisingly, it takes her until the second page of search results to find any information regarding the shooting. She should be relieved, but it only serves as a reminder of just how influential these people really are. People don't often think about what real power is anymore. Money has always bought a certain amount of influence and protection. There was a time when power was seized through bloodshed and artillery. Now, power—real power—belongs to those who control information. Entire swaths of the population could be emboldened or hamstrung by the flow of information. That had always been true to an extent, but now it is even more critical with its immediacy.

People have been falling victim to cultism and propaganda since the beginning of time, but the world is smaller now. These individuals were written off as extremists at one time—a fable used to keep people tethered to reality. But the current implementation has been so surgical it has infected entire families. It is no longer a matter of rolling your eyes and having a good laugh. Extremists are sitting at your holiday table and sharing custody of your children.

"What is it that we're really trying to save?"

Thor stares at her blankly. But what does she really expect? She doesn't have the answer either. The only reason she continues to push forward is because it feels like the right thing to do. Shining a light on this extraordinary betrayal is the only option, but to what end? Some would be perfectly happy if the system is rigged as long as it's in their favor. Others may be so despondent it may completely disenfranchise them. It may very well lead to an all-out civil war. But she can't let herself spiral into the endless whirlpool of what-ifs. She could no more regulate the reaction of millions than she could spin the world on her fingertip. All she has the power to do is her job.

The tablet dings, pulling her from dreadful compilation. She opens the camera and recognizes Hunter's car, along with Hunter driving and Leo beside him. She's relieved they're okay and here to help and disappointed that her time alone with Cassidy is over. It's hard to figure out where to put that contradiction, so she shoves it to the back of her mind, where she puts everything else she doesn't want to deal with. She thinks of Cassidy's glitter theory and nearly laughs. Her mind must be a giant glitter ball.

Hunter grabs her as soon as he gets out of the car. "I'm so glad you're okay. Things are getting a little squirrely."

She pats his back. "Don't go soft on me now."

Leo pulls several latched boxes from the back of the car. "If you two are done, I could use some help with these."

Alex snorts. "Always so sentimental."

Leo heaves two boxes over his shoulder. "Want me to tell you I'm happy you're okay?" He pushes past her. "Okay. Thanks for not dying and making my life harder."

She pulls a suitcase from the car. "I think that's the nicest thing he's ever said to me."

Hunter grabs the last box and closes the trunk. "You should start writing poetry."

"Fuck off," Leo yells from the porch as he opens the door.

"Such a sweet kid." Hunter walks next to Alex. "Seriously though, are you okay?"

"Did you hear about Edwards?"

Hunter adjusts the seemingly heavy box. "Your dad said someone came after you at your house, but I didn't realize it was Edwards. Shit." He shakes his head. "I can't believe he got himself caught up in all this."

Alex sighs. "I don't know if he understands what he's caught up in. Hell, we don't even know the full extent of who's involved."

"Gregory asked me today if I've been in contact with you." He shrugs. "I asked him if he really wanted to know, and he just walked away mumbling under his breath."

Alex pauses briefly. "Do you ever wonder what we're really doing all this for? Maybe the whole thing needs to break to be fixed again. You know, like a bone or something."

Hunter looks at her contemplatively. "I don't know about all that. I do know that I don't want anything breaking on my watch. What if they're teaching this in some history class fifty years from now? I know which side I want to be on, and it's not theirs."

Alex snorts. "It may not be enough."

Hunter opens the screen door with his foot. "Let's make sure it is."

It's too bad Hunter's confidence isn't contagious because she could sure use a dose of it now—even if it is false bravado.

CHAPTER SEVENTEEN

Cassidy grabs the glass of whiskey from Hunter's hand and takes a swig. "Explain it to me again, but slower."

Leo puts his hands over his face. "Which part?"

Cassidy points to his screen. "Let's go with all of it."

Leo turns in his seat to face the computer. "I hate being the smartest person in this group. You all are dragging me down."

Hunter holds up her finger. "But we have all the guns."

Leo scoffs. "Let's check with, oh, I don't know, all of human history to see how well that's worked." He waves him off. "Okay, I think the only way we'll get anywhere with all of this is to get the information to the public. The FBI has proven unreliable because we don't know who's involved. They're already trying to get rid of Alex." He points to her. "I mean, seriously, it's a flipping miracle you're alive." He points to the computer screen. "I've traced the money as well as the algorithm and any emails, and they lead to one person. Jack Jorgenson. He's the one pulling all the strings."

Alex pinches the bridge of her nose. "Are you seriously telling us that the founder and CEO of the largest company in the world is who we're dealing with? Not even a real politician?"

Leo shrugs. "Technically, Abracadabra is the second largest company in the world." He holds his hands up. "But I understand that's not the point." He opens several windows on various screens. "Jack Jorgenson has been leveraging and manipulating the world economy for several years. Sure, he throws money at pet projects here and there, sets up a few scholarships, but make no mistake—his wealth puts him in a different stratosphere than anyone else on the planet." He scrolls further down the page. "You can see it starting here, three years ago." He points to the screen. "He acquired several companies that manufacture voting machines, but he did so with a few of his smaller corporations. It didn't raise any flags because he kept all the employees in place and made no changes. But he's listed as the owner under all the schematics, although you have to dig through a pile of paperwork and encryption to get to his name." He opens another window. "After he started tucking those away, he started buying up media companies. Again, he left management in place and made no significant changes. But he has the ultimate say in what is published." He scratches at the stubble on his chin. "I'm not sure the media acquisitions were part of the plan. He was cheating on his wife, and one of the outlets reported it. He was so pissed that he couldn't stop it that he bought it. But now it seems a happy accident morphed into a potential propaganda machine." He points to another area on the screen. "He had spread his money around to several politicians over the years, but he's consolidated those efforts in the last three, focusing primarily on one side of the voting coin. Senator Christie played a major role in getting him tapped by the previous president for the Defense Innovation Board, but he very publicly turned it down. I also found payments and business dealings between him and Fletcher."

Hunter downs the rest of his whiskey. "So basically, we just have to take down the master of the universe. Sounds easy enough."

Leo nods. "Yup. We're fucked."

Cassidy studies the different images on the screen. She wants to see the human angle. He isn't motivated by rage, bloodlust, or revenge. His motives can't be picked apart to try to identify the next victim because he didn't want victims—he wanted subjects.

"You're not wrong about the master of the universe title," Cassidy says.

Hunter snorts. "The one time she admits I'm right."

Cassidy ignores him. "He wants to be king. I think he got bored with conquering business and now wants to take over politics and policy." She grabs the mouse from Leo and opens up the window that holds his biography. "He's notorious for overworking his employees, and in the early days, he expected them to practically sleep at his house to get Abracadabra off the ground. It was like a drug to him—the need to succeed. He pushed and sacrificed until he reached the top of the mountain. Now that he's there, he wants to climb another. The country is like another business acquisition to him."

Alex sighs. "Literally, none of that is making me feel any better."

"It shouldn't." Cassidy keeps scrolling. "But there's good news. Public opinion matters very much to him. It's not enough for him to simply be number one. He wants people to *want* him to be number one. Adoration is imperative."

Hunter looks confused. "I understand what you're saying, but how can we use that in our favor?"

Cassidy slaps Leo on the back. "Exactly what Leo said. Get the information to the public."

Leo smiles. "I knew I kind of liked you."

"I wouldn't get too excited. We're going to have to be very circumspect in releasing this information. We can't just open the floodgates and expose everyone. If we do that, we're at the whim of public perception and a bunch of really powerful people playing the spin game. We need an outright admission of guilt if we're going to try and slay Goliath," Cassidy says.

Hunter crosses his arms. "You're not wrong, Cassidy. We need a confession. It has to be solid. Also, we still don't know what those city blueprints were for, and I have a feeling it's not for something good."

Cassidy paces. "Leo, can you release the information to show the public the voting machine plan, but not who's involved? If we can draw them out, that may be our opportunity to get the confession. They're going to want to get their hands on what we have."

Leo cracks open a Red Bull can. "You should really stop using phrases like 'can' and just start asking, 'will you.' I'm a proud member of Anonymous, so this is very on brand for me." He sighs. "I suppose you'll tell me when to release it?"

Alex stands. "Obviously." She points to the door. "I need some air." Thor hops up and follows her.

Hunter nods in Alex's direction. "Is she okay?"

Cassidy watches her walk away. "I'm not sure."

Alex is a bit of a puzzle. She can be open and vulnerable, and funny. But there are times like this when she seems to need to escape into her own world. Cassidy fully understands the need to process information, but she hoped they'd reached a point where they could share their concerns—especially over this situation. They're a team, and they need to know if she's having doubts.

"I'll be right back."

Alex skips the stone across the river and watches the small ripples until they lap against the shore edge. She's still trying to wrap her head around the revelation that Jack Jorgeson is responsible for this whole situation. It's disappointing, to say the least. She learned long ago not to idolize people, but that's not where the disappointment stems from.

"Hey," Cassidy calls from a few feet behind her.

"Hey." She shields her eyes from the sun when she turns to look at her.

"You okay?"

"Yeah, just thinking." She turns back to the river and throws another stone.

"Want to share?" There's a tinge of annoyance in Cassidy's voice.

Alex isn't used to having someone pay attention to her comings and goings. She never considered what Cassidy would think about her abrupt exit, and she should've.

"I'm okay. Sometimes I just need a change of scenery to clear my head."

Cassidy bumps her. "Dragging any information out of you is like pulling teeth."

Alex takes her hand. "I'm sorry. I was thinking about what would drive a man who already has everything to want more. What is so fundamentally flawed about humans that we're never satisfied? We keep taking and taking until we've depleted everything, even at the risk of civil war and the deaths of innocent people. It's depressing and disappointing on every level."

"I don't think everyone is like that. It's been my experience that the people who are never satisfied are trying to fill a hole. Unfortunately, those people usually try to fill that hole with the wrong things. It's like trying to pour water into a leaking glass. I don't think most people are inherently bad. I think most just lost their way."

"Have you always been so relentlessly optimistic?" She puts her arms around Cassidy's waist.

Cassidy smiles. "No, actually." Her face gets serious. "I think it's because I've seen the very worst of humanity. I spend hours interviewing people who want to tear everything beautiful apart." She chuckles. "I guess it should've had the opposite effect on me, but it made me realize what connects them all. Every single person I've sat across the table from is broken at their core. Something happened to them that took a hammer to their last shiny piece of humanity." She kisses Alex softly. "I simply decided to protect all my shiny pieces."

"I like your shiny pieces." Alex kisses her again and lets her lips linger against Cassidy's. "Who knows, maybe it will convince me to polish my own every once in a while."

Cassidy puts her forehead against Alex's. "I think you're already shiny."

Hunter yells from the porch. "We need to show you two something."

Alex doesn't let go of Cassidy's hand as they walk back to the cabin. She isn't usually one for public displays of affection, but she can't bring herself to break their connection—no matter how small.

Leo points to the screen. "Peterson is on his way here. We have an hour."

Alex looks at the screen. "How do you know that?"

Leo looks at her as if she just asked a stupid question. "I put a tracer on his car. Obviously." He shakes his head. "Thanks, Leo. That was a great idea, Leo. Wish we'd thought of that, Leo." He points at all of them. "If there's a weak link on this team, it isn't me."

"What do you want to do? We can cut him off before he gets here," Hunter says.

Alex shakes her head. "Let him come here. This may be the opportunity we need to get a confession. Leo, I assume you have more cameras with you. Let's get a few set up. I want to make sure we get this whole exchange on camera. However this shakes out, we'll be able to use it later one way or another."

Hunter nods his approval. "We should hide Leo before Peterson gets here."

"Agreed."

Leo raises his hand. "What do you mean hide me? I'm not being stuffed under the floorboards like some kind of bridge troll."

"There's a small fishing shack at the back of the property," Alex says. "You and Thor can stay there until he leaves."

"Do I get a gun?"

"No," Alex and Hunter say in unison.

"Wow. Take your time and think about it." Leo pulls a few cameras from one of the open boxes. "Trust me to help you save the world, but not with a firearm."

Hunter nods. "Yeah, that pretty much sums it up."

Leo mumbles under his breath as he walks away. "Yeah, pretty much sums it up. Dicks."

"I'm going to go check the camera feeds and give Leo a hand if he needs to reach anything above five foot eight," Hunter says. "I'm around if you need me."

"How are you feeling about this?" Cassidy rests her palm against Alex's cheek.

"If he's coming here, he thinks he has a play. I'd rather know than be left wondering."

Cassidy hugs her. "If you change your mind and want to talk, let me know. I'm going to walk Thor around a bit and get some energy out of him, so he doesn't drive Leo nuts." She pauses. "More nuts. Nuttier?"

Alex can't help but smile. Cassidy always finds a way to ease her, even when she doesn't think it's possible. "Hard to say. I'm a hard pass on all nuts, but I know you like to dabble."

Cassidy's face scrunches. "Let's stop this while we're barely ahead." She scratches Thor's chest and heads to the door.

Alex busies herself by checking her gun and hiding a few in different locations around the room. She never wants to use one, but it makes her feel better knowing they're there. She tries to imagine what she'll do in the various ways this may play out. She likes having a plan. She needs a plan. Cornered animals are unpredictable, and people with nothing to lose are even scarier. If Peterson thinks his whole life and career are about to be flushed down the toilet, he will fall into both those categories. And Alex isn't about to let him hurt the people around her. Whatever it takes.

CHAPTER EIGHTEEN

Alex checks her watch for the fourth time in fifteen minutes. Peterson should be here any minute. She focuses on controlling her breathing as she leans against the doorjamb—gun ready.

"Stop checking the time," Hunter whispers.

Alex rolls her shoulders. "You don't need to whisper. This isn't a library."

Hunter continues to peer out the window. "Smartass. I'm listening for wheels on the gravel." He mumbles something under his breath. "He waited until nightfall. Smart."

"We have cameras." Alex tries to sound informative and not condescending.

Cassidy tosses the tablet on the table. "We had cameras. They just went black."

Hunter moves to the other side of the window. "Leo anticipated the possibility of a scrambler. They'll be up and running in a few minutes."

The crunch of the gravel under wheels make Alex's heart pound in her throat. This is it. Whatever happens next, however it happens, there's no going back. She'll either be the person who took down a corrupt FBI assistant director, or he would put her down. There were no shades of gray.

Peterson gets out of the car, gun at his side. He spends a few moments looking around and then walks to the passenger door.

Alex's head pounds and her palms start to sweat when he reaches in and grabs someone from the front seat. He tosses the person to the ground. Alex can tell by how they struggle to get to their feet that their hands are bound.

"Alex." Peterson draws out the last part of her name in a sadistic tone. "Alex, we need to talk, and I'm not going in there. Come outside, and we can work this out."

"Stay where you are. Make him come to you."

Alex would recognize that voice anywhere—her father. She reaches for the door but stops herself. Questions start peppering her mind. Is he hurt? Is her mom okay? What the hell is the next step?

She looks over at Hunter, and he shakes his head. "You need to come in here if you want to talk," she yells.

He looks up at the sky and groans. "I can't do that. I don't know what you have set up in there. Anything could be waiting for me." He knocks the gun against his leg. "How about this?" He points the gun at her father's head. "You come outside, or I put a bullet in his head." He starts laughing. "Can you imagine the guilt you'd feel?" He taps the gun against the side of her dad's head. "See, I know you. That will eat you alive. What would you say to your mother? I've always been fond of your mother. Pretty little thing."

Cassidy puts her hand on her shoulder. "I'll go outside with you." She glances at Hunter. "The cameras are working again. Make sure you get all of this. He won't be intimidated by two women, but it'll put him more on edge to see you. Only come out if things go off the rails."

Hunter gives her a look that indicates he doesn't like the idea. "Fine, but if he so much as flinches the wrong way, I'm coming for him."

Alex opens the door and immediately trains her gun on Peterson. "It didn't have to be like this."

"You're right. It didn't, but you made it this way." He grabs her father around the neck and pulls him closer. "You had to go poking your nose around in places it didn't belong. I would've given you that promotion."

Now that she's closer, she can see the violence inflicted on her father. His face is swollen, bruised, and covered in dried blood. Her stomach turns, and she prays that her mother is in better condition.

"It was never about the promotion." Her voice is drenched with fury. "You're a traitor."

Cassidy is beside her a moment later, gun in the same position. "What is it that you want, Peterson? You didn't come all the way out here to get a rise out of Alex."

He shakes the gun at Cassidy. "See? I told you to spend more time with her. She's smart." He moves the gun back to her father. "I'm going to need that flash drive back, and please don't insult me by telling me you don't know what I'm talking about."

"Fuck you, Peterson. How about that?" Alex takes a step closer.

He tilts his head slightly and stares. "Alex, I've known you most of your life. I know you care about your father more than whatever is on the flash drive."

This is the first time it's occurred to Alex that Peterson doesn't think they were able to crack the encryption. His arrogance won't allow it.

"If we agree to give it to you, will you let Tom go?" Cassidy moves slightly to the right. They now have him flanked on both sides.

Peterson is quiet for longer than Alex is comfortable. "Why do you think I brought him? I needed a bargaining chip."

The rage that pumps through Alex's body reaches her legs, and she takes another step closer. "Liar. You aren't going to leave any loose ends." Her father struggles against the arm around his neck. "He's your best friend, and he needs medical attention."

Peterson ruffles her dad's hair. "He's fine. As far as loose ends, there aren't any. This will all be over in a few weeks, and nothing you have to say will matter. In fact, I hope you scream it from the rooftops. Help sow the chaos. It will be the final blow. Why do you think I came here alone? I want you to live. I just need a little more time." He sighs. "Do you want me to apologize for Larry? Fine. I'm sorry I sent someone to kill you. That's on me. But once you got away, I realized it was far less messy to just keep you alive." He shrugs. "So there it is, an apology."

Her father pushes harder against him. "What happened to you? I don't know who you are anymore."

Peterson looks at him in shock. "What happened to me? What happened to you?" He pushes the gun into her father again. "We used to think we were going to change the world. We talked about righting wrongs and keeping the evil people locked away. Then we got bogged down in bureaucracy, red tape, and all the other bullshit that comes with our thankless fucking jobs." His eyes are wild as he searches her father's face. "This is my chance to be remembered."

"Is this really how you want to be remembered?" Her father's voice is laced with anger and worry. "All the good you've done will be erased. This is all that will be associated with your name for the rest of time."

Peterson laughs. "Not likely. John Adams hated criticism so much that he made it illegal to talk negatively about the president. He quite literally had people jailed or beaten up because of it. George Washington promised to free all the enslaved people who worked for him, but even in death, only one was released. John Hancock was a smuggler. Thomas Jefferson owned and raped children." He shrugs. "I mean, let's be honest, these are just a few things we know. There are probably worse stories lost to the annals of time. These men founded our country, and they're revered as gods. Greatness eclipses wrongdoing through the lens of history." He squeezes her father's cheeks forcefully. "I'm not going to let you or anyone else get in the way of that."

"Is whatever is on that flash drive more important than your best friend?" Cassidy's voice sounds much calmer than Alex feels.

Peterson smiles. "It's more important than anything. It's the key to saving what's left of our country."

"Did you lift the nuclear codes or something? What can possibly be so important?"

Peterson stares and he pulls her father closer. "Better than nuclear codes. It's given us the power to change what people are too stupid to do for themselves. It gives the power back to those who should have it, to those of us who really understand what's going on—not a bunch of barely literate bleeding hearts. When this is all over, you'll all be thanking me for what I've done."

"You keep saying 'we' and 'us.' We found your ledger. We know you're working with Christie, Fletcher, and Jorgenson. What exactly is three million dollars buying these days?" Alex tries to mimic Cassidy's calm demeanor, but she's likely falling short.

The side of his mouth twitches. "It buys freedom for you and everyone else in this country. It's quite the steal if you ask me. You should be thanking us."

"I'm not letting you leave here," Alex says. She's tired of listening to him rant like a madman.

"Alex, these choices aren't yours to make." His smile is sadistic. "Looks like we've come to an end in our negotiations then." He puts the gun to her father's head again. "I'm going to count to three." He kisses the side of her father's head. "One."

Alex takes a deep breath and steadies herself. She will take this shot and won't care about the consequences.

"Two."

The probability that he shoots precisely on three is low. She can get the shot off when he moves away to pull the trigger. Then this will finally be over.

"Wait." Cassidy puts her gun on the ground and digs in her pocket. "Here." She holds out the flash drive. "Let him go, and I'll give it to you."

Alex's heart starts pounding at a speed she's never experienced. "Cassidy, what are you doing?"

Cassidy doesn't look at her. "Take the flash drive." She walks up to him so it's within reach.

Peterson looks at Alex and then back at Cassidy. In a split second, he releases her father and grabs Cassidy. "I think I'll trade him for you." He turns to Alex. "If you don't let the plan come to fruition, I will kill her." He puts his hand around Cassidy's neck. "I'll kill her and deliver her in pieces to your front door—bit by bit."

Consequences and choices fire through her head like spears. There are only so many options and none of the outcomes are favorable. He walks backward to the car, still holding Cassidy. Alex keeps her gun trained, waiting for any opportunity. But the darkness is unforgiving, and she isn't confident she has a clean shot.

Hunter comes crashing through the front door with his weapon drawn. "You got what you came here for, Peterson. Don't be stupid." He shoves Cassidy into the driver's seat and forces her to move over. "I'm many things, Agent, but stupid has never been one of them."

Alex takes several steps forward in an attempt to improve her line of vision, but it's pointless. Cassidy isn't completely settled before he's in the car and pulling away. Hunter chases the car, but she knows he won't take a shot. He won't risk hitting Cassidy either.

Alex wants nothing more than to get in the car and chase him down, but then what? Shoot at him on a highway? Run him off the road with Cassidy in the car? Call the police for backup? This isn't a movie. No, she needs to be smart about this.

She runs over to her father and helps him off the ground. "Are you okay?"

There are tears in his eyes. "I will be. Can you help me get inside? We have a lot to discuss."

Alex and Hunter get him inside and set him on the couch. Hunter runs to the kitchen and grabs several bags of ice. Alex touches different parts of his body, looking for broken bones or internal bleeding.

Leo races through the screen door with Thor on his heels. "Jesus, that guy is off his rocker."

Her father stares, and she sees his jaw clench. "Leo Parker. You're wanted in fourteen states for hacking."

Leo slides his hands into his pockets and rocks backward. "It's technically sixteen, but not anymore. I help out the CIA." His head rocks back and forth. "And I guess the FBI." He points to himself. "One of the good guys now."

"He went to college with Brooke," Alex says quietly. "He's the reason we figured out what Peterson was doing."

Leo sits on the couch. "Plus, Jack Jorgenson. Which I mean is like the real big news." He uses his hands to simulate his mind exploding. "Talk about being good at my job." He laughs and then clears his throat. "Which isn't important right now." He stands. "I'm going to go." He motions around the room. "Somewhere else to track Peterson."

Hunter hands her father an ice pack, and he winces when he puts it against his cheek. "You need to tell me everything."

Alex nods. "I will. But before I do, I need to know if Mom is okay."

Her dad nods. "She's at your brother's for the weekend babysitting. I'm sorry I brought him here. He ambushed me, looking for you. I wouldn't have told him where you were, but he saw the calendar and threatened to go to your brother's. I couldn't put the kids in danger. I figured this was the only way to keep the rest of the family safe."

Alex grabs his hands. "You did the right thing. I'm sorry I put you in this position."

"Don't you ever apologize to me for letting me be your dad. It's the best job I've ever had."

Alex's eyes well with tears. The deliberate compartments she's spent so much time curating seem to be cracking at every opportunity. She chews the inside of her cheek, preferring physical pain to emotional.

She takes a deep breath. "I guess it's best to start at the beginning."

An hour later, her dad stares at her in stunned silence. "So you have evidence implicating Senator Christie, Jeffery Fletcher, Dave Peterson, and Jack Jorgenson." He leans forward. "Jesus Christ."

Leo raises a hand. "I've actually been able to implicate a few more with the flash drive."

"Which Peterson has again," Alex says.

Leo shakes his finger. "Tsk, tsk. That was a copy, and I corrupted the file. He can open it, and it will look legit, but the files are slightly scrambled. He'll never be able to figure it out. He would need me, and versions of me are in short supply."

"Maybe you aren't all that bad, Leo." Her dad eyes him.

"Friendly neighborhood hacker at your service." He salutes.

Hunter scoffs. "You're neither friendly nor happily at anyone's service."

Leo shrugs. "One out of three is still more than any of you."

Alex rubs her eyes with her palms. "Okay, I need to get you home, and then I'm going to get Cassidy back."

Hunter points between them. "We're going to get Cassidy back."

Her dad stands shakily. "It can't just be you two. I'm sorry, but you have no idea where she is or what is waiting for you when you get there."

Leo tosses a tennis ball down the hall for Thor. "He's at an Abracadabra warehouse in Sterling, Virginia." He takes the ball from Thor and throws it again. "Who do I talk to about getting a raise when this is over?"

Alex stares out the window. "My dad is right. We're going to need more than just the two of us." She turns and looks at Leo. "Give me your phone."

Hunter looks confused. "Who in the fresh hell are you going to call?"

Alex dials the number from memory. "The only two people in the world we can trust. Brooke Hart and Tyler Monroe."

Her nerves sing with each passing ring. "Please pick up, Brooke. Please."

After a few more rings, a sleepy voice answers. For the first time in days, relief spreads through her body. This may turn out to be a hail Mary, but it's the only play she has left.

CHAPTER NINETEEN

Cassidy spends the whole ride politely agreeing with Peterson or staring out the window. Her decision had been spontaneous but necessary. She could tell by the look in Alex's eyes that she was getting ready to take the shot. As much as she hates to admit it, they need Peterson alive. They need him to get Jorgenson, and this is the most direct path. Peterson was tempting fate by bringing Tom Derby into this whole mess, but it's clear now that he did so to kickstart the chaos.

Alex had been on the brink. Not that she blames her. Quite the opposite. Cassidy was trying to protect her from a rash decision that could have gone terribly wrong. She wouldn't let Alex go down that road—not if she could help it.

They pull up to a gate in front of a large warehouse, and he punches in a series of numbers. "Now, remember, I don't want to hurt you. That was never my intention. You're just security for me. So there's no reason to do anything reckless when we get inside. Do you understand?"

Cassidy nods.

"Say it."

"I understand."

Peterson drives the car around to the back of the warehouse. A large loading bay opens, and he parks the car inside. There are dozens of pallets along the back wall with a tall box on each. A table large enough to sit twenty people sits in the center. Lights shine on it, and two people lean over the top. She looks around for any other security. A few people are milling around, but it's hard to tell if they're armed from this distance.

She hears them before she sees them. Their voices bounce off the walls like instrument chords in a chamber. It doesn't take her long to place the thundering vocals—Jeffery Fletcher and Senator Miles Christie. They're coming from the other side of the warehouse and are visibly irritated when they see Peterson has brought her along. Christie's plump face flushes an even darker shade of red, and Fletcher mumbles under his breath.

"What the fuck?" Christie bellows. His angry baritone jumps from one wall to the next.

Peterson puts his hands up, telling them to relax. "She's our insurance policy."

Fletcher glares at her. "We wouldn't need an insurance policy if you'd done what you were supposed to do."

Cassidy considers her next play. Either one of these men could decide Peterson made a miscalculation and kill her on the spot. Peterson won't put up much of a fight. She has no weapons. The only tool she has at her disposal is her intelligence. If there was ever a time she needed to be smarter than a group of men, this is it.

"I'm not here to do anyone any harm. On the contrary, I'm actually rather intrigued. You don't have to tell me what's really going on, but I have to be honest—Dave made quite a compelling case." She touches his shoulder. "This country is broken, and you all want to start something new. Something better." She smiles. "I understand you don't trust me. If it makes you more comfortable, I can wait in the car." She points to Peterson's pocket. "Obviously, you can hold on to the keys."

Peterson squints at her. "Are you fucking with us?"

She laughs and shakes her head. "No. Not at all. Listen, I want to be on whatever side will come out of this on top. I have no interest in being part of a civil war or whatever else may happen." She points to the pallets. "Let's be honest. With those voting machines, the odds are in your favor. You're going to have half the country on your side, and the rest aren't going to know what to do. I'm just playing the odds."

A voice from the back of the building echoes. "What is your name?"

"Cassidy Wolf." She tries to see who is speaking, but they're still too far away. "I'm a profiler at the FBI."

He continues to approach. "That's a useful skill." It takes him several more seconds to reach her. He cocks his head and looks her up and down. "Tell me, Agent Wolf, what do you think of me?"

Cassidy blinks slowly. Blinking too fast unconsciously signals to people that you're nervous or lying. We don't always understand why we recognize deception, but it has something to do with your brain processing dozens of micro indicators. In the first few seconds of conversation, the brain decides whether it perceives a person to be a friend or foe.

She softens her eyes. "Jack Jorgenson. I can't profile you. I don't know enough about you. That wouldn't be fair."

He slides his hands into his pockets and stares at the ground before looking back up at her. Putting your hands in your pockets typically indicates insecurity. Her initial assessment is correct—he cares very much about what people think of him.

She matches his position to put him more at ease. "Okay, I'll give it a shot. You're the most successful businessman on the planet. That means you're not just a genius but a bit of an artist." She smiles. "You pride yourself on your work ethic, so you have high expectations of yourself and others. You value loyalty and honesty. You have a vision of what the world should look like, and you'll stop at nothing to see that dream come to fruition."

His smile is faint as he takes a deep breath. "You didn't say whether or not you think I'm a good person." He takes a step closer and into her personal space. "Do you think I'm a good person, Agent Wolf?"

Cassidy doesn't take a step backward. She stays rooted in her spot, allowing their closeness. "I don't believe in things like good and evil. I think people are complicated and messy and sometimes beautiful and sad and lonely. I think people are a little bit of everything, a splendid mosaic of broken glass and healed wounds."

He hesitantly pushes a piece of hair behind her ear. "And why shouldn't I just have you killed right now?"

She maintains eye contact but keeps her eyes soft and calm. "You have no reason not to kill me, except one." She smiles. "You don't want to, and you never do anything you don't want to do."

He stares at her, studying her eyes and lips. "No. I don't." He points to the massive table. "Would you like to see my vision of the world?"

She nods but says nothing. She doesn't want to seem too eager. As she approaches, it all clicks into place. She understands exactly why there were city blueprints on the flash drive. He intends to rebuild the country after they burn it to the ground. Acid slides down her throat, but she smiles and attempts to look confused. His personality type needs to be in control, to be the one to explain his brilliance. Take that away, and he'll become petulant and unstable.

"What is all of this?"

His face lights up with excitement. "This is what the world will look like very soon." He points to an Abracadabra statue in the center of the model city. "We're going to build a world that is entirely interconnected. Everyone will work in a sector of Abracadabra. We're going to build hospitals, schools, transportation, and homes. There will no longer be any homeless. Everyone will have access to health care. Every person will have the option to go to college and enter corporate operations or start at tech school and immediately go to work." His pupils change as if he's looking at someone he loves. "There will be no crime because everyone will have what they need. There will be no poverty, no drug addiction, no pain." He points to the people in the room. "The entire government can be made up of just a few people. There will be no more wasteful spending. We can fix the planet. It will be utopia."

Cassidy watches him. He means every single word he says. He's so singularly focused on this world he wants to create that he doesn't care who has to die to make his utopia happen. Irony at its finest.

He strokes the side of a helix glass tower. "What do you think?"

She touches the same building. "I think it's a beautiful concept worthy of praise. But what are you going to do about the people who won't come willingly?"

He shrugs. "I don't concern myself with such matters. We're on the precipice of evolution. They'll either evolve or fall victim to their own poor decisions. After this election, when the nation is steeped in despair and chaos, people will beg for a better system and a better life. They are now, and no one listens. No one but me. I'll listen, and I'll fix it."

She keeps her voice even and as light as possible. "I'm sure you've run the numbers. How many people will we lose?"

He picks a piece of lint off one of the buildings. "Millions, probably. But I promise it will be worth it. Are you familiar with Jean Rostand?"

"No."

"He was a biologist. He said, 'Kill one man, and you are a murderer. Kill millions of men, and you are a conqueror. Kill them all, and you are a God.'" He straightens his suit jacket. "You should be relieved that I'm content to be a conqueror. But a conqueror with only the true good of humanity in my focus."

Cassidy smiles and waits for him to return the facial gesture. People are more open to listening if you've removed that slight barrier. "This is quite the vision, and I agree. Our system is fundamentally broken, but change takes generations if you want it to stick. No matter how good, these ideas you have will cause people to rebel against you. The war you're about to start could go on for decades. It's difficult to solve all these problems when people are willing to tear their neighbors apart."

He pulls a cloth back from another section of the display and reveals rows of model tanks and soldiers. "Do you know how much the United States spends on its military?"

"Seven hundred and seventy-eight billion."

He points at her and smiles. "Smart girl." He looks at her calmly. "Imagine if those forces were used in our country instead of all over the world. People would have no choice but to fall in line."

Bile rises in the back of Cassidy's throat, but she keeps her voice calm and interested. "That's true, but it's illegal to use the Army or the Air Force. Ignoring the Posse Comitatus Act could splinter those already willing to follow you."

"True." He shrugs. "But we already have precedent for suspending that. President Bush did so from 2006-2007. All the president has to say is that it's in the public's best interest." His eyes twinkle, and she has the sudden urge to hit him. "Americans don't realize how much they've already allowed or how much they've already given up in the name of security. We still talk about this country like it's a democratic republic, but it hasn't been for quite some time."

She has nothing to say in response. The silence that hangs between them is smoldering, but she does her best to keep her expression neutral, as though she's genuinely considering his words.

He points to Peterson. "Take her to the break room in the back and lock her inside." He checks his watch. "I have a meeting to attend, but when I return, we'll decide if she stays insurance or becomes the first of my conquests." He touches her face. "Wouldn't that be poetic?"

Peterson grabs her by the arm and drags her into a room. He pulls the phone off the wall and throws it into the warehouse. There are beads of sweat trickling down the side of his face. His arrogance has never been a matter of debate, but the cruelty surprises her.

"Do you have any guilt about what happened with Tom?" She sits at one of the circular tables. "That must have been hard for you."

He pulls a bottle of water from the fridge and tosses it to her. "Sacrifices need to be made in the name of achieving greatness."

She takes a sip from the bottle. "I understand that, but what about your humanity? Does that need to be sacrificed as well?" When he doesn't answer, she continues. "You mentioned the founding fathers earlier. You think their sins are overlooked because their achievements were much grander. I don't think that's what happened at all."

His eye twitches, and his stare is intense. "They were a product of their time. Their accomplishments eclipse everything else. They weren't monsters. They were visionaries. Just like us."

"Maybe. They also would've been branded as losers and traitors had a few elements gone differently." She takes another sip of water. "Also, let's say for a minute that none of their infighting, misogyny, racism, or hypocrisy matters—that they were, in fact, a product of their time. What do you think they'd say about the kingdom you're setting up here? And make no mistake, it is a kingdom."

His neck flushes. "It's much better than the corrupt and broken system we're stuck living in now."

She nods slowly. "Maybe you're right. Hell, what do I know?" She leans forward. "Although it is interesting. You're all supposed to be the new founders, but the one with all the plans, say-so, and power is Jorgenson. As he said himself, he's the conqueror." She looks up at him. "Maybe he'll share the glory when it's all over." She smiles. "He wouldn't want it all for himself, right? There's plenty of room at the top." She looks at the ceiling as if she's contemplating. "All that talk about the president taking down Americans and ridding the country of defectors…He'll need someone to blame. Will it be Christie or Fletcher? I'm sure he wouldn't put you in that position."

He says nothing else as he angrily slams the door behind him. Her comments won't be enough to derail their plans, but she planted a seed. A seed that may sow some discourse and hopefully buy them all a little extra time.

She's willing to do anything and everything to help the rest of the team. It doesn't matter if she's tempting fate. She owes it to all of them—to Alex. *Alex*. It's possible that she's making well thought out and intricate plans. It's also possible that she's devising a way to burn the whole warehouse down. She hopes it's a combination of the two.

CHAPTER TWENTY

"So you're just going to break into all the television broadcasts and air that video?" Tyler leans over Leo's shoulder.

He stares at her before leaning around to talk to the others. "Television? Brooke, where did you find her? Nineteen ninety-five?" He pushes her backward. "That's right. Then I'm going to take an ad out in a local paper." He shoos her away. "I'm going to upload it to the Anonymous platform. We'll reach hundreds of millions of people in a matter of minutes, and networks like CNN and the BBC are always on the lookout for our posts."

Alex ties her boots and grabs the duffel bag Tyler brought and opens it on the counter. "Did you get all these weapons from Homeland?"

Tyler winks at her. "The less you know, the better."

Alex grabs an M27 and throws it over her back. "Thanks for coming when I called. I didn't want to bring in all our agencies until we can get Cassidy back. I don't know how long Peterson will keep her, and I didn't want to waste time by having to run the gambit."

Tyler tucks a 9mm into her waistband. "No thanks needed. This is what we do." She smacks her on the back.

Brooke heaves a duffel bag over her shoulder. "You guys ready? We can go over logistics when we get in range."

Leo claps. "This is very exciting. It's my first real mission."

Hunter straightens his ballcap. "You aren't going."

Leo puts his hand behind his ear as if he can't hear. "I'm sorry. What? I'm absolutely going." He points to Brooke. "She's good, but

I'm better. You need me." He pulls at his shirt. "I put on a black shirt and everything."

"He's right," Brooke says. "We'll need all the help we can get, and no one is better at breaking into security systems than Leo."

Leo dusts off his shoulder. "Having a change of heart?"

Hunter shakes his head. "No, but if she wants you there, I guess you're coming." He pushes past him. "Just keep the bullshit chattering to a minimum."

Brooke cackles. "Oh, I'm not giving him a mic."

"Thank God for small miracles," Alex says as she walks across the room to her father. She hugs him. "The Uber will be here in fifteen minutes. They'll take you to Clark's. You need to be with Mom."

"When did you become the parent?" His smile is faint.

"I just need to know you're all okay."

He hugs her. "I've never been more proud of you." He pats the side of her face. "Promise me you'll be careful." His voice cracks slightly. "If the worst happens..." His voice trails off.

"I love you, Dad."

"I love you too, kiddo. Every single day of your life. I love you." He pats her back. "Get out of here."

Her dad grabs Brooke next. "Watch their backs out there."

"Always. We'll bring them all back safe."

Her father raises an eyebrow when Leo extends his arms to him. "Absolutely not."

"Worth a try," Leo says and heads for the door.

Twenty minutes later, they park a quarter-mile from the Abracadabra warehouse. Alex, Tyler, and Hunter check their vests and weapons one last time. They take turns checking their earpieces and syncing up their watches.

Leo pulls up the schematics of the building. He points to the vent on the roof. "This is the easiest access location."

Alex smacks his shoulder. "For fuck's sake, Leo. None of us are Batman. How the hell would we get up there?"

He taps heavily on the keyboard. "Fine. I think it's the coolest way to enter, but I'll find a different access point." He squints at the computer. "There's a fire exit on the second floor. You'll have to go up the fire escape. I'll unlock it from here, but I can only cut the power for a few seconds before it notifies the fire department." He rotates the monitor so they can see. "Is that boring enough for you?"

"What about cameras?" Tyler squats next to her. "What kind of control can you get?"

He bites his lower lip and types faster. "He has the indoor cameras wired on a triple security circuit. I have to isolate them in order. The order they need to be cut changes every few minutes. I can't cut them permanently, or an alarm will sound." He sighs. "It's actually kind of brilliant. But I guess that isn't surprising given who we're dealing with. Jorgenson is the ultimate tech guy."

Brooke takes the keyboard and types for several seconds. "We can patch through the cameras and use them to see through. It looks like the outside cameras won't see you if you stay pressed against the walls. We'll be able to help you with any security in the area, but the actual time we can cut the indoor cameras will be brief. The best we can give you is six minutes with no indoor cameras. When the cameras are cut, we won't be able to see anything either. Is that enough time?"

Tyler smiles. "Sounds like a challenge."

Leo whistles. "She's so much cooler than either of you." He shakes his head. "No wonder you can't keep your hands off her."

Hunter hits the back of Leo's head. "Six minutes. We go in, get Cassidy, and get out. As soon as we tell you we're clear, release the video."

Leo salutes him. "Dodger that."

Alex sighs. "It's roger, Leo."

"Who's roger?"

Alex stares at him and then at Hunter. "Is he fucking with us? I can't tell if he's fucking with us."

"Who cares? Let's go." Hunter slides the van door open.

The streets shine from the recent rainfall. They shimmer and reflect the dim streetlights that light their way. There's no traffic this time of night, and their footsteps make the only noise Alex can hear. They reach the back of the warehouse and stop when they arrive at the chain-link fence.

The three of them duck behind a shipping container. Tyler clicks the radio link on her chest. "We're here. Is there security in the area?"

"Two guys patrolling the perimeter. You'll have about forty-five seconds with no eyes on your location. I'll tell you when you're clear."

Tyler pulls out a small set of shears and waits. It takes a full minute for the clearance to crackle through their earpieces. They run to the fence, and Tyler snips the bottom eight links. She pulls it up, and the three of them crawl under. They hurry to a dark corner.

"Stay in the shadows. Wait ninety seconds and go to the fire escape."

The air is eerily quiet. Alex can't hear the guards walking, she hears no breathing, and no one dares adjust their gear on the off chance they make a slight noise.

"When you get to the fire escape, Leo will set off one of the motion floodlights on the other side of the warehouse. It should draw the guards in that direction. We'll tell you when you're clear." There are several seconds of silence. "Go."

The three of them stay as close to the wall as possible as they move toward the fire escape. It's only about two hundred feet, but it feels like five miles. They stay hidden in the darkness provided by the massive walls and wait for clearance.

"Light on, go."

The three of them hurry up the stairs. Tyler unholsters her sidearm, and Alex and Hunter do the same.

Alex pushes her radio link. "We're in position."

Tyler puts her thumb against her watch. "Six minutes when they say. I go left. Hunter, you go right. Alex, you go down."

"Go."

They push the buttons on their watches and enter the building. Alex takes the stairs as the other two make their moves above her. Voices are echoing off the walls, but the hollow sound indicates they're far away. There are several office spaces, and Alex peeks into the window of each, searching for Cassidy.

She catches a glimpse of Hunter. He's on the catwalk above, his gun trained toward the ground in the opposite direction of her. He must be clocking the voices. He's watching her back. A slight pang of relief travels through her chest as she continues down the wall of half-windows. She maintains her crouched position and moves as quickly as possible.

A door ten feet from her opens, and she ducks into a narrow inlet. She holds her breath as the guard passes her. She checks her watch—three minutes left. The guard makes another pass but heads toward the other side of the building. She's almost to the end when she sees Cassidy pacing inside a room. There have only been three times in Alex's life where she believed that there was a God with every fiber of her being. The first was when she was a kid and her brother almost drowned during summer vacation. The second was in college when she hit every green light, found a parking spot close to the building, and made it on time for her final exam. And now, this. She found Cassidy.

She opens the door. Cassidy looks at her with wild eyes. "Come on, let's get out of here." She waves. "We only have one minute to make it to the door. We have to leave now."

"No." Cassidy's eyes are blank. There's no emotion.

Confusion and anger swirl through her body. "What do you mean, no?" She tries to grab her. "We have to go now."

Cassidy shakes her head. "I'm not going anywhere. I saw their plans. It's a better life. Everyone will be better off if we let this play out."

"Have you lost your fucking mind? Were you drugged?"

"My mind has never been clearer. I'm not coming with you." She folds her arms and steps back, her face still blank. "Leave, Alex."

"But—"

"Leave. Now. There's nothing more between us."

The thrumming in her head is so loud that she almost doesn't hear Brooke yelling through her earpiece to get out. It takes several seconds to make her body move after feeling her heart crack. It isn't something she's ever felt before. It isn't so much alarming as it is all-consuming. Her cheeks have no tears, and her body doesn't hurt. All she feels is numbness.

Her body moves on autopilot. She follows the instructions in her ear and stays against the wall, but she has no idea how she makes it back to the van. Everything is a blur. People are talking to her, and she knows she needs to give an answer—they're all waiting.

"We'll go back in and try again." It's Hunter's voice. He's staring at her. "We'll get her back."

Tyler is pulling off her gear. "Now we know how many people are inside. We can make another run at it. We've already covered half the area. There aren't that many places left to check."

The humid air from the earlier rain feels like sap on her hot skin. Her mind is telling her to remove her gear. It will help with the feeling of suffocating, but she can't move. She can't reconcile what Cassidy just said to her with the woman she knows.

"How many rooms do you think are left? Did you see any evidence of where they're keeping her?" Hunter is shaking her, but she can't bring herself to look at him.

"I found her. She refused to come with me."

Hunter's hands are on his waist. His stance is defensive. "That's not possible. You must've heard wrong. We have to go back."

Fresh tears slide behind her lids, but no moisture falls. It's like her body won't let it happen. "She said their plan is solid, and everyone will be better off if we let it play out."

Alex continues to replay the words in her head while they all mumble their disbelief and whatever other patronizing phrases they feel necessary to exchange. But she knows what she heard, and she saw the determination in Cassidy's eyes. She wanted Alex out of that room.

Leo rocks slightly back and forth. He seems agitated, but she can't bring herself to offer him a single platitude. He turns toward the computer and pulls the keyboard into his lap. She knows instinctively what he's going to do, and she wants to stop him. Her mind screams at her body to move, but her fractured heart holds her limbs in place.

He pushes a single button and tosses the keyboard back onto the desk. "It's done."

Hunter scrambles to the monitor. "What did you do?"

"What had to be done."

Hunter grabs the keyboard and starts pushing buttons. "You could've just signed her death warrant." He breaks the keyboard over his knee and tosses the pieces at their feet. He leans against the small table and shakes his head. "If anything happens to her, it'll be on you two."

Hunter looks like he may hit her. Maybe he should. Maybe she'll feel it. Maybe it will pull her out of this abyss it feels like she's floating in. Maybe it will hurt more than what she's feeling now, and that will be lovely.

Words hammer her head. *Betrayal. Guilt. Love.* She wants to rush back into the building and pull Cassidy out, regardless of her protest. But she can't bring herself to move. She can't do anything but wallow in her sadness and quiet desperation. Her heart beats loudly in her head as if screaming at her that she's wrong. But her brain can't reconcile what it saw against what she feels. Any ability she has to reason is cloaked in a fog she can't see through. Despite the confusion, she knows one thing to be unequivocally true—if anything happens to Cassidy, the guilt and regret will keep her unmoored from her heart for the rest of her life.

CHAPTER TWENTY-ONE

Peterson swings the gun over his back and comes out of the shadows where he'd been hiding. "Nice job. Even I believed you."

Cassidy holds her tears at bay. She won't let him see her cry. "You have no idea what you've done. You'll be in jail before any of those voting machines are delivered. Everyone will know what you've done."

He pulls out the chair next to her and sits. "If she releases any information, she knows what will happen to you. Do you think she'll risk it?"

"I know she will. She thinks I betrayed her."

He smiles. "But you didn't betray her. I would've killed her had you not done what I said."

"She doesn't know that." She crosses her arms. "I don't understand why. If you knew they were here, why not just move me? Why not kill her? Why play all these games?"

He rubs the back of his hand against his chin. "You said something earlier that got me thinking. Jorgenson doesn't have any loyalty. He just wants power. He isn't going to give me power. I have to take it. I'm not going to be anyone's fall guy."

She played right into their hands in her attempt to buy them more time. She thought she was putting doubt in his head when all she's done is give him a reason to move forward in his own way and remove Jorgenson from the equation.

She closes her eyes. "You want her to release the evidence early. You want him out of the way."

He smacks the table, laughs, and shakes his finger at her. "See? I knew you were the smart one. I always saw the potential in you." He leans forward on the table. "Alex is about to light the fuse to the exact chaos I need. Even when I'm implicated, I'm going to say that I was acting deep undercover. I'm going to end up being a hero. They're going to throw the presidency at me. They'll beg me to take it. Jorgenson won't be anyone's savior. It will be me."

She squeezes her hands closed, wanting to relieve some of the tension. "Then why tell me everything? We can all implicate you. The evidence will back up what we say. There's no way you come out of this unscathed."

He stands and smiles at her. "Sweet, innocent Cassidy Wolf. None of you are getting out of this alive. I'll see to that. But don't worry. You'll all be regaled as heroes. I couldn't have done it without you, after all."

She looks up at him. Hot tears stream down her cheeks. "How did you know I'd protect her, but she'd still expose all of you?"

"Because I know Alex. That feeling of betrayal will send her into a vengeful rage. She'll act without thinking. She'll ignore everything she knows about you and act on the hurt because, underneath all her confidence and courage, she's a scared little girl who doesn't believe someone like you could love someone like her."

"But I do love her," she whispers.

"And that's how I knew you'd protect her."

He closes the door behind him, and Cassidy turns herself over to the fury. She screams into her lap and lets the tears flow freely from her cheeks. He still got the best of them for all their planning, intent, and knowledge. He used their feelings and emotions against them to gain his advantage. She wants to chase after him, hit him, shake him, hurt him. But to what end? They'd played right into his hand, and they have no one to blame but themselves.

CHAPTER TWENTY-TWO

Alex watches the second hand tick on the clock in her boss's office. Her head hasn't stopped pounding, and her body aches with the remnants of adrenaline and stress. She's exhausted. She's also finding it difficult to sit still. It's like every part of her body and mind is in opposition.

Hunter hasn't stopped clenching and unclenching his jaw since Leo uploaded the video. She doesn't blame him. She could've grabbed Cassidy. She could've forced her out, but she did nothing. She walked out and left her behind. He's sitting next to her, but his subconscious body language says he's trying to stay as far away as possible. He clicks the pen in his hand over and over. The repetitious sound is like nails on a chalkboard. It's shredding the last scrap of her sanity.

"There had to have been another way." His voice is smoldering with anger.

"You didn't see her. She meant what she said. I made the only decision I felt I had available to me at that moment."

He looks at her, and his eyes are like hot pokers against her skin. "It wasn't your decision alone."

"Believe me when I tell you that I've been second-guessing myself every single second since we walked out of that building."

"I would've found another way," he says through gritted teeth.

"I guess we'll never know."

She wishes it had been Hunter who had found her. The image of Cassidy telling her she was staying will be etched into her mind for the rest of her life. It will be a bad dream that reoccurs night after night. The possibilities of what could've happened have piled up since she closed that door. Was Cassidy being threatened? Drugged? Or is it an Occam's razor situation—she simply meant what she said. The unknown tangled with the guilt has left her with constant nausea and a fierce headache. Hunter is lucky he's just mad and worried. He isn't being strangled with guilt so fierce Alex knows it will never leave.

Gregory walks into the room and drops several files onto the desk. "You two are on my last fucking nerve. What were you thinking?" He holds up a hand. "On second thought, don't tell me. I don't give a shit." He puts his hands over his face and shakes his head. "The number of rules and regulations you either ignored or outright violated is extraordinary."

"Sir, we—"

"Nope. I'll tell you what you're not going to do; you're not going to give me a bunch of half-baked excuses and reasons. Because I'm going to be honest, I don't give a shit. We have a serious shitstorm on our hands and we need to fix it." He points to the door. "Let's move." When they don't jump up immediately, he smacks the door. "Why are you two still sitting here?"

They follow him down the hall and into one of the large control rooms. There are dozens of monitors on the walls. People are hurrying around, answering phones, and looking at satellite images. People are moving around in uniforms she doesn't even recognize.

She walks over to one of the monitors airing the video Leo uploaded. A news anchor comes on describing what this means for the country and the worldwide implications. Other news programs are interviewing US citizens and leaders from different parts of the world. She hears about the tanking stock market on a different screen, and there's a hunt for Jack Jorgenson.

She focuses on a different screen. A middle-aged news anchor straightens his papers on the desk in front of him. "We're bringing you information as it unfolds. So far, we know that there was a massive plot to change Democratic votes to Republican in the upcoming election. CEO and founder of Abracadabra, Jack Jorgenson, Senator

Miles Christie from Florida, and business mogul Jeffery Fletcher are the masterminds of the operation. There have also been several high-ranking GOP officials implicated in the operation. We'll keep you updated on the story as it unfolds. Right now, we're going live to Los Angeles, California, where Governor Newport is—"

Alex can't listen anymore. She needs to find Gregory. Are they keeping Peterson a secret from the media? She sees him across the room and hurries over.

Gregory is putting folders in a line on a long table. He sees her coming and shakes his head. "In a minute, Derby."

She ignores him. "Do we have a location on Peterson? He wasn't mentioned in the news reports."

He glares at her. "Our more pressing issue is finding Fletcher, Christie, and Jorgenson." His face turns red. "If you'd gone about this the right way, we could've set up an actual operation instead of chasing our tails. We could've had all these assholes in custody. Instead, we're closing down airports and highways, looking for people who have access to more money than God." He slams the folders down. "But please, I'd love to hear your insight on how to do my job."

Jack Jorgenson's voice comes through every monitor in the room. "Good evening, my fellow Americans and the rest of the world. I'm sorry to hijack your programming, but I need to get my message out as quickly as possible."

Alex studies the screen. He's in a nondescript location. There's only a black screen behind him, and no one else is with him. He could be anywhere.

"It seems that our esteemed FBI is trying to make me out to be some kind of traitor. I want to assure you that's not the case. I want nothing but good things for my country and the rest of the world. I want to end poverty, give everyone medical care, and provide free quality education to everyone." Images of the cityscapes she'd seen on the flash drive appear. "I want to give everyone the gift of innovation, accessibility, and reliability. Imagine a world with no homelessness, no poverty, no pain and suffering. I can give that to all of you. You just have to let me."

He's still talking when she feels a tap on her shoulder. She turns around to see Leo standing there with a knowing grin. He points to the tablet he's holding.

"Leo? How the hell did you get in here?"

He lifts his badge. "I made it. Cool, huh? Nobody gives you a second look if you have a badge."

She doesn't have time to question him further. "What did you find?"

He zooms in on the map. "He's at a small private airport near Petersburg, Virginia."

Alex grabs the tablet. "How did you find him?"

Leo grunts. "He can't stay that hidden broadcasting live. He needs a strong signal for that. It's actually pretty stupid."

"Leo Parker?" Gregory turns him around. "How in the hell did you get past security?"

Leo flips up his badge. "I just made one of your crappy security badges. It scans and everything."

Gregory's nostrils flare. "Please tell me he hasn't been the tech guy who's been helping you."

Leo puts his hands on his hips. "I'll have you know that I've been helping the CIA for the last year. They wiped my record."

Gregory stares at him and blinks. "You want me to believe the CIA made you an informant?"

Leo holds up his finger. "Technically, I'm an independent contractor."

"I don't care if you're the actual son of God. What are you doing in my war room?" Gregory grabs the tablet.

Leo points to the screen. "I found Jorgenson. Not that I should be helping you with an attitude like that." He looks at Alex. "How do you function in this hostile work environment every day?" He shakes his head. "You should take this to the union."

Alex pulls him away. "Okay, you aren't doing anyone any favors right now."

Leo pulls his arm away. "I beg to differ. I do nothing but favors, and for what? You all are the most ungrateful people I've ever met." He looks around. "Are there seriously no snacks in here?"

Gregory stands on a chair. "Gather around, everyone."

A young agent runs up to him. "We managed to find Jorgenson's location, sir."

Gregory's face flushes a shade of red Alex has never seen. "Get away from me right now." He points to the tablet. "I have it right here. You should've had it fifteen minutes ago."

Leo nudges Alex. "See." He leans closer and whispers, "Also, Cassidy is still alive. I have a monitor on her. All her vitals are strong."

Her ears burn from the information, and a lump lodges in her throat. She's painfully grateful that Cassidy is still alive. Alex wants answers to the questions plaguing her soul since they last saw each other. She needs to see that she's okay. She needs to tell her how she feels and see if there's anything left between them, no matter what's happened.

Gregory continues. "We've isolated Jorgenson's location, and the likelihood is that Peterson is with him. He won't be there long. We're going to set up a strike team. Alex Derby and Hunter Nagle will lead the strike. Tactical Operations will be on the scene, but they will report to Derby and Nagle. Everyone else set up for communications and tactical assistance. We need to leave here like yesterday."

He hops off the chair and grabs Alex and Hunter. "This is it. Make sure I don't regret this. We'll call the airfield and instruct them to act like nothing is wrong but to stall for as long as possible."

They nod their understanding and take off for the garage. Her heart shudders at the possibility of seeing Cassidy at the airfield. She wants answers, but she can't afford any more regret, so she pushes it back. It needs to stay in its place, in the special box she created for it somewhere in the back of her mind—labeled Cassidy. But it's not possible. Cassidy is everywhere. She's all over her, and that's not going to change.

Chapter Twenty-three

Cassidy watches Jack pace up and down the hangar, yelling at no one in particular. "Something is wrong. Christie and Fletcher should be here by now." He storms over to her. "This isn't how any of this was supposed to happen." He pushes several buttons on the tablet he's carrying. "We only have an hour. I scrambled the broadcast signal through several different routers, but time is ticking."

Cassidy flashes on Leo but doesn't dare say anything about their super-hacker. She grits her teeth at the pain in her arm from his grip and stays focused on his other observation. "They probably took off with Peterson the moment the story leaked and all of you were implicated in a coup attempt." She pulls her arm away. "You didn't pick very reliable people to try to overthrow an entire government."

"Stop saying that. I wasn't trying to overthrow anyone. I was trying to save everyone. People have no vision. You can't see what's good for you."

She watches the airport employees. They're moving at a pace that can only be described as lethargic. Jorgenson broadcasted his little manifesto across every available signal. Leo undoubtedly figured out where they are by now. They're probably moving on the location. All of this sluggish work is to buy time. She tries to make quick work of counting the security guards Jorgenson has brought with him. She can see twelve, but that doesn't mean there aren't a few sprinkled in other parts of the airport. The FBI will show up with three times that. Her odds are improving by the second.

"For what it's worth, I don't think you're wrong. This country has a lot of broken systems. People are going bankrupt with healthcare costs. College puts people in debt for the rest of their lives, and corporations pass money out like candy to their shareholders and don't give a shit about their workers. The whole thing is rigged."

"Yes, exactly." He grabs the arms of her chair and leans on them. "Why can't they see I'm trying to save them?"

She's bone tired. This whole situation came to fruition because these men needed their already extraordinary egos stroked. And for what? She's stuck here waiting to see what a madman decides to do with her. She doesn't have it in her to play their games anymore. She's given everything she has to give.

Cassidy sighs. "Because you aren't trying to save them. If you were, you would've already. You would've paid your employees a living wage. You'd be spending your billions on lobbying the politicians for universal health care. You'd go ahead and just set up those free universities and tech schools you're talking about without having to kill and conquer to do so." She leans forward and holds eye contact. "You tried to rig the people's only voice, and hoped they'd tear each other apart. You don't want to fix anything. You want to be king. And the fact that you don't see the difference is why you'll just be a footnote in history."

His breathing becomes more labored, and he shoots daggers with his eyes. "And why are you still sitting here?" He grabs her face and squeezes. "All this adoration for doing the right thing—all these courageous people you defend, no one came to save you."

She sees the airport employees run out of the hangar, and she winks at him. "Looks like you spoke too soon."

The guards run into the hangar and make a barrier between him and the armored cars as they arrive. He grabs her and moves behind one of the large steel storage boxes. The irony of a person who declares themselves fit to run an entire country hiding behind a single storage container is comical.

She shakes her head. "You are quite literally everything that's wrong with the world."

He peeks around the side of the container. "Having a death wish doesn't equate to being brave. I'm not an idiot."

"Then go turn yourself in and make your case. You know damn well your trial would be publicized on every media outlet in the world. You hiding, having a hostage, trying to flee—that's not leadership, that's criminal."

He shakes his head. "If I go out there, they'll shoot me on sight. I'm not going down for treason."

"Then send me. I'll tell them you're surrendering."

Her breath catches when she hears Alex's voice on a megaphone echo through the hangar. "Jorgenson, you're surrounded. Tell your guards to put their weapons down and come out with your hands up, and no one will get hurt."

He bangs the back of his head on the container. "Fuck, fuck, fuck."

She softens her voice. "This doesn't have to end badly. You can still get out of this."

He stares at her. His eyes are cold and resolute. "And then what? Spend the rest of my life in some hole like Carol O'Brien? I can't live like that. I've been to space. I have a yacht that's worth more than some countries." He wipes at his mouth. "No, I can't go to prison."

She grabs his arm, hoping the physical contact will snap him out of whatever decision he's about to make. "It's still better than dying."

He smiles, and it's clear by the look in his eyes that he's made up his mind. "No. It's not. I'm not going to do either."

He stands and holds her in front of him, gun pressed to her side. She sees the FBI tactical team flinch as they move. Every one of the people behind those trained weapons is now trying to calculate if they have a clear shot. This whole situation is a powder keg waiting to be ignited by one mistake. Cassidy is playing every scenario in her head. Despite what the movies portray, she knows she can't move faster than a bullet if she tries to fight. She wishes she could see Alex, but all she sees are guards in full gear.

He drags her up the metal stairs and opens the door to the small plane. Jorgenson's guards are getting nervous. They shuffle back and forth in front of the hangar. They're outnumbered, and they know it. They also know their boss will leave them to die.

Alex's voice booms out again. "Jorgenson, don't do anything foolish. We will shoot that plane down. You are *not* leaving here."

Jorgenson holds her more tightly and yells from behind her. "I'd rethink that, Agent. If you take me down, she's coming with me."

He backs inside the plane and slams the door shut behind them. The engines are deafening. This plane wasn't designed to be started inside a hangar. Various items that Cassidy can't make out fly against the walls. Jorgenson's guards struggle to stay in their position. As one is forced to the side, he fires off a single shot.

Cassidy doesn't hear the gunshot, but she recognizes the kickback against the guard's shoulder. The next ninety seconds feel like slow motion. She knows what will happen before it occurs because it's entirely predictable.

The rogue shot hits the armored tactical vehicle at the front line. She sees the sparks fly off the steel. She watches the agent on the left closest to the disturbance fire back at the guard. The bullet hits him square in the chest, and he drops his weapon as he hits the ground.

There's no more warning. There will be no more conversation. There goes the powder keg.

Bullets are exchanged in rapid succession. The guards are terribly outnumbered and not as well trained. Agents fire strategically as guards duck behind any barrier available, firing bullets like they're spraying the grass on a Sunday afternoon. There's no rhyme or reason. Their only goal is to hit something.

She sees Alex and Hunter duck behind a ten-foot ballistic shield. The fleeting relief she feels from knowing they're safe is quickly replaced with raging panic when she sees Alex emerge with a small ballistic shield. She's moving into the hangar. The guards turn their attention to her. Each spark shreds Cassidy's already frayed nerves. With the guards' focus pulled, the agents take them down with ease.

Jorgenson slips into the pilot seat and puts his hand on the throttle just as Alex makes it to the stairs. Cassidy takes advantage of the fact that the gun is no longer trained on her, threads her fingers together, and hits Jorgenson in the nose with every bit of strength she has. Blood sprays onto the controls and Cassidy. He grabs his nose and screams.

He stands and grabs the back of Cassidy's hair. He pulls the gun from his waistband and tries to grab Cassidy again, but she knees him in the stomach.

He grabs the pilot's chair to steady himself while he wheezes. "You fucking bitch."

"It's over, Jorgenson," Alex says from where she stands in the plane. "Put the gun down."

He spits a mouth full of blood onto the floor. "I say when it's over." He points the gun at Alex.

She sees Jorgenson fall to the ground before she realizes what the sound of shattering glass means. She looks out and sees the sniper on top of the armored tactical vehicle. She looks back at Jorgenson and sees the pool of red spreading out from under him. Just like that, it's over. She should be feeling nothing but relief and elation, but all she feels is rage. Rage that she's in this position. Rage that people like this exist in the world, and rage that it had to get to this point. She wants to scream, but her ability to do so is lost. She's so overwhelmed and exhausted that her legs grow weak. She kneels and tries to control her breathing.

"Are you okay?" Alex moves toward her.

Cassidy has difficulty finding the words she wants to say, so she settles on a single syllable. "No."

Alex is kneeling in front of her a moment later, checking her for injury. She grabs her hands and holds them. Cassidy isn't experiencing any physical pain, but explaining that to Alex right now just isn't possible.

Alex's voice is timid. "Can you stand?"

Cassidy nods. "Thank you for coming back for me." The last thing she wants to do is cry, but her body doesn't care. Tears immediately start burning her cheeks. "Please get me out of here."

Cassidy nods and lets Alex help her to her feet. She leans on her for support because she can. Alex is solid and there, and she's so grateful.

Alex helps her sit on the back of the armored tactical vehicle. "What happened when I showed up? Why didn't you go with me?"

She watches all the people moving around her. Scenes like this are like an orchestra. Everyone knows their part to play, and if even one is missing, it's felt through the whole ensemble. Ambulances begin to arrive on the scene, and she absently considers whether there are wounded or only dead.

"Cassidy?"

She shakes her head and blows out a long breath. "I was never with them. Peterson was in the room when you arrived. He told me to tell you I was staying or he'd kill you. He was standing right behind you."

Alex shifts her weight from one foot to the other and won't make eye contact. "I should've known that." She runs a hand through her hair. "I don't know what I was thinking. I should've stopped Leo from releasing that video. We could've gotten you killed."

"I would never betray you." Cassidy reaches for Alex's hand, but she pulls away. Cassidy's heart hurts with the pain of watching Alex torture herself. "You did the right thing. What else were you supposed to think?"

Alex shakes her head. "I should've trusted you and figured I was playing into some plan. But I didn't. I was blinded by my bullshit." She turns away. "I have to go. I'm sorry."

Cassidy tries to call after her, but her voice catches in her throat. It snags on anger and exhaustion. Cassidy can't absolve Alex of her regret—only Alex can do that.

CHAPTER TWENTY-FOUR

Alex wakes up to Briggs tapping the side of her face. His little purr is almost enough to undo the last several days—almost. Her chest burns with the same dull ache that has been there since Cassidy told her to leave, but today is worse.

Today she knows the truth. Cassidy did it to save her life. Cassidy had been ready to risk everything to protect her, and she immediately thought the worst. Even if there were a version of this world where they could find a way to work through something like that—Alex would never forgive herself. She'd be reminded of the decision she made every time she looked at Cassidy. The failure would never leave her.

She drags herself out of bed and to the kitchen. The contents of the fridge are disappointing, to say the least. She grabs an apple from the counter and starts the coffee. She's halfway through her first bite when there's a sharp knock on her door.

She isn't even halfway there when Leo comes bursting through. "Have you seen the news reports?"

Alex takes another bite of her apple. "Several things." She puts up a finger. "Number one, when you knock on a door, you're supposed to wait for the person to open it." She puts up another finger. "It's seven in the morning. No, I haven't seen anything." He tries to interrupt, and she shakes her head, putting up a third finger. "How did you get in?"

He sighs and stares at her with fierce annoyance in his eyes. "I made a key in case of an emergency—which this is." He pushes past her and grabs the remote. "You're going to want to see this."

She stands next to him. "When did you make a key?"

He shoos her away. "That's not important." He turns up the volume. "Here we go."

None other than Dave Peterson is on the television. He's giving a press conference, wearing a suit—as if he didn't just try to dismantle the entire government. "For the last two years, I have been part of a deep undercover investigation. The objective of this investigation was to uncover a plot to rig our precious elections. Through my work and the support of other agents, we were able to identify the traitors behind this nefarious attack on our country. Jack Jorgenson may have been the money and mastermind, but he had help. Today, I arrested Senator Miles Christie and Jeffery Fletcher, along with several high-ranking politicians. It's a sad day for our country, but rest assured, there are people on your side fighting for you every single day. I won't be taking questions, but I will be releasing a more detailed report to the media later today. Thank you."

Leo turns off the television. "Fucking wild, right?" He shakes his head. "What a time to be alive."

"I can't believe this is happening." She sits down on the couch.

Of all the reasons someone may be pounding on her door at seven in the morning, this wasn't on the list. Briggs walks by again and rubs up against Leo. Leo's eyes soften as he reaches down to pet him. Another thing to add to her inventory of surprises for the day—Leo is a cat person.

There's another knock at her front door, and Hunter comes in. "Did you guys see the news?"

Alex throws her hands up in the air. "Seriously? Does no one understand how doors work?"

Hunter brushes past her to get to Leo. "We're going to completely out this guy right? There's no way anyone actually believes this horseshit. Undercover? Please. There would be a paper trail a mile long. Who does he think he's fooling? There has to be early communication between all of them to prove that he's been in on this from the beginning."

Leo snatches the apple from Alex's hand and sits on the couch. "Let me see what I can find. It should be easier now since we have definitive suspects and know exactly what he's trying to pull." He shoves the apple in his mouth and starts typing.

"This can't be real life," she says as she walks back to the kitchen for another apple.

"Is the coffee ready?" Hunter calls from the living room.

"Unbelievable," she says under her breath while pulling cups down from the cupboard.

She hands them their coffee. "I'm going to take a shower."

"Good. I called Cassidy, and she's on her way over." Leo gives her a disgusted look. "You look terrible. You don't want her seeing you like that."

She squeezes the back of the couch. "It's not like I knew you guys were coming over."

He takes another bite of her apple. "Tick tock."

She closes her bedroom door and takes a shaky breath. She wasn't planning on seeing Cassidy. She knew they'd see each other at work, but she'd thought it would be in a team environment while closing this case. Granted, that was what they were doing today, but her house is very different from the office. The office has countless eyes, standards, and an understood professionalism. There weren't any of those protections here.

Fuck.

Cassidy must have been sitting in the driveway long enough for someone to notice because Hunter eventually comes out and heads in her direction. She gets out of the car to wait for him and so Thor can adequately greet him.

"Whatcha doing out here?" He leans against her car.

"I shouldn't be here. Alex doesn't want to see me." She points to the house. "She needs more time."

He scratches at his beard. "Alex is a great agent. Seriously, one of the best I've ever worked with." He slings his arm around her. "But if she can't get over this, she doesn't deserve you." He kisses her temple. "She may need time, but that doesn't mean you aren't a part of this team. We need you. You two will sort the rest out."

She takes a deep breath. "Okay. Let's finish this."

Hunter opens the door, and Thor makes a beeline for Briggs, who looks surprisingly excited to see a creature who wants to do nothing but play with him by carrying him around in his mouth.

"Good morning." Cassidy rubs Leo's shoulder.

Leo puts his computer down and stands. He wraps her in a hug. "I was sure you were going to die. I'm almost never wrong. You're so lucky this was one of those times."

She stands in shock for a brief moment before patting his back. "Glad I didn't die too."

He immediately sits back down and starts typing.

Cassidy is in the process of pouring herself a cup of coffee when she hears a familiar voice behind her. "Morning."

Cassidy steadies herself. Her impulse is to pull Alex against her. She misses the smell and feel of her skin. She wants to smell her shampoo and feel the little tap on her lower back that Alex gives her when they hug. She wants all of it, but it's not hers to take—it has to be given.

"Hi," she says as she turns around. "I don't want this to be weird. I'm sorry if it is."

The corner of Alex's mouth turns up in a smirk. "You're just as much a part of this team as anyone else. I'm glad you're here."

"Alex, I—"

Alex shakes her head. "I can't right now. Let's just get through this. Can we do that?"

Cassidy nods because she doesn't trust her voice. She follows Alex to the table and takes a seat.

Leo rubs his hands together. "Okay, so we have that video from the cabin—"

"He'll just say it was part of his deep cover. He'll tell everyone that he couldn't divulge his position and risk the case. We need more than that," Hunter says.

Cassidy sips her coffee. "I'll testify against him. He basically told me his whole plan. I know when and why he changed his mind and turned on the other conspirators. My testimony undoes his."

Alex chews on her finger. "It's still he said, she said. We have to find a smoking gun to outshine all the bullshit he's spewing.

It's pretty clear that he's setting himself up for political office, and people are eating it up. They think he's a hero."

"We have the flash drive that was literally in his house when we found it. He still doesn't know that we have the original. That's another nail in the coffin," Hunter says.

Leo holds up his finger. "What if I told you that I have a recording of him saying all of that to Cassidy?"

Alex pops out of her chair and shakes Leo. "I'd say you're a damn miracle worker who should have said that sooner so he didn't have a chance to have a fucking press conference."

Leo moves Alex's hand off his arm. "I am a miracle in general, but I don't have it yet." He sighs. "It pains me to say this, but I need help. Does anyone know someone at the NSA? I haven't been able to crack their firewall in over a year." He sucks his lips in. "Not that I've tried that hard, but they've definitely improved their security. I need someone on the inside."

Hunter pushes Leo's laptop screen down. "Did you seriously just admit to a group of FBI agents that you were trying to hack the NSA?"

Leo slowly reopens his computer. "Not on purpose?"

Hunter exhales loudly. "That's not a defense."

Cassidy puts her hand on Hunter's forearm. "Okay, we can have a stern conversation with Leo later. But, right now, let's see if we can get him what he needs."

Alex holds up her phone and walks out of the room. "I'm on it."

"Okay, good. Alex is on it." She looks at Hunter, who is glaring at Leo.

"What?" Leo puts his hands up.

"You're the smartest dumb person I've ever met."

"Don't hate the player. Hate the game." Leo goes back to typing as Hunter walks out of the room.

Well, they were off to a great start. Cassidy pats Thor, and he follows her to the backyard. As soon as the air hits his face, he's thrilled to chase the few birds perched on the table's edge. She scolds him for disturbing their morning, but he pays her no attention.

She sits in the sun and tries to enjoy the crisp morning heat. The air is still damp from the night before but not stifling. It's lovely. It's almost pleasant enough to forget the pit in her stomach caused by the distance between her and Alex.

"Brooke has someone who can help us." Alex sits next to her.

Cassidy laughs. "Brooke has someone for everything."

Alex nods. "Her team is awe-inspiring. Emma Quinn is the best the NSA has to offer, and she was a bridesmaid at Brooke and Tyler's wedding. They're on their way over now."

"Then we should count ourselves lucky."

Alex looks like she's turning something over in her head. Her expression looks pained, and she's kneading her hands together. She rubs the back of her neck and bites on her thumbnail.

Cassidy reaches to touch her but changes her mind and pulls back. "Are you okay?"

Alex looks like she may cry. "I don't know how to answer that."

"I'd prefer the truth."

Alex nods and looks up at the sky. Her leg moves up and down in a nervous motion. "I, umm…" She shakes her head. "I'm going to go inside and order some food for everyone."

As she walks by, Cassidy grabs her hand. "I miss you," she whispers.

Alex stands there briefly but then pulls away and continues inside.

Thor wanders back over and looks around, confused. "She went back inside, buddy."

He flops down at her feet, apparently deciding that she needs comfort more than he needs to play. It's amazing how animals can be so attuned to their humans' needs. They give what's needed and ask for very little in return. They accept with their whole heart and forgive without question. If only Alex could do the same.

CHAPTER TWENTY-FIVE

Alex watches as Emma Quinn unpacks several devices and places them on the table. She's meticulous and careful. She sits down and adjusts one of the black boxes millimeters to the left. She opens a small journal and scribbles down several notes before closing it again.

Leo is tracking her every movement like she's the most mystical creature he's ever seen. "Is there anything I can help you with?"

Emma raises her eyebrow. "I'm familiar with your work, Mr. Parker. If you weren't a friend of Brooke's, I wouldn't want you within ten feet of my gear."

Leo pulls his pockets inside out and holds up his hands. "I don't have any trace tech on me. I swear."

She lightly blows on her keyboard. "Even if you did, I have four different scramblers running to keep you at bay."

Leo puts his hand over his heart. "I think I'm in love."

Brooke pushes him into the kitchen. "Okay, Casanova. Help me get something from the kitchen."

"What?"

Brooke keeps pushing him. "I don't know, anything."

Emma puts on glasses and turns her attention to Alex, Hunter, and Cassidy. "Brooke has filled me in on what happened. I understand we're looking for a particular conversation in one of the Abracadabra warehouses." She checks her notes. "You don't by chance have the coordinates to the location, do you?"

"I can get that for you. One second." Hunter starts tapping on his phone.

"We really appreciate you doing this, Emma. I'm sure you have better things to do than help us on a Saturday morning."

"More important than making sure this asshole gets what's coming to him? I don't think so. Plus, there's nothing I wouldn't do for Brooke, including helping all of you."

Hunter hands her a piece of paper. "Here are the coordinates."

She pulls a pencil from her blond bun and sticks it between her teeth. "Now, please, go anywhere else. I can't handle all of you staring at me like a bunch of puppies waiting for their treat."

There's another knock at the door, and Alex looks around. "I can't imagine who that can possibly be."

Hunter moves toward the door. "I called Gregory." He shrugs. "I don't want my ass chewed again."

Alex grabs his arm. "We don't know what side he's on."

Hunter puts his hand over hers. "Trust me. It's ours." He takes off toward the door without waiting for a response.

Alex pulls the fridge door open. "I'm drinking a beer, and I don't want to hear a single thing about it only being eleven in the morning."

Cassidy rubs at her eyes. "Grab me one."

Alex grabs the six-pack and heads to the backyard. Cassidy is already sitting down. Her sleeves are rolled up, and her head is tilted toward the sky. She's heart-stoppingly beautiful. A memory of Cassidy arching on top of her flashes through her mind, and she pushes it away.

Alex sets the six-pack on the table and sits next to her. "Did you know Hunter called Gregory?"

Cassidy straightens her aviators and shakes her head. "No, but it may be for the best. He hears more than us. He may have some information that can be helpful."

Alex leans back in her chair. "Or it's another part of Peterson's plan?"

Gregory walks out the screen door and grabs a beer from the table. "I assure you, Derby, Peterson can fuck all the way off to the deepest pits of hell as far as I'm concerned." He tips his beer toward the kitchen. "How do you have so many connections?"

Alex smiles as she takes a pull from her beer. "What can I say? I'm a people person."

He snorts. "We all know that's bullshit. Why don't you tell me what's really going on here? I'd like to help." He pulls a toothpick from his pocket and sticks it in the corner of his mouth. "I saw the internal report from Peterson. It doesn't make any sense. There's no way he was undercover, and no one knew about it. Unfortunately he came out of the woodwork to hold that press conference. He surrendered his passport to the director and has agreed to fully cooperate. The powers that be are worried about public perception. We had mud all over our face after the last debacle with the FBI and the last president. People are already accusing us of a cover-up, including several members of congress. We need this to be ironclad." He shakes his head. "I hope you have something that will hold up against serious scrutiny." He pulls out the toothpick and takes a sip of his beer. "Even then, I don't know if it will be enough."

"It has to be enough. He can't get away with this." Alex rubs her eyes with the palms of her hands. "I won't let him get away with this. If it's the last thing I do, the world will know what he is."

Brooke takes a seat at the table and grabs a beer. "Oh, the FBI is way more fun than the CIA. I could get into this."

Gregory absently taps the side of the bottle with his wedding ring. "What do you think, Hart? I know you've been up against something like this before. Are we going to be able to make something stick to Peterson?"

Brooke wipes a bit of the beer on her lip away with her thumb. "I can tell you that if there's a conversation to find—Emma will find it. That in combination with the flash drive and Cassidy's testimony will be enough. Whether that's enough to turn public perception?" She shakes her head. "I don't have an answer for that."

Brooke's words roll around in Alex's head. The truth of it is hard to swallow. Even if they can get all the evidence together, there's no guarantee that the public will buy it. The American people have become increasingly unpredictable in the last few years. Lies have been spun into reality, and reality has taken on cartoonish characteristics—depending on who you ask. Overall distrust in systems is at an all-time high, and people are ready to disregard everything they've ever known to follow cultist leaders if it allows them to point the finger of blame at anyone else.

People she once considered friends now hurl slurs at her that cut to the bone. Talking points taken directly from the mouths of political pundits who've become filthy rich by sowing fear, hatred, and malice directed at neighbors and family members. And for what? The only ones winning are the people cashing in on hatred.

"It doesn't matter who believes us. We're going to do the right thing. We're going to do our jobs. We can't control what happens after that." Alex pulls at the label on her beer bottle. "But if we lose, and we're all out of a job next week or next month, it's been my pleasure." She takes a sip of her beer.

Gregory taps his bottle against hers. "Here's to going down fighting."

Leo pops his head out the door. "No one is going anywhere. Emma is a genius. I don't say that lightly. I think she may be the smartest person I've ever met."

Alex unconsciously touches Cassidy's leg under the table and doesn't realize what she's done until Cassidy covers her hand with her own. She pulls her hand away and tries to ignore the look of pain on Cassidy's face.

She stands quickly to try to hide her misstep. "I can't wait to see what the smartest person Leo has ever met has come up with."

Cassidy smiles at her comment, but it doesn't reach her eyes. They can't continue like this. They can't remain in each other's orbit when they just keep hurting each other. It's not fair to anyone.

Emma is using words and phrases that Cassidy doesn't understand. She understands them separately, but not as they are, strung together in what she can only assume are sentences. Finally, she starts on something she can comprehend.

"So typically, the packets from the personal media devices are stored on the cloud servers, but that isn't the case in the Abracadabra buildings. They're smart enough to know that information is easily hackable. They have their own server, which is hilarious." She smiles. "They think keeping these on a hidden server will keep people like Leo and me from finding them. They're wrong."

"A packet of what?"

"Packets are bits of information sent from one device to another," Emma says. "If it were a message, they would—"

Gregory cuts her off. "Let's not get into the weeds with this one."

Emma nods. "Right. Sorry." She turns her screen around. "These personal devices are designed to give you updates, news, play music, whatever. They're voice activated, which means they're actually always listening. Those snippets are kept to improve speech pattern awareness and develop a greater contextual understanding for the AI. Illegal? Not necessarily. Legal? Not completely." She looks around as if she's checking to make sure everyone is still paying attention. "So, once I finally isolated and cracked the system, it was just a matter of pulling different files until I found the one Cassidy described." She pushes the play button on the computer.

Peterson's voice starts projecting from the speakers, followed by Cassidy's. Their whole exchange was right there, available for everyone to hear. The sudden laugh that bursts from deep in Cassidy's belly isn't intentional, but she couldn't stop it if she wanted to. Of course everything they were saying was being recorded by those little devices. Jack Jorgenson was never concerned because he thought he was the only one with access. But why would Peterson have ever thought about it?

"So we have him on audio admitting to everything." Alex looks partially shocked and partially elated.

Emma grins. "Actually, I have him on camera too. These devices are voice and video activated." She starts the video recording. "They're kept in two separate areas, but it wasn't difficult to dig out once I knew it was there."

Leo points to Emma again. "Fucking brilliant, right?" He shakes his head. "I can't believe you cracked those servers in under an hour. I've never seen firewalls like that before."

Emma stands and stretches. "That's what they pay me for." She pulls the flash drive out of the computer and hands it to Alex. "Your golden ticket, ma'am."

Alex takes it and hugs her. "Thank you. I don't know what we would've done without this." She kisses her cheek. "Seriously, a million times, thank you."

Emma blushes adorably. "It was nothing." She looks at Leo. "I don't know how you're all going to use that, but I left the authentication code on there in case you need to prove its validity." She pats his arm. "I've changed my mind about you. You're okay, Leo Parker." She turns to Brooke. "I need to get over to Dylan's. I promised I'd kick her ass at her new video game."

"What game?" Leo looks excited.

Emma shrugs. "I don't know, and it doesn't matter. I always kick her ass."

Leo watches Emma walk out the door. "That's the girl of my dreams."

Brooke snorts. "Her girlfriend is way hotter than you."

Leo glares at her. "Don't ruin this moment for me."

Hunter snatches the drive out of Alex's hand. "So, what are we going to do with this? Turn it over to the bosses?"

Cassidy listens as different ideas are tossed around. None of them are bad, but none of them are great. Their biggest obstacle in this volatile environment is public opinion. They need to win a significant portion to get anyone to really bring the hammer down on Peterson. She absently glances at the news broadcast in the background, running its typical filler stories when the idea comes to her. It may take some convincing, but she hasn't heard a better alternative yet.

CHAPTER TWENTY-SIX

G regory ends the call. "Well, it took every favor I had up
my sleeve, but I pulled it off. Peterson will be interviewed
tonight on Maddox. Cassidy will be brought on halfway through the
interview to answer questions about what it was like to be taken by
Jorgenson. Then, Maddox will air the video."

"When do we need to get them the drive?" Alex squeezes the
small device in her pocket like a precious stone. "I don't want them
to have access too early." Alex dislikes the idea of Cassidy being
anywhere near Peterson again, but she reminds herself that Cassidy
is an agent too. This is the job.

"I told them we'd deliver it when we arrive. We'll be there to
make the arrest as soon as it's over." He checks his watch. "We need
to be in New York by six. We should leave here in two hours. We
need to take two cars. One to transport him back to DC and one for
everyone else. Let's go get them and meet back here."

"I'll go with you." Hunter steps forward like he's volunteering
for service.

Gregory nods. "Perfect." He looks Cassidy up and down. "You
may want to change your clothes. You need to look official, and
those sweatpants aren't it."

Cassidy leaves to go home and change, and she stops to hug
Alex before she goes. Though she doesn't make eye contact, the
move leaves Alex off balance. Alex is left with Leo and an hour
to fill while she waits for the rest of her life to unfold. The typical

excitement she feels before collaring a suspect should be emanating through her, but it's not. Dread, worry, and loss are the only feelings working through her cluttered mind.

Leo props his feet up on the table, and Alex doesn't bother correcting him. "You seem bummed. I figured you'd be bouncing off the walls with excitement."

"Hmm."

He taps a pen against his temple and looks at her contemplatively. "Do you want to talk about it? I can't promise that I'll give good or even helpful advice, but I can listen."

She eyes him. "I don't think there's anything to be done. I just need to get through this."

"Listen, I've worked with much smarter people than the three of you. Seriously, like significantly smarter."

Alex takes a deep breath. "Thanks, Leo."

He frowns. "I didn't get to finish. I've worked with more intelligent people, yes. But I've never worked with people so committed. You three are all heart, and that isn't something that can be taught. We're going to get Peterson because you're all willing to go balls to the wall every time. It's impressive."

"Thanks, Leo." She heads toward the bedroom. "I'm going to go change."

She doesn't have the heart to tell him that he's completely off base. He's also unintentionally insulting, but that's a moot point. She isn't worried about finally getting Peterson. Their plan is solid, and she knows they'll leave with him in handcuffs tonight. The part she can't reconcile is her feelings about Cassidy.

The pull is stronger than ever. Her heart reaches for her while her mind slaps it away. The hardest part is that she knows Cassidy feels it too. She could feel it when she grabbed her hand. If this were up to Cassidy, they'd pick up where they left off. It's mind-boggling that she can feel that way after Alex left her in that building. Sure, she did what Cassidy had asked, but she should've known better. She should've known something was off and that Cassidy would only behave that way to protect Alex. Cassidy risked everything to save Alex, but she didn't return the same loyalty. She should've known better. It's easy to say she doesn't deserve her. That part is categorically true, but it is more than that. Alex knows how this will end. A part of Cassidy will always wonder why Alex didn't trust her that day, and Alex will never fully get over her choice. In the end, they'll be left with resentment and anger. And Alex can't bear the thought of Cassidy looking at her with disdain in her eyes. That, she knew, would break the last bit of her heart.

❖

Cassidy has been interviewed dozens of times for her job. People with microphones don't scare her. She's always thought it was important for people to see the government working for them and helping them. This won't be one of those interviews. She's about to reveal something that will make half the country mad at her, a part of the country will think she's outright lying, and who knows what the upper echelon of the FBI will think.

The makeup artist puts the finishing touches on her lips. "I think you're all set. The stage manager will send word when they're ready for you. You can wait in the green room until then."

"Thanks."

She opens the door to the green room and is relieved to see Alex waiting inside for her. "Where are Hunter and Gregory?"

Alex crosses her arms. "They're talking with NYPD downstairs. They'll be up here in a few. I didn't want you to think we all abandoned you, so I agreed to come up and keep you abreast of the situation."

Cassidy takes a step forward. "You sound so official."

"Well, this is official."

Cassidy grabs her hands and holds them in place when she tries to pull away. "I'm just going to say what I'm feeling because I don't know when you'll allow yourself to be alone with me again." She continues when Alex tries to interrupt. "Just let me say this. I'll regret it if I don't." Alex closes her eyes and nods. "I've been a lot of things in my life. A daughter, a student, a wife, an FBI agent, and for a while, I thought I'd be yours. I feel more like me when I'm with you because I don't have to be anything else. When you look at me, I feel like I'm enough." She pushes past the marble that's forming in her throat. "I'm not going to pretend to know what's going on in your head. We all have baggage, and if you don't want help with yours, I can't change that. But we can sort through it together. If you want me, I'll give you everything in me. I trust you with the good, bad, broken, lost, and found parts of me. I trust you." She kisses her forehead. "I love you, and even if you don't feel the same, I want to thank you for giving me the chance to feel that again." She puts her hands on either side of Alex's face. "Even if you don't give us a chance, promise me you'll let someone in. You're worth it."

The stage manager comes into the room. "We're ready for you, Agent Wolf."

Alex's eyes are filled with pain and confusion. It hurts to look at her, but Cassidy waits, hoping she'll say something. When no words come, she turns and leaves. She put her heart out there for Alex to take or kick to the ground. She'd hoped it would be the former, but she regrets nothing. She'll always wonder what they could've been, but she's done her part.

CHAPTER TWENTY-SEVEN

The lights are brighter than Cassidy had anticipated. They're hot and uncomfortable. Then again, maybe her broken heart has more to do with it than lighting. She pushes the thought away and focuses on the two people in front of her. Peterson looks smug and confident. His body language reeks of ego, and she wants to smack the pretentious smile off his face.

Raquel Maddox looks between them. "Thank you for coming on the show. I'll ask you both a series of questions, and you'll do your best to recall the event." She winks at her. "They'll count us in. Don't forget we're live. You two will do great."

Peterson straightens his tie and flashes her a sadistic smile. She makes a great effort not to clench her jaw. He thinks he has this in the bag. There are few things she hates more than being underestimated, and Peterson has ticked off every box.

Music starts playing, and Cassidy does the same thing she's seen every guest on this show do and smiles. The cameras move, and people hustle behind the scenes. The teleprompter starts moving, and Cassidy takes a breath to settle herself.

"Welcome back to our show. We're fortunate to be joined tonight by FBI Assistant Director Dave Peterson and FBI Profiler Cassidy Wolf. They were both involved with the hostage situation that led to Jack Jorgenson's death." She turns her attention to Peterson. "You've already stated that you'd been deep undercover in Jorgenson's plot to rig the upcoming presidential election. Tell me, how did you first discover what was happening?"

Peterson paints a sad look on his face that Cassidy could see through even if she wasn't sitting three feet from him. "I had to be open to the evidence. No one wants to think that one of our most extraordinary businessmen, our senators, or our citizens could be involved in something like this. But the evidence said otherwise, and I knew I owed it to the American people to follow my gut. So, I reached out to Senator Christie and started poking around. I saw an opportunity to inject myself into the plot, and I took it. I'm sure any agent would've done the same."

Raquel nods. "Who knew about your mission? I assume you had to inform your immediate supervisor. What about the president?"

Peterson shakes his head. "No, I couldn't tell anyone. I wasn't sure who was involved at that point, and I didn't want to risk the investigation." He chuckles. "To be honest, I'm still not sure if I'll have a job next week. There were a lot of people really upset with me, but I had to do the right thing. The soul of our country was at stake, and I couldn't sit idly by and watch it crumble."

"Oh, I'm sure you're safe," Raquel says with a smile. "You saved democracy after all. It would be hard to fire you after that."

Peterson takes a deep breath and intertwines his fingers. "As defenders of democracy, we have to stay vigilant. If no one is there to protect it, to do the right thing, we're in jeopardy of losing it. I'm proud to be one of those people."

Raquel points to an image of one of the cities Jorgensen had designed. "When you heard Jorgenson was planning on leveling our greatest cities and replacing them with Abracadabra facilities, what was your first thought? Were you ever concerned it would come to fruition?"

Peterson glances up at the picture, but he doesn't let his eyes linger. "I know there are people out there struggling. I know this is appealing in many ways, but it's a trap. He wanted to make everyone utterly reliant on him. If he supplies your salary, home, groceries, health care, and schools, no one is left to keep him in line.

He essentially wanted to be king, and this country decided a long time ago that isn't for us."

Cassidy practically chokes on the bullshit he's spewing. He's landing applause line after applause line. He's expertly playing to people's insecurities and fears, and the punch line is—he's the only one who can protect them. He wants people to believe he isn't like the others when the truth is—he's worse.

Raquel turns her attention to Cassidy. "Special Agent Wolf, you were on another team investigating the same coup. Tell me, what was it like to think Assistant Director Peterson was involved? What went through your head?"

Cassidy studies Peterson. His demeanor is cool and calm, but Cassidy knows better. She sees his pulse quicken at his neck and how he rubs his hands together. He's scared. The video is queued up and ready to play, but she intends to make a few points first.

She leans forward and smiles at Peterson. "Honestly, Raquel, I wasn't all that surprised. See, Assistant Director Peterson can sit here and pretend that he cares about the people of this country and the people he works with, but that isn't who he is. The sense of entitlement, the need for admiration, manipulative tendencies, lack of empathy, and arrogance are all textbook examples of a narcissist. Special Agent Derby is the agent who picked up on this case, and she's the one who deserves the credit. She's been investigating it on her own for several years, and she brought in a team when she had enough information to move forward. Dave Peterson is as guilty as they come. He wanted pure unadulterated power, and anything he says to the contrary is an outright lie. He didn't care who he had to hurt, step on, or kill to get it." She knocks on the table. "As a matter of fact, Raquel, I think we have the proof the American public needs to see."

The video starts playing, and Peterson looks like a trapped animal. His eyes fix on Gregory and Hunter to the left of the stage and then move to Alex on the right. He has nowhere to go, and it's more beautiful than Cassidy had imagined. The sound of his voice admitting to everything, including his plan to say he was undercover, reverberates throughout the room. Angry rumblings come from the audience and crew, and when it ends, there's stunned silence.

She leans over Raquel to look at Peterson. "I think it goes without saying, but you're under arrest. Don't worry; I have an excellent hole picked out for you right next to Carol O'Brien. I think you're really going to enjoy it."

Sweat starts to bead at his temples. "You aren't going to get away with this. I have public opinion on my side. I won't spend more than a week in jail."

Cassidy shrugs. "We'll see, but I wouldn't count on it. This is live, Peterson. You just said public opinion will save you. I don't think it will."

Gregory jerks him out of the chair and slaps handcuffs on his wrist. "You're a disgrace. You're under arrest for treason."

Peterson spits on the ground at Gregory's feet. "And you'll be lucky if you don't get fired over this. I know you didn't get this cleared."

Gregory jerks him toward the side of the stage. "I'll still be better off than where you're going."

"Any chance you want to stay for a follow-up interview? Eight million people just watched what happened. There are lots more questions to be answered." Raquel looks hopeful, but Cassidy can't think of anything she'd like to do less right now.

"The FBI appreciates your help, but all other inquiries need to be routed through the proper channels." Cassidy looks at the camera focused on her. "But we hope people see the truth. These entitled, arrogant men thought the public would be foolish enough to support them and their lies. We know differently, don't we? We know better than to let them control us using their money and fake desire for better things. We know our nation is a democratic republic. Flawed, yes, but also beautiful. And we can't let liars and evil men who would take that away from us win."

Raquel smiles. "Maybe you should run for office."

"Not a chance," Cassidy says as she leaves the stage.

Hunter pulls her into a hug. "You did great."

Cassidy looks around. "Where's Alex?"

"Taking Peterson back to DC with Gregory." He throws an arm around her. "She'll come around."

"Yeah, maybe."

It's easy to agree with Hunter at the moment, but she doesn't fully believe it. She may have to accept that wanting and loving Alex will never be enough to cross the bridge between them.

CHAPTER TWENTY-EIGHT

"So you weren't fired? You aren't on administrative leave? You just took a vacation?" Brooke lifts her sunglasses and stares at Alex from her lounge chair by the pool.

"Brooke, you invited me here. I accepted the invitation." Alex fans her face with the magazine sitting next to Brooke's drink.

Brooke lies back down. "I've invited you to my parents' beach house a hundred times, and you've never come before."

Alex pulls off her shoes and lies down. "Well, I came this time. I can go if you don't want me here."

Tyler's head pops up from the pool. "Stop interrogating her." She grabs her sunglasses off the ground and slides them onto her face. "It's obviously girl trouble."

This seems to get Brooke's attention. "What did you do? Please tell me this isn't still about the night at the warehouse."

Alex grunts. "Why do you automatically assume I did something wrong?"

Brooke snorts. "Because I've known you most of my life. At first sight of something good, you take off for the hills like a scared forest animal."

Alex scoffs. "I do not." She turns to Tyler. "She's referencing Julia Fest, and I didn't take off for the hills. She was leaving for college."

Brooke sits straight up and takes off her glasses. "In two years. You were juniors in high school. She adored you."

Alex shrugs. "Better to end it before someone gets hurt."

"You're unbelievable, Alex Derby. Cassidy is as good as they come, and you're being an idiot." She points at Tyler. "Tell her I'm right."

Tyler pushes off the wall and floats on her back. "Brooke is right."

"Your big point is to have your wife agree with you?" Alex closes her eyes and sighs. "That would hardly hold up in court."

"For fuck's sake, Alex. This isn't court. Cassidy is beautiful and funny and smart. For some reason that I can't think of right now, she wants you. If you keep messing this up, you'll regret it for the rest of your life."

Anger and hurt bloom in Alex's chest. "You think I don't know all of that, Brooke? I already regret it."

"Then fix it."

"I can't." Alex pushes the tears away with the back of her hand. "I'm not as brave as you, Brooke. There will always be this thing between us, and I'm terrified it will always be there. I left her behind, you guys. I left her there, with a maniac, instead of pulling her out and damn the consequences. I thought there was the slightest chance she'd actually bought into the bullshit, and what does that say about me? How will she ever forgive me, or trust that I won't let her down again? It will push against us until we finally break. The only thing scarier than not being with her is having her and then losing her. I couldn't handle it."

Brooke strokes her back and kisses the side of her head. "If all of that is true, then you're right, you shouldn't be with her. Cassidy deserves someone who will give her everything they are. You don't deserve her."

Alex nods. "Glad to know what you really think of me."

Brooke shakes her head. "We've never had a sugar-coating type of relationship, hon. You came here because you knew what I'd say. The only question now is if you're going to use it for pity-party validation or let it kick your ass into gear."

"Want to know what I think?" Tyler pushes herself out of the water and perches on the edge of the pool.

"Sure." Alex waves for her to continue. "Can't be any worse than her." She nods at Brooke.

"When I joined the Marines, I thought I knew everything. I wasn't scared of anything. I spent years operating like that. My only goal was to be the best. No mission was too dangerous, no situation held too much uncertainty." She laughs to herself. "Then I met Brooke, and I was confronted with fear like I'd never felt before. Would she get tired of me? What would happen if our careers moved in different directions? Would I be enough?"

Alex's heart lurches at the familiar thoughts. It's hard to believe Tyler ever had any doubts about Brooke, but here she is, admitting to the same thoughts that prick at Alex's mind.

"How did you get over it?" Alex leans closer. It's like someone is giving her an answer key she never knew existed.

Tyler smiles. "You never really get over it. We could wake up tomorrow and Brooke may tell me she's tired of me. I have no way of knowing with absolute certainty how she'll feel. So, I make every effort, every day, to give her reasons to stay. Brooke goes to sleep every night knowing just how much I love her. That's not an accident." She winks at Brooke. "I do it because she's worth it. We're worth it."

Brooke's ears are red, and she's trying to suppress a smile. "It turns out Tyler is better at this than me."

Alex snorts. "Well, you've set a really low bar."

Brooke sighs. "Listen, if you're in this much pain, it's already too late. You're already in love with her. The rest is just semantics."

Alex lets her head rest in her hands but hope begins to bloom where despair had made her cold. "I don't even know how to go about fixing any of this. It might be too far gone. I've done some pretty extensive damage."

Tyler smiles at her. "That's not how it works. She'll either forgive you, or she won't. If she doesn't, you won't be in any worse shape than now." She shrugs. "Doesn't seem like you have a whole lot to lose at this point."

Alex sighs. "Can you do me one more favor, and I'll never ask for anything again?"

Brooke laughs. "I doubt that, but sure."

Alex takes a deep breath. "Will you invite Cassidy here?"

Brooke stares at her. "If I'm going to do that, I need to tell her that you're here too. I'm not going to blindside her. I really like her. I'll help you, but she needs to agree to see you too."

"I understand. I don't want to make her uncomfortable."

Brooke bumps her with her shoulder. "Look at us, all grown up and making adult decisions."

Alex smiles. "Who would've thought?"

She excuses herself to go unpack her bag and change into her swimsuit. There's no point in letting the sun, pool, and ocean go to waste while her entire love life hangs in the balance. Besides, no one has ever said that salt air and sunshine were bad for their mood. It will do her some good and give her a chance to clear her head before explaining to Cassidy what she's feeling.

Alex heads down to the beach with a chair, towel, and sunscreen. The afternoon sun glints off the ocean, giving it the look of diamonds trailing into the distance. The only noise is the sound of crashing waves against the sand. She understands why people seek refuge in places like this. It's an easy way to remember how small you are in the grand scheme of things.

"Hey," Cassidy says from somewhere behind her.

Alex's heart pounds, her newly found peace scattered against the sand. "Hi. I'm glad you came. You got here pretty quick."

Cassidy smirks. "I was already on my way here when Brooke called to say you wanted to talk. She'd invited me up a few days ago."

"So Brooke had this planned already, even before I agreed?" She snorts. "Typical."

Cassidy sits on the towel Alex has laid out. "If you want to talk just to reiterate that you don't want to see me anymore, it's unnecessary. I can take a hint."

It hurts to hear the words, especially because Alex wants to tell her the opposite. "Believe it or not, I don't want to hurt you."

Cassidy straightens her sunglasses and looks out at the ocean. "So, what's up?"

Alex takes a deep breath. "I've never known anyone like you. I don't think I've ever felt more like myself than when I'm with you. You bring out the best in me." She hops off her chair and sits next to Cassidy. "It's like I was waiting for the other shoe to drop when we were together. It felt too good to be true, and I didn't think it could last." She grabs her hand and almost cries when Cassidy doesn't pull away. "I convinced myself that you'd never forgive me for leaving you there because I didn't think I could forgive myself. But for you, there was never anything to forgive. I finally realized that I can hold space in my head for more than one truth. I can still wish I'd made a different decision, *and* that doesn't have to be the defining moment of our relationship."

Cassidy runs her thumb over the back of Alex's hand. "But you didn't change your mind when you knew what happened. You still didn't want me."

Alex shakes her head. "There hasn't been a single minute since I've known you that I haven't wanted you. I let my fear and embarrassment control my actions. I convinced myself that I was beating you to the punch of leaving. I figured it was inevitable. But I realize now that was based on my own nonsense and wasn't based on anything you'd shown me or how you'd treated me."

Cassidy slides her glasses up on top of her head. "Don't you know how much I care about you, how much I want you, how much I love you?" She tips Alex's face up to look at her. "It would be easier to be mad at you. I've tried, and my heart won't let it happen because it knows the truth." She runs her thumb over Alex's bottom lip. "We could leave here and pretend that it's over. We could try to be friends and act like we never had a chance. We could do all those things, and it still wouldn't change reality."

Alex grabs her palm and kisses the inside. "I don't want to pretend it's over. I don't think it ever would be for me. I love you."

Cassidy moves from her position on the sand and wraps her legs around Alex's waist. "Say it again."

Alex takes off her sunglasses and kisses Cassidy's jaw and neck. "I love you."

Cassidy pushes into her and pulls her closer. "Show me."

Alex looks down the other side of the beach, and Cassidy turns her face back to her.

"No. Don't think." She presses Alex's mouth back against her neck. "It's just us."

Alex doesn't need any more convincing. She kisses Cassidy's neck and revels in the feeling of Cassidy's arm tightening around her neck. Alex moves down to her collarbone and rakes her teeth against the soft skin. Cassidy's hands are in her hair, guiding her mouth along her body. She pauses briefly to remove Cassidy's shirt and moves her mouth against her breasts.

Cassidy pushes herself against Alex's mouth and whimpers when Alex pulls at her nipple with her teeth. Cassidy slides her hand down Alex's stomach and under the waistband of her swim shorts. Her stomach clenches as Cassidy moves her hand farther down into her wetness.

Cassidy smiles against Alex's lips as she continues to kiss her. "Touch me."

Alex does as she's told and matches Cassidy's movements, sliding her hand between Cassidy's thighs. Cassidy shivers when Alex finally makes contact and pushes against her harder. Cassidy lifts her hips against Alex's hand, and Alex matches her speed with her own. Cassidy slightly speeds up when she feels Alex shudder against her neck. Alex uses her thumb to apply pressure to Cassidy's clit as she slides her fingers inside.

Cassidy groans and bites Alex's lip. "Harder."

Alex does as she's told through the haze of arousal that is becoming harder to navigate by the second. She's so close, and with each expert movement of Cassidy's hand, it's getting more difficult to maintain control. Cassidy's hips move against her hand while she continues to match Alex's thrusts.

Alex feels Cassidy's body clench around her fingers in spasms. Cassidy bites down on Alex's shoulder, sending Alex over the edge. They're a tangled mess of short breaths, groans, and quick kisses. The ripples of pleasure continue to vibrate through Alex for several seconds after. It doesn't matter that there is sand stuck to the sweat on her legs and back. She doesn't want to move until Cassidy releases her.

Cassidy pushes the hair out of Alex's eyes and kisses her slowly. "I may still need more convincing."

Alex smiles and kisses her again. "I think I can manage that."

"I love you, Alex. Don't ever forget that."

"I love you too. I always will."

Cassidy puts her forehead against Alex's. "I'm going to hold you to that."

Something Alex has never felt explodes in her chest at that moment. The fears and anxiety fall away, and all that remains is Cassidy. She understands exactly what Tyler was talking about. She may not be able to guarantee Cassidy's feelings about her five, ten, or fifty years from now, but she knows it will never be because Alex doesn't show her how she feels. Loving Cassidy is the only thing she's sure will remain of her, even after she's gone.

EPILOGUE

"Thor, get away from that waffle, or I'll rehome you," Cassidy yells from across the kitchen.

Thor begrudgingly removes his paws from the counter and moves over to the corner of the room and flops down next to a sleeping Briggs. She can't prove it, but she swears she hears him let out a loud huff as he flops to the ground.

Alex scratches his head as she walks past. "Don't listen to her. I'll share my waffle with you."

Cassidy grabs her by the shirt and pulls her closer. "Whose side are you on?" She kisses her. "Congratulations on your first day in the Counterterrorism Division, honey." She smacks her in the butt. "But if you feed him any of that waffle, you'll be on the couch for a week."

Alex shrugs at Thor. "Sorry, buddy. She's the boss."

Cassidy takes a bite of the waffle. "What time is Hunter coming to pick you up?"

Alex checks her phone. "He should be here any minute." She shovels several bites into her mouth. "You're going to meet us there, right?"

"I wouldn't miss it for the world." She kisses Alex and wipes a speck of whipped cream from the corner of her mouth.

Alex kisses her. "I love you. I'll see you in a bit." She runs out the door as a car honks outside.

Cassidy flips open the journal she's been writing in since they arrested Peterson. She skims several sections as a way to remember this chapter of her life before she closes it out for good. The passages are a mixture of factual events and her feelings on the subject.

They've been waiting for this day for eighteen months—Dave Peterson's sentencing. The trial had been long and painful. As they'd expected, a lot of people had a lot of different feelings about what had taken place. A swath of the country had thrown their support behind Peterson. They held rallies and signed petitions to help aid with his release. There were millions of think pieces written on the topic, and every political pundit in the world had to grab their fifteen minutes and weigh in on the subject.

Several political figures tried to hitch their wagon to the ideals Jorgenson had presented, and a few of them even won their elections. How that will eventually work out for them still remains to be seen. As the trial dragged on, it was impossible not to include the details of the plot Jorgenson had cooked up. Peterson tried his best to take credit for the perceived good aspects of the plan and lay the bad at a dead man's feet. The debate that followed still hasn't died down, but Cassidy has no regrets about that. Some things need to change, and maybe it will be the silver lining of the situation.

The American populous has a relatively short attention span, and without the constant influx of Peterson's deranged musings working its way into the social conscious, it will be difficult to make it stick long-term.

Cassidy moved into Alex's house after a year of dating, and it has been better than she ever imagined. She feels truly settled for the first time since leaving California. She carries a constant sense of peace that only comes from being truly loved by someone you love in return.

She closes the journal and places it in the desk drawer. It's time to start a new chapter, and all signs point to it being the best yet. She gives Thor a treat and scratches Briggs behind the ears on her way out of the house.

The courthouse parking lot is overflowing with cars, news vans, and people. She passes that lot and goes to the back, where she stops at the guardhouse and hands them her badge. They wave her through.

Brooke and Tyler are outside waiting for her. Tyler looks impeccable in her suit and sunglasses. Brooke is gorgeous in her pencil skirt and blouse. They're undoubtedly a gorgeous couple, but more than that, they're some of the best people Cassidy has ever met. She's lucky to count them as friends.

"Hey," Cassidy says as she approaches them.

Brooke kisses her cheek. "Where's Alex?"

Cassidy hugs Tyler. "Oh, you know her. She's been here for hours. She didn't want to miss anything."

Tyler nods. "That's understandable. This is a big deal."

Brooke rolls her eyes. "Those two are cut from the same cloth. Tyler would get to the airport three days before a flight if I'd let her."

"I don't like being rushed," Tyler says and pulls the door open.

Brooke puts her hand on Tyler's face. "I understand that, honey, but it's excessive."

Cassidy smiles at their typical banter as she walks past. The courthouse is bustling with excitement. It's a shocking contrast from the quiet of the parking lot. They push their way through several groups until they finally find Alex and Hunter.

Tyler smacks Alex on the back. "Congrats on the promotion. Hell of a way to spend your first day as the DSAC of the Counterterrorism Division."

Alex beams with excitement. "First day or not, there was no way I would miss this."

Hunter nods to the courtroom. "We got us all seats. We should get in there before it starts."

They don't have to wait long, and Alex grabs Cassidy's hand when Peterson walks in. He looks about ten years older than he did the last time she saw him. It's not surprising. He knows what's waiting for him.

The judge walks in, and order is called. "Calling the case of the United States versus David Theodore Peterson, here for sentencing today. If counsel will identify themselves for the record, please."

Cassidy squeezes Alex's hand while the lawyers go through their normal introductions. "I love you."

Alex looks at her. Her eyes are filled with excitement and anticipation. "I love you too."

The judge clears his throat and shuffles through several papers. "Mr. Peterson, you've been found guilty of treason, seditious conspiracy, misprision of treason, and conspiracy to levy war." He pushes his glasses up his nose. "I know you've requested to make a statement before my sentencing, but I'm going to deny that request."

Peterson's lawyer stands. "Your Honor."

"Sit down, Mr. Boardman. I'm not interested. No one is interested in hearing what he has to say at this point. He's had his time. Mr. Peterson, please rise."

The judge takes a deep breath and swivels in his chair for a moment. "Mr. Peterson, I've sat on the bench for the better part of twenty years, but I've been a citizen of this country for sixty. I've never been more disappointed in a person in all that time. You were entrusted with extraordinary responsibility during your tenure at the FBI, and I won't sit here and pretend to understand what you were thinking for a single second. You're a disgrace to this country, your fellow FBI agents, and your family. I'm well within my rights to sentence you to death." He pauses. "But I'm not going to do that. Death is too good for you. I'm sentencing you to four life sentences with no possibility of parole, to be served at a location determined by the government." He rubs his face and shakes his head. "On a personal note. You're everything that is wrong with this country. Instead of wanting to fix something that you believe is broken, you tried to burn it down and didn't care who had to pay the ultimate price. You're a shining example of what we pray our children and grandchildren will never become. May God have mercy on your soul, sir, because I do not have it in me." He bangs the gavel and walks out of the room.

Peterson turns and looks at Alex. "You did this. This is your fault."

Alex smiles and slides her hands into her pockets. "Take care of yourself, Dave. I'll be sure to come by and visit."

Tyler leans forward. "He'll be a few cells down from Carol O'Brien."

Alex smiles. "Perfect."

Cassidy walks Alex to her car and kisses her. "Have a good day, babe. I love you."

Alex hugs her and picks her up off the ground. "I love you too."

Cassidy watches her drive away, and the same butterflies that have always bounced in her stomach when she's near Alex erupt. She's grateful to be with someone who still affects her after almost two years, with no sign of stopping soon. Alex is everything she ever wanted and a few things she wasn't aware she needed. Cassidy is precisely where she's supposed to be—with Alex, always.

"So how's it feel to be in charge?" Hunter smiles at her as he turns onto her street. Their first day in their new positions had been exhilarating.

Alex shrugs. "Not any different. I feel like I've always been in charge of you."

Hunter raises his eyebrow. "Interesting. See, I thought I was always kind of the leader between us."

Alex sighs. "Well, our ranks say differently."

Hunter laughs and gets out of the car. "Do you mind if I run in and say hi to Cassidy, real quick?"

Alex grabs her bag from the back seat. "Not at all. We don't have any plans tonight."

She opens the door to her house and almost pulls her gun when a loud screeching welcoming erupts.

"Surprise!"

Alex is still holding her chest when Cassidy grabs her hand. "Did we surprise you?"

Alex stares at her. "Did you surprise me?" She grabs her face and kisses her. "I still can't feel my feet."

Alex is greeted by all her friends and family. Each takes their time congratulating her on her promotion and the close of the Peterson case. She's overwhelmed by the generosity and love each of them is emitting. If you would've told her two years ago that this would be her life today, she wouldn't have believed you. So much has changed, and every single bit of it is for the better.

Cassidy has helped push her out of her comfort zone, both personally and professionally. She opens her eyes to new wonders every day, and there is no way Alex could ever repay her for everything she's done.

She grabs Cassidy by the hand and pulls her into their room. "I love you." She kisses her. "I'll love you forever."

Cassidy smiles against Alex's mouth. "I like when you say stuff like that to me." She hugs her. "Don't ever stop."

"Never."

About the Author

Jackie D was born and raised in the San Francisco, east bay area of California. She lives with her wife and their son. She earned a bachelor's degree in recreation administration and a dual master's degree in management and public administration. She is a Navy veteran and served in Operation Iraqi Freedom as a flight deck director, onboard the USS *Abraham Lincoln*.

She spends her free time with her wife, friends, family, and incredibly needy dogs. She enjoys playing golf but is resigned to the fact she would equally enjoy any sport where drinking beer is encouraged during gameplay. Her first book, *Infiltration*, was a finalist for a Lambda Literary Award. Her fourth book, *Lucy's Chance*, won a Goldie in 2018.

Books Available from Bold Strokes Books

A Haven for the Wanderer by Jenny Frame. When Griffin Harris comes to Rosebrook village, the love she finds with Bronte de Lacey creates a safe haven and she finally finds her place in the world. But will she run again when their love is tested? (978-1-63679-291-0)

A Spark in the Air by Dena Blake. Internet executive Crystal Tucker is sure Wi-Fi could really help small-town residents, even if it means putting an internet café out of business, but her instant attraction to the owner's daughter, Janie Elliott, makes moving ahead with her plans complicated. (978-1-63679-293-4)

Between Takes by CJ Birch. Simone Lavoie is convinced her new job as an intimacy coordinator will give her a fresh perspective. Instead, problems on set and her growing attraction to actress Evelyn Harper only add to her worries. (978-1-63679-309-2)

Camp Lost and Found by Georgia Beers. Nobody knows better than Cassidy and Frankie that life doesn't always give you what you want. But sometimes, if you're lucky, life gives you exactly what you need. (978-1-63679-263-7)

Felix Navidad by 'Nathan Burgoine. After the wedding of a good friend, instead of Felix's Hawaii Christmas treat to himself, ice rain strands him in Ontario with fellow wedding-guest—and handsome ex of said friend—Kevin in a small cabin for the holiday Felix definitely didn't plan on. (978-1-63679-411-2)

Fire, Water, and Rock by Alaina Erdell. As Jess and Clare reveal more about themselves, and their hot summer fling tips over into true love, they must confront their pasts before they can contemplate a future together. (978-1-63679-274-3)

Lines of Love by Brey Willows. When even the Muse of Love doesn't believe in forever, we're all in trouble. (978-1-63555-458-8)

Manny Porter and The Yuletide Murder by D.C. Robeline. Manny only has the holiday season to discover who killed prominent research scientist Phillip Nikolaidis before the judicial system condemns an innocent man to lethal injection. (978-1-63679-313-9)

Only This Summer by Radclyffe. A fling with Lily promises to be exactly what Chase is looking for—short-term, hot as a forest fire, and one Chase can extinguish whenever she wants. After all, it's only one summer. (978-1-63679-390-0)

Picture-Perfect Christmas by Charlotte Greene. Two former rivals compete to capture the essence of their small mountain town at Christmas, all the while fighting old and new feelings. (978-1-63679-311-5)

Playing Love's Refrain by Lesley Davis. Drew Dawes had shied away from the world of music until Wren Banderas gave her a reason to play their love's refrain. (978-1-63679-286-6)

Profile by Jackie D. The scales of justice are weighted against FBI agents Cassidy Wolf and Alex Derby. Loyalty and love may be the only advantage they have. (978-1-63679-282-8)

Almost Perfect by Tagan Shepard. A shared love of queer TV brings Olivia and Riley together, but can they keep their real-life love as picture perfect as their on-screen counterparts? (978-1-63679-322-1)

Corpus Calvin by David Swatling. Cloverkist Inn may be haunted, but a ghost materializes from Jason Dekker's past and Calvin's canine instinct kicks in to protect a young boy from mortal danger. (978-1-62639-428-5)

Craving Cassie by Skye Rowan. Siobhan Carney and Cassie Townsend share an instant attraction, but are they brave enough to give up everything they have ever known to be together? (978-1-63679-062-6)

Drifting by Lyn Hemphill. When Tess jumps into the ocean after Jet, she thinks she's saving her life. Of course, she can't possibly know Jet is actually a mermaid desperate to fix her mistake before she causes her clan's demise. (978-1-63679-242-2)

Enigma by Suzie Clarke. Polly has taken an oath to protect and serve her country, but when the spy she's tasked with hunting becomes the love of her life, will she be the one to betray her country? (978-1-63555-999-6)

Finding Fault by Annie McDonald. Can environmental activist Dr. Evie O'Halloran and government investigator Merritt Shepherd set aside their conflicting ideas about saving the planet and risk their hearts enough to save their love? (978-1-63679-257-6)

Hot Keys by R.E. Ward. In 1920s New York City, Betty May Dewitt and her best friend, Jack Norval, are determined to make their Tin Pan Alley dreams come true and discover they will have to fight—not only for their hearts and dreams, but for their lives. (978-1-63679-259-0)

Securing Ava by Anne Shade. Private investigator Paige Richards takes a case to locate and bring back runaway heiress Ava Prescott. But ignoring her attraction may prove impossible when their hearts and lives are at stake. (978-1-63679-297-2)

The Amaranthine Law by Gun Brooke. Tristan Kelly is being hunted for who she is and her incomprehensible past, and despite her overwhelming feelings for Olivia Bryce, she has to reject her to keep her safe. (978-1-63679-235-4)

The Forever Factor by Melissa Brayden. When Bethany and Reid confront their past, they give new meaning to letting go, forgiveness, and a future worth fighting for. (978-1-63679-357-3)

The Frenemy Zone by Yolanda Wallace. Ollie Smith-Nakamura thinks relocating from San Francisco to her dad's rural hometown is the worst idea in the world, but after she meets her new classmate Ariel Hall, she might have a change of heart. (978-1-63679-249-1)

A Cutting Deceit by Cathy Dunnell. Undercover cop Athena takes a job at Valeria's hair salon to gather evidence to prove her husband's connections to organized crime. What starts as a tentative friendship quickly turns into a dangerous affair. (978-1-63679-208-8)

As Seen on TV! by CF Frizzell. Despite their objections, TV hosts Ronnie Sharp, a laid-back chef; and paranormal investigator Peyton Stanford, have to work together. The public is watching. But joining forces is risky, contemptuous, unnerving, provocative—and ridiculously perfect. (978-1-63679-272-9)

Blood Memory by Sandra Barret. Can vampire Jade Murphy protect her friend from a human stalker and keep her dates with the gorgeous Beth Jenssen without revealing her secrets? (978-1-63679-307-8)

Foolproof by Leigh Hays. For Martine Roberts and Elliot Tillman, friends with benefits isn't a foolproof way to hide from the truth at the heart of an affair. (978-1-63679-184-5)

Glass and Stone by Renee Roman. Jordan must accept that she can't control everything that happens in life, and that includes her wayward heart. (978-1-63679-162-3)

Hard Pressed by Aurora Rey. When rivals Mira Lavigne and Dylan Miller are tapped to co-chair Finger Lakes Cider Week, competition gives way to compromise. But will their sexual chemistry lead to love? (978-1-63679-210-1)

The Laws of Magic by M. Ullrich. Nothing is ever what it seems, especially not in the small town of Bender, Massachusetts, where a witch lives to save lives and avoid love. (978-1-63679-222-4)

The Lonely Hearts Rescue by Morgan Lee Miller, Nell Stark, Missouri Vaun. In this novella collection, a hurricane hits the Gulf Coast, and the animals at the Lonely Hearts Rescue Shelter need love, and so do the humans who adopt them. (978-1-63679-231-6)

The Mage and the Monster by Barbara Ann Wright. Two powerful mages, one committed to magic and one controlled by it, strive to free each other and be together while the countries they serve descend into war. (978-1-63679-190-6)

Truly Wanted by J.J. Hale. Sam must decide if she's willing to risk losing her found family to find her happily ever after. (978-1-63679-333-7)

A Good Chance by Ali Vali. Harry, Desi, and Desi's sister Rachel are so close to getting everything they've ever wanted, but Desi's ex-husband is coming back to get his revenge and rip apart their chance at happiness. (978-1-63679-023-7)

A Perfect Fifth by Jaycie Morrison. Streetwise pianist Zara Keller and Lady Jillian Stansfield couldn't be more different; yet their connection brings a new awareness of who they are and what they truly want in their lives—including each other. (978-1-63679-132-6)

Catching Feelings by Ana Hartnett Reichardt. Andrea Foster expected to catch a lot of pitches from the Alder Lion's star pitcher, Maya, but she didn't expect to catch feelings. (978-1-63679-227-9)

Defiant Hearts by Lee Lynch. In these stories, you'll find your lovers, friends, and lesbians you wish you knew—maybe even yourself. (978-1-63679-237-8)

Love and Duty by Catherine Young. All Princess Roseli wants is to marry her three lovers, but with war looming, she must instead marry Princess Lucia to establish a military alliance between their planets. (978-1-63679-256-9)

Murder at Union Station by David S. Pederson. Private Detective Mason Adler struggles to determine who killed a woman found in a trunk without getting himself killed in the process. (978-1-63679-269-9)

Serendipity by Kris Bryant. Serendipity brings jingle writer Annie Foster and celebrity pop star Bristol Baines together, and their undeniable attraction keeps them close, but will their different paths drive them apart? (978-1-63679-224-8)

The Haunted Heart by Jane Kolven. A ghost, a ring, and a quest to find a missing psychic—it's a spell for love. (978-1-63679-245-3)

The Rules of Forever by Nan Campbell. After reconnecting at their high school reunion, Cara and Lauren agree to embark on a textbook definition friends-with-benefits relationship, but trying to keep it uncomplicated is harder than it seems. (978-1-63679-248-4)

Vision of Virtue by Brey Willows. When virtue and desire come together, be prepared for sparks in this next installment of the Memory's Muses series. (978-1-63679-118-0)

Cherry on Top by Georgia Beers. A chance meeting leaves Cherry and Ellis longing for a different life, but when Ellis's search for truth crashes into Cherry's insta-filter world, do they have any hope at all of a happily ever after? (978-1-63679-158-6)

Love and Other Rare Birds by Angie Williams. Ornithologist Dr. Jamie Martin and park ranger Rowan Fleming are searching the Alaskan wilderness for a bird thought to be extinct and they're about to discover opposites really do attract. (978-1-63679-108-1)

Parallel Paradise by Mayapee Chowdhury. When their love affair is put to the test by the homophobia of their family, community, and culture, Bindi and Rimli will need to fight for a chance at love. (978-1-63679-204-0)

Perfectly Matched by Toni Logan. A beautiful Cupid named Hannah, a runaway arrow, and just seventy-two hours to fix a mishap that could be the best mistake she has ever made. (978-1-63679-120-3)

Royal Exposé by Jenny Frame. When they're grouped together for a class assignment, Poppy's enthusiasm for life and love may just save Casey's soul, but will she ever forgive Casey for using her to expose royal secrets? (978-1-63679-165-4)

Slow Burn by Missouri Vaun. A wounded wildland firefighter from California and a struggling artist find solace and love in a small southern town. (978-1-63679-098-5)

The Artist by Sheri Lewis Wohl. Detective Casey Wilson and reclusive artist Tula Crane are drawn together in a web of passion, intrigue, and art that might just hold the key to stopping a killer. (978-1-63679-150-0)

The Inconvenient Heiress by Jane Walsh. An unlikely heiress and a spinster evade the Marriage Mart only to discover true love together. (978-1-63679-173-9)